Bang

SABRINA STARK

CHAPTER 1

Cami

I was practically screaming now. "For God's sake, will you *please* stop the car!"

The roads were slick with snow, and I was in the middle of the back seat. In the *front* seat were two strangers in ski masks – one male and one female.

The male was behind the wheel, and the female was in the passenger's seat, craning her neck to stare behind us.

And the vehicle? Technically, it belonged to my boss – one Mason Blastoviak, who wasn't known for being a nice guy.

Whether these idiots realized it or not, they'd picked the wrong vehicle to car-jack.

I took a deep, calming breath and tried again. "Seriously, just stop the car, alright?"

With a sarcastic snort, the female said, "It's not a car. It's an SUV, remember?"

Of course I remembered. It was, after all, the vehicle I drove as part of my job. But that wasn't the point.

I told her, "You called it a car first." And she *had*, like ten minutes ago when she and her companion had caught me by surprise.

"Yeah, well you called it one *last*."

"It doesn't matter what we call it," I said. "You still need to stop."

From the driver's seat, the guy said, "Shut up! You've got no say in this."

The female turned to face him. "You'd better be talking to *her*."

"I'm talking to both of you," he said. "Now, zip it! I'm trying to drive."

Oh, for God's sake. Did I really need to say it? "You wouldn't *need* to drive if you'd just pull over."

He glanced in his rear-view mirror and cursed under his breath. "I can't. He's gaining on us."

Of course he was. Mason's car was a sleek turbo-charged sedan with eight cylinders and a lot of horses under the hood.

But this vehicle? It was a big orange SUV with a whole lot of safety features, but not a lot of power. On the upside, it *did* have four-wheel drive, which gave us a huge advantage on the slick roads.

Mason would've surely caught up with us already, if only his own vehicle weren't more suited for hot dry pavement – and *not* a snow-covered country road in the middle of a raging blizzard.

Still, it was only a matter of time.

I told the driver, "You can't outrun him, you know."

He yelled back, "Didn't I tell you to shut up?"

"Don't you get it?" I said. "He thinks *Willow's* in the car."

"Willow who?"

"Willow Blastoviak. His little sister."

Willow was only eight years old and as cute as a button. *Man, I loved that kid.*

I said a silent prayer of thanks that she *wasn't* in the vehicle.

And she *would've* been, if only my best friend – who happened to be the fiancée of Mason's brother – hadn't taken Willow for an impromptu bake-a-thon earlier this afternoon.

And me? I was Willow's nanny – not because it was my final career choice, but because teaching jobs had been thin on the ground, especially for recent college grads with more heart than experience.

As far as the nanny job, it wasn't *all* bad. *Willow was terrific.* But her brother, the billionaire who signed my checks? *He was something else entirely.*

And that *wasn't* a compliment.

Still, I knew one thing for certain. Mason would've braved a hundred slick roads – and whole lot more – to save his little sister.

But me? I was expendable. I knew this, just like I knew that Mason was the most impossible person I'd ever met. Rude, abrasive, and cold as ice – except when it came to his own family.

I wasn't family. Ask Mason. *He'll* tell you.

Repeatedly.

In the SUV, the female looked to me and said, "Can't you just call him? Tell him Willow's not here?"

"Suuuuure," I said. "Just turn back and retrieve my purse." I gave her a sarcastic smile. "You know, the one you tossed out the window?"

From the driver's seat, the guy said, "We're not goin' back for nothin'."

I made a sound of frustration. "Well, you can't drive forever. Eventually, you'll run out of gas." *Assuming we didn't slide into a ditch long before that.*

He gave the rear-view mirror another glance. "Yeah, well maybe *he'll* run out first."

"Or *maybe,*" I said, "he'll catch up with us and beat you senseless for kidnapping his little sister."

This wasn't as far-fetched as you'd think. Mason was six-foot-two and packed with hard muscle. He looked amazing in a suit – *and* in jeans, too.

He was no pampered pussy cat. He hadn't always been rich. His tool company, Blast Tools, had been founded with grit and determination, along with a firsthand knowledge of his products.

The guy could swing a hammer with the best of them – *and* looked very good doing it, as millions of cable TV viewers already knew.

The driver shot back, "But his sister's not even here."

"I know," I said through clenched teeth. "But Mason doesn't know that, does he?"

The guy glanced toward his female companion and said, "Why'd you throw out her purse for?"

It wasn't the purse that was the issue. It was everything inside the purse – my wallet, my phone, and my little cannister of pepper spray, which would've come in extra-handy right about now.

"Don't blame *me*!" the female yelled back. "It was *your* idea!"

The guy made a sound of disgust. "Since when do you listen to me?"

As they bickered back and forth, I whirled in my seat to study the road behind us. Snow was falling so hard, I could hardly see anything. Even Mason's black sedan – it was a gray, hazy blur amidst the swirling snow.

As far as the road itself, we were on a long country stretch, with very few houses and no other vehicles in sight.

And why? It was because only an idiot would be out in these conditions.

Correction. *Four* idiots. Me, the two masked wonders, and the guy who was hot on our heels.

Through the rear window, I was still eyeing the fuzzy outline of Mason's car. The way it looked, he was having a hard time keeping it on the road. Every once in a while, the sedan would begin to fish-tail before straightening out again.

But he wouldn't give up. I knew this, just as sure as I knew my own name – Camille Josephine O'Neal, aka Cami the Nanny.

One thing about Mason, he always got what he wanted. *Including me.*

And I meant that literally.

God, I'd been such an idiot.

But that was a story for another time, when I wasn't in the middle of grand-theft nanny-mobile.

The driver said, "Fuck! He's not giving up!"

I couldn't resist. "Told ya."

The funny thing was, we weren't going terribly fast. The slick roads made it literally impossible – not to mention, the visibility was horrendous, like driving thorough a sea of swirling cotton balls.

In reality, we were driving barely above the speed limit. Still, we were going a lot faster than was safe – especially Mason. *He* didn't have four-wheel drive. No, what *he* had was a reckless disregard for his own safety.

Idiot.

But I guess I said that already, didn't I?

And even though our history had been on the rocky side, I knew in my heart, I'd be crushed if anything bad happened to him.

So who was the idiot now?

Me.

That's who.

As I watched, the sedan lurched forward, as if Mason had abandoned all reason. My stomach clenched. *Oh, God.*

I whirled forward and yelled to the driver, "Seriously, just stop, alright?"

"No way," he said. "I told you, that guy's fucking nuts."

I whirled again to look behind us. *Oh, yeah.* Mason had definitely lost his mind. Already, the sedan was closing in on us fast, like he was putting the pedal to the metal in spite of a million fluffy reasons to do just the opposite.

Suddenly, his sedan shifted lanes and roared forward. Within mere moments, it passed us in a blur of speed and disrupted snow.

The guy in the driver's seat said, "What the fuck?"

But then, a split-second later, Mason's car swerved directly in front of us. The female screamed, and I might've too.

It was like Mason *wanted* us to hit him.

The thought had barely crossed my mind when that's exactly what happened. With a sickening crash, our SUV slammed into the back of Mason's sedan and sent both of our vehicles spinning.

I heard a series of bangs as airbags deployed all around us – in the front and even on the sides. The guy in the driver's seat gave a girlish scream as we spun like five times before coming to a slow stop in the shallow ditch.

Frantically, I glanced around.

I was okay.

And so, apparently, were the two idiots in front, because already, they were arguing about whose fault it was.

The female yelled, "You should've swerved!"

He yelled back, "I *did* swerve!"

"Yeah, but you swerved too much!"

"What? *You* wanna drive?"

"I can't *now*," she said. "The car's toast."

Was it? I wasn't so sure. Yeah, maybe the front end was severely crumpled, but it's not like we were in a twisted heap of burning metal.

My heart clenched. *But what about Mason?*

I yanked off my seatbelt and lunged toward the side window. The side airbag had deployed at hip level, leaving my view unobstructed. *Thank God.*

And yet, thanks to the swirling snow, I still couldn't see beyond a few feet.

But then, the snow cleared barely enough for me to spot Mason's car on the opposite side of the road, where it had apparently found a ditch of its own. The rear of his sedan was a banged, crunched-up mess.

As far as the front, I couldn't be sure either way.

As I took in the damage, something squeezed at my heart. *Was Mason alright?*

I reached for the door handle and gave it a frantic tug. *Nothing happened.* In the front seat, they were still arguing.

The guy was saying, "Oh yeah? Then next time *you* drive!"

"I *wanted* to drive," she yelled back. "But you wouldn't let me!"

"Yeah, because you drive like shit in the snow."

"Yeah? Well so do you!"

Ignoring them, I gave the door handle another tug. *Still nothing. Stupid safety features.*

I hollered out, "Unlock the door!"

Both of them ignored me and kept on bickering.

Great. Already, the snow was kicking up again, hiding Mason's car from my desperate view. With growing anxiety, I stared through the swirling snow.

And then I saw him, striding forward like a gladiator heading into battle. He wore a dark business suit, a red necktie, and a look so ominous, I felt myself swallow.

In his right hand was a hammer – silver on the business end with a blazing orange handle. I couldn't make out the logo, but of course, I didn't need to.

Blast tools were famous worldwide. And *this* was their trademark Blast Demolition Hammer, which he was wielding like a weapon.

I murmured, "Oh, my God," before hollering out to the idiots in front. "At least roll down the window!"

I wasn't even thinking of escape. I knew I'd make it out eventually. But now more than anything, I needed to let Mason know that his sister wasn't here, before he killed someone in a brotherly rage.

But did they listen?

No.

They kept on bickering.

As I watched in growing horror, Mason strode to driver's side window and lifted the hammer high. A split second later, the window shattered in a hail of broken glass that instantly silenced the bickering.

Mason used the sharp end of the hammer to puncture the driver's airbags. And then, he tossed the hammer aside and reached into the car with both hands. He grabbed the guy in the driver's seat and yanked him out through the now-open window.

The guy hollered out, "What the fuck?"

As for his companion, she practically dove for the passenger's side door. Unlike me, she shoved *her* door open with no trouble.

How nice for her.

As for myself, I was still trapped by the child safety locks.

I watched in stunned disbelief as the masked female bolted from the vehicle and headed *not* for her companion, but in the opposite direction, sprinting toward the nearby woods.

Well, so much for loyalty.

As for Mason, he slammed the driver up against the side of the car, just inches from my face. He hauled back and hit the guy in the dead center of his ski mask.

With my face pressed against the back window, I hollered out, "Willow's not here!"

Mason called back, "I know," just before hitting the guy again, this time in the stomach.

Huh?

By now, the masked car-jacker was babbling and cussing up a storm. *And so was I.*

Obviously, Mason still wasn't getting it. I scrambled over the center console and dove into the driver's seat. As I did, Mason called out, "What the hell are you doing?"

"I'm trying to get out!"

"Don't," he said. "There's broken glass."

As if I didn't know.

I glanced down at my hands and thanked my lucky stars that I'd worn gloves today, along with my warmest winter coat and sturdy denim jeans. My clothes were thick, and if the shards of glass were cutting me, I sure as heck didn't feel it.

Or maybe I was just too numb to feel anything but desperation.

I needed to stop Mason before he murdered the guy.

I grabbed the front door handle and gave it a hard yank. The door wasn't locked, but when I tried to push open the door, I was met with hard resistance in the form of the guy's backside, which was apparently blocking the door just enough to keep it from swinging open.

I stuck my head out the front window and yelled, "Didn't you hear me? I *said* Willow's not here. She's with Arden."

Now Mason was gripping the guy by his shoulders, holding him firm against the vehicle. Without letting go, he looked to me and said, "And I told *you*, I know."

"Yeah, but—"

"Hang on." And then, almost as an afterthought, he tossed the guy aside, sending him stumbling toward the road. The guy regained his balance for only a moment before slipping and falling hard on his backside.

With a string of curses, he scrambled up and then bolted through the snow, heading in the same direction as his female companion.

I watched for only a moment before I looked back to Mason. As I did, the wind momentarily died down, even as the snow kept falling in big fluffy blobs, lending a Christmas card quality to our surroundings.

The picture would've looked quite serene, if only there weren't two banged-up vehicles and a very ticked-off guy standing just outside the SUV.

He didn't look serene. *Far from it.*

His gaze locked on mine as he said, "I didn't come for Willow. I came for *you*."

My breath hitched, and my mouth fell open. I hardly knew what to say. I wasn't even sure what he meant, not for certain.

After all, this wasn't the *first* time he'd caught me by surprise. It wasn't even the first time he'd come for me, even if that *other* time – just three months ago – had been a whole lot different.

CHAPTER 2

Cami

Three Months Earlier

"Oh. My. God." In front of me, Livia's eyes widened as she stared across the small, crowded nightclub.

She was facing the main entrance. *I wasn't.*

When I turned to look, she lunged for my arm. "Cami, don't!"

At the sound of my name, I stopped in mid-motion. "Don't what?"

"Don't look," she said. "I think he's coming over."

"He?" I turned back to Livia. "He who?"

Her voice grew dreamy. "A total freaking hottie."

"Let me guess," I laughed. "Tall, dark, and handsome? Like the *last* three guys you mentioned?"

"Forget *them*," she said. "They're chopped liver compared to *this* guy."

Now, I *really* wanted to look – not because I was here to meet someone, but rather because the *other* guys had been nothing to sneeze at. This meant the latest "hottie" must be something truly spectacular.

Livia was still gripping my arm. With a little squeeze, she said, "Quick. Laugh like I just said something funny."

At this, I actually did laugh, not because she'd commanded me to, but rather because the request was so ridiculous, I couldn't help but laugh. "Seriously?"

"Louder," she urged. "And *better*. Like this." And then, right on cue, she threw back her head and laughed with such wild abandon that several people turned to look.

Then again, people always looked at Livia. She was undeniably gorgeous, with long dark hair and a figure to die for.

And me? Well, I wasn't *quite* chopped liver, but I was no Livia, that's for sure.

I stood several inches shorter, with long auburn hair that was nearly impossible to tame, especially during humid weather – or when I'd been dancing for too long in a crowded nightclub.

But Livia? She still looked picture-perfect. She and I were probably the same dress size, but with her impossibly long legs, she looked three sizes smaller and ten times more fashionable in her little red dress with matching heels.

She was holding her fifth mojito – not because she'd consumed the other four, but rather because a long parade of guys had been vying for her attention *and* buying her drinks whenever she expressed the least bit of thirst.

As I watched, she placed the latest mojito onto the bar beside us and smiled winningly over my shoulder. Under her breath, she urged, "Hurry up."

"Sorry, what?"

"Laugh, like I said."

Oh, God. I didn't want to. But the truth was, I owed Livia a favor, and I couldn't afford to tick her off.

Just yesterday, she'd gotten me a job interview with her dad's jewelry store, and if there was one thing I needed now, it was gainful employment.

So, feeling like a total idiot, I threw back my head and laughed like Livia had done just a few moments ago. Or at least, I *thought* it was the same – except the reactions were totally different.

Where people had stared at *her* with obvious interest, they stared at me like I'd like just farted at the dinner table.

Livia frowned. "That sounded totally fake."

Heat flooded my face. In a near-whisper, I said, "Yeah. Because it was."

I wasn't good at faking things, especially orgasms. Ask my last boyfriend. *He'll* tell you.

Livia was still frowning. "You'll never get any better if you don't practice."

"Practice what?"

"Laughing."

I didn't *want* to practice. I laughed when I was amused. I smiled when I was happy. And about the orgasms, well, let's just say it was better to fake it than to let Russell fumble around for any longer than was necessary.

It wasn't that I didn't love sex. *I did, truly.* It's just that my last couple of partners had been perfunctory at best, which probably explained why I was in the middle of a long, self-imposed dry spell.

Until I met someone who truly rocked my world, I figured it was better to wait.

As for Livia, she looked primed to get naked *now* as she stared toward the club entrance. Like someone in a trance, she murmured, "You really *should* see him."

Again, I turned to look.

"Don't!" Livia said for the second time. And then, in a lower voice, she added, "I mean, I don't want him to think we're talking about him or anything."

Reluctantly, I returned all of my attention to Livia. "But I thought he was coming over."

"He was," she said. "But a couple of hoochies jumped in the way." She made a sound of disgust. "Sluts."

I'd gone to high school with Livia. In her world, *any* girl was a slut if they put the moves on someone she liked. From the look in her eyes now, she liked this new guy the way lions liked antelope.

With a little laugh, she said, "Boy, did he give *them* the brush-off." Her eyes were gleaming now. "Now he's *really* coming over." As she spoke, she tossed another smile in his direction as if to say, *"Come on in, the water's fine."*

By now, I was dying of curiosity. "Can you at least describe him to me?"

"My pleasure," she said, sounding like she meant it. "Six-foot two, rocking hard body, thick dark hair, dark dangerous eyes."

I almost snickered. "Dangerous how?"

"Oh, he's seen things. I can tell." With another long, appreciative look in the guy's direction, she sighed, "And the way he's dressed, it's like his suit was custom-made."

I shook my head. "Wait, so he's wearing a business suit?"

This was Petoskey, Michigan, not some urban fashion center. As far as the club itself, it was nice for what it was – a popular hangout where locals and tourists could mix and mingle on Saturday nights.

It wasn't a suit-and-tie sort of place.

On the stage, a local band was jamming some tune that had hit the charts maybe three or four years ago. The place was packed with adults of all ages, some of them probably triple my own age of twenty-four.

It was late-September, and fall colors were approaching their peak, turning the green of Northern Michigan trees into a glorious display of yellow, orange and gold. People from all over the state and beyond had flocked northward like they always did, bringing with them enough money to keep the shops and restaurants open for another season.

In front of me, Livia practically purred, "I'll give *him* some business, alright." She cocked a hip and gave a toss of her long dark hair. With a flirty smile, she said, "Now shush. He's almost here."

Shushing was easy. By now, I hardly knew what to say. But sure enough, the guy finally strode into view and stopped directly beside us, just as Livia had predicted.

With a little gasp, I stared up at the guy. His hair was dark, and his eyes were too compelling for words. He wasn't smiling, but he wasn't frowning either as he looked from me to Livia and back again.

I felt myself swallow. He was everything Livia had claimed and then some. But this wasn't the reason I was staring. It was because I actually knew the guy.

I didn't like him.

And he sure as heck didn't like me.

He was Mason Blastoviak – my least favorite billionaire.

And hey, the feeling was totally mutual, because I knew one thing for darned sure. I was his least favorite *something*. I just didn't know what.

CHAPTER 3

Cami

As I craned my neck to stare up at him, I stammered, "What are you doing here?"

Mason frowned. "You declined my offer."

"Yeah, so?"

"So, I'm here to give you another shot." He flicked his head toward the main entrance. "And a ride if you need it."

"Wait, a ride where?"

"To Bayside," he said. "Where else?"

My jaw dropped. Bayside was where Mason lived, *and* where he worked, running a global tool company along with his two brothers.

Thanks to some seriously sexy publicity, Blast Tools had become a household name all over the globe, just like the company's three founders, who'd become obnoxiously famous for reasons unrelated to their business acumen.

They were hot, single, and *very* sure of themselves, as evidenced by Mason's rude assumption that I'd simply get into his car on a moment's notice.

Talk about arrogant.

Bayside was nearly three hours away. The time was almost midnight, and I hadn't packed a single thing. I wasn't planning to either. *And why?* It was because I wasn't going anywhere. Not with *him*.

Just yesterday, he'd offered me a job, by email, no less. I'd submitted no application, which made the offer doubly surprising. As far as the job itself, heaven knows I needed one. But I'd seen the offer for what it was. It was a pity-job, plain and simple, which meant the only decent thing I could do was decline.

So that's what I'd done.

By email.

I'd been polite, professional *and* appreciative. But I'd *still* declined, because it had been the right thing to do – and yes, because Mason Blastoviak would be the worst kind of boss, especially in close quarters.

And I *do* mean close, considering that the job was a nanny position for his much younger sister. *Her*, I liked. *Him, not so much.*

After I'd declined his surprising offer, I'd received no response at all. Then again, I hadn't expected one, which made his sudden appearance here in Petoskey all the more unsettling.

I was still trying to process it all when Livia sidled closer to him and practically purred, "You can give *me* a ride any time."

Oh, for God's sake.

With barely a glance in her direction, Mason replied, "I know."

Livia blinked. "What?"

"I know," he repeated. "But I'm not interested. So beat it."

I felt my gaze narrow. *Beat it? Seriously?*

It was vintage Mason.

As millions of strangers already knew from watching him on the Home Network, he could be a real jerk sometimes. But me? I'd seen him be a jerk in person, and I *hadn't* appreciated it.

I didn't appreciate it *now* either, even if Livia *was* coming on a little strong.

I was just about to tell him what he could do with his rudeness when Livia gave a happy shriek. "Oh, my God!" she squealed. "It's you!" Looking nearly orgasmic, she announced, "You're Mason Blast."

His jaw clenched. "I know," he said yet again.

Livia whirled to me and said, "You know him? Seriously?"

I did. But it wasn't something I liked to brag about. Until tonight, I'd met Mason exactly one time.

Our encounter hadn't been friendly.

With a giggle, Livia turned back to Mason and said, "I just *love* your act. I can't believe I didn't recognize you."

I could.

The so-called act was Mason's regular appearance on *Blast*, a weekly cable show on the Home Network, where the Blastoviak Brothers used their own tools to remodel older homes or sometimes build new ones.

Already, *Blast* was the network's number-one hit show of all time. With its massive ratings and subsequent publicity, it was already a cultural icon, with millions of rabid fans including yours truly, even if I'd never admit this to Mason.

On the show, Mason wore work clothes – T-shirts and flannel mostly, along with jeans that showed off his long legs and tight ass.

Yes, I'd noticed. So sue me, okay?

Just because he was a jerk, that didn't mean I was blind to his appeal. The funny thing was, he looked just as good in flannel as he did in the pricey business suit he was wearing now.

As I watched, Mason turned cold eyes on Livia and said, "An act?"

"Oh, *you* know," she giggled. "How you pretend to be such a hard-ass."

As the two of them locked gazes, my eyes dipped lower toward Mason's hips. I couldn't see his ass *now*. But I'd seen enough of it on the TV screen to know that it was, in fact, quite firm. *Or at least it sure looked that way.*

As I eyed his pelvis, my fingers clenched with curiosity. If his ass *looked* firm, would it *feel* firm, too?

My pulse quickened. *Oh yeah.* It definitely would.

Horrified, I jerked my gaze upward. *Why was I thinking of his ass? I didn't even like him.* And I *knew* the feeling was mutual.

But apparently, Livia liked Mason enough for the both of us. With a playful hip bump, she told him, "But I can tell you're just a big ol' softie on the inside."

I couldn't help it. I laughed long and hard.

Mason? Soft?

Oh, please. I'd seen bricks with softer edges.

Mason looked to me and said, "You wanna share the joke?"

Under his withering gaze, I stopped laughing. "Not particularly."

Next to him, Livia gave me an accusing look. "Why didn't you laugh like that earlier?"

I wasn't following. "What?"

"*You* know," she said with a sly wink. "When I told you that really funny joke?"

Oh. Then.

My gaze shifted to Mason, and something in his eyes suggested that he knew exactly what Livia was doing. With a look that was *almost* devious, he turned to her and said, "You wanna share it?"

She swallowed. "What?"

"The joke," he said with no trace of a smile. "Go ahead. Hit me."

Her mouth opened, but no sound came out. After a long, awkward silence, she looked to me and suggested, "Why don't *you* tell it?"

I froze. "Um, well…" I knew lots of jokes, but all of them were more suited to grade schoolers than to adults. I'd look totally ridiculous if I repeated any of *those* in a nightclub.

Around us, the music was rocking, glasses were clinking, and people were talking. And yet, my own silence felt loud in comparison. Desperately, I tried to think. *A joke, a joke…*

I was still trying to think of something that was age-appropriate when Livia made a sound of annoyance. "Hurry up," she urged. "He's waiting."

Oh, screw it. I looked to Mason and said, "Actually, I don't remember it either."

He gave a curt nod. "Good."

I felt my brow wrinkle in confusion. "Wait, why is that good?"

"Because we're wasting time."

Now *that* was a joke. "You do realize we're in a nightclub, right?"

"Yeah, so."

"So, by definition," I said, "that's why we're here. To waste time."

Next to him, Livia said, "*I'm* not wasting any time." She made a show of licking her lips. "I can be *quite* productive, if you know what I mean."

I stared in stunned silence. She wasn't suggesting what I *thought* she was suggesting.

Was she?

Mason turned to face Livia head-on. Looking less than flattered, he asked, "Is that so?"

"Oh yeah," she said, giving his crotch a long, lingering look. "And I'm so *very* thirsty."

Oh, God. I wanted to die of embarrassment, although for the life of me, I couldn't imagine why. I mean, it's not like I cared what Mason thought of me. And even if I *did* care, he'd surely realize that Livia and I were two very different people.

As I watched, Mason reached across Livia and picked up the mojito she'd discarded earlier. He shoved it vaguely in her direction and said, "Here. Now go drink that somewhere else."

She drew back. "What?"

He shoved the drink closer. "You heard me."

"But…" She summoned up a shaky smile. "That's, um, not what I meant, actually."

Watching from the sidelines, I didn't know whether to laugh or sympathize. I'd known Livia since kindergarten, and I'd never seen her so rattled. Then again, I'd never seen her rejected before.

Mason was still holding the drink. "I know what you meant," he told her. "And like I already said, I'm not interested." He flicked his gaze toward the mojito. "Now do you want this or not?"

Yikes.

By now, *I* almost wanted the thing. Livia had barely touched it, and the glass was still nearly full. Oh sure, the ice had gone all melty, but I didn't care. Suddenly, the thought of *any* drink, watery or not, sounded shockingly good.

I was still eying the mojito when Livia practically ripped it from Mason's hands. Not bothering with the straw, she lifted the glass to her lips and downed the whole thing without coming up for air, not even once.

I had to admit, it was pretty darn impressive.

When she finished, she thrust the empty glass toward Mason and said, "There. You happy?"

"Not really," he said, making no move to take the glass. "You were supposed to do that somewhere else."

Her eyes narrowed. "You are *such* an asshole. You know that?"

"No kidding." And with that, he turned back to me and said, "About the job offer, let's talk."

CHAPTER 4

Cami

Mason's two final words hung between us. *Let's talk?*

I didn't *want* to talk. By now, I was so unsettled, I could hardly think. Plus, Livia was still refusing to leave, which made this conversation doubly awkward.

Just yesterday, I'd interviewed with the manager of her dad's jewelry store.

The job was for weekends only, which was better than nothing, especially given the sorry state of my finances. Even so, a part-time job in retail was a long way from where I'd hoped to be by now.

I'd graduated from college several months ago, but I still hadn't found full-time employment. So a few weeks ago, I'd done the only thing that made sense. I'd registered for more classes, looking to make some headway on getting my master's degree.

This wasn't my first choice. Still, it was my only smart choice, considering that my degree was in primary education, and the schoolyear had started nearly a month ago. This meant that my odds of getting a teaching job *now* were practically non-existent.

Barring some miracle, I'd be waiting almost a full year before any decent teaching jobs opened up again. Until then, I needed to find something else, if only to stem the tide of student debt.

And yet, none of this explained Mason's surprise arrival. Yesterday, he'd offered me a job. I'd declined. Surely this meant that his obligation had been met – meaning an obligation to my best friend who was almost certainly behind the sudden offer.

I gave him a perplexed look. "You didn't come all this way for *that*, did you?"

"For what?" he asked.

"To talk to me." Quickly, I clarified, "About the job, I mean."

"So what if I did?"

I made a point of looking around. Not only was Mason almost three hours away from home, he was standing in a small-town nightclub. Around us, everyone was staring, including Livia, who looked like she didn't know whether to jump his bones or pelt him with the empty drink glass.

I looked back to Mason. "I'm just saying, you could've called instead."

"Yeah. And you could've declined on the phone."

"You mean the job offer?" I said. "I could *still* decline. In fact, I already did. You received my email, right?"

"Yeah, so?"

"So, like I said in the email, I *can't* take the job." I straightened to my full height, which barely reached his shoulders. "No. What I *mean* is, I *won't* take the job." I paused. "Even though I do appreciate the offer."

And I did, truly. I appreciated it more than words could express. But it wasn't Mason who received the bulk of my gratitude. It was my best friend, Arden, who was engaged to Mason's brother.

I wasn't quite sure how she'd managed it, but I just *knew* that Arden was the driving force behind the sudden opportunity.

And how did I know this?

Two reasons. Reason number-one – just three days ago, Arden had promised to help me find a job. And reason number-two? Mason disliked *me* just as much as I disliked him, which meant that he was only doing this as a favor to his brother.

In front of me, Mason said, "If you're so thankful, take it. You can start tomorrow."

I made a sound of frustration. "Just because I'm thankful, that doesn't mean I should take it."

"Alright. Then take it because it's a good offer."

Good? Actually, it was *better* than good – which was yet another reason I'd declined. The pay actually exceeded what I'd make as a first-year teacher. It included living expenses, too. *And a vehicle.* Not for keepsies, but to drive whenever I wanted.

When I'd received the offer, I'd been so tempted, I'd almost said yes without thinking. But just in time, I'd come to my senses.

It was a pity job, plain and simple.

Plus, there was the matter of the employer himself. *Mason was a total nightmare.*

Mentally, I ran through his least desirable traits.

He was condescending.

Rude.

Abrasive.

Arrogant.

And, on top of *that*, he was too darn sexy for his own good, which was a huge distraction.

Like now, I was utterly distracted by his amazing eyes – *and* how good he looked compared to anyone I'd seen in, well, forever, actually.

The lunk-blaster.

And, as awful as he was, I could only imagine how he'd treat an employee he'd hired *only* out of obligation.

Even so, I still might've accepted, if not for one sobering fact. Taking the job would be cruel, and I didn't mean to myself.

"Listen," I said, "I can't take it, because it wouldn't be fair to Willow."

Mason frowned. "Why not?"

"Because," I said, "don't you think she needs some stability in her life?"

His frown deepened. "You don't think she has that now?"

According to Arden, Mason was a surprisingly good dad to his little sister. Willow, who'd just turned eight, even called him "Dad" – not because Mason had asked for such a thing, but rather because Willow had apparently *begged* to call him that, after she'd been the only girl at her preschool to not have a dad of her own.

Both of Willow's parents were dead, which meant that she was technically an orphan, just like her three older brothers.

My heart went out to her. It went out to *all* of them, even Mason, whose *own* heart went out to no one, well for except his own family.

He was notoriously protective when it came to *them*.

But to strangers? *Not so much.*

So yes, I was sympathetic. And heaven knows I needed the money – but not so badly that I'd solve my own problems at Willow's expense.

To Mason, I clarified, "I meant stability with a nanny."

"So you're unstable, huh?" He gave me a look. "You mean mentally, or…?"

Oh, for crying out loud. "No. That's not what I meant, and you darn well know it."

I swear, his lips curved ever so slightly as he said, "Do I?"

"Of course you do," I said. "I'm just saying that even if I did accept – which I can't – I'd only be there 'til next fall."

"So? That's a year from now."

"Nooooo," I said in my overly patient voice. "It's eleven months."

"Which is eleven times longer than the *last* nanny lasted."

I blinked. Maybe four or five months ago, he'd fired the only nanny *I'd* been familiar with. But according to Arden, she'd been replaced right away.

And yet, the way it sounded now, the replacement nanny had been fired, too. *Or had quit. Or whatever.*

So she'd lasted only a month?

I heard myself say, "Seriously? What happened?"

His jaw clenched. "Trust me. You don't want to know."

He looked so disgusted that I felt the blood drain from my face. "She didn't do anything to Willow, did she? Because if she did—"

"She didn't."

"Oh." I blew out a relieved breath. "Well, that's good."

"No kidding," he said. "So, the job's yours if you want it."

Next to us, Livia spoke up. "But she already *has* a job."

I did a double take. "I do?"

With a tight smile, she replied, "Yes. With my dad's jewelry store. Remember?"

"Well, I remember interviewing," I said. "But the manager, he said he'd let me know next week."

"Screw *him*," she said. "You're hired."

I frowned. I wasn't sure Livia had the authority to make such an offer. "Um, seriously?"

She nodded. "Oh yeah. Trust me. I'll make it happen."

Still, I hesitated. "*Make* it happen? Meaning it hasn't happened already?"

She made a sound of annoyance. "Well, you only interviewed yesterday."

"I know," I said. "And I'm really thankful. I just mean, without an actual offer—"

She sighed. "It's handled, okay?" And with that, she smiled up at Mason. "So you need a nanny, huh?"

He gave her a long, cold look. "Me? No."

At this, Livia threw her head back and laughed, just like she had earlier, except *this* time, she couldn't quite pull it off. And when she finished, she got the same funny looks *I'd* gotten from the people around us.

Even Mason looked a little disturbed. In a tight voice, he told her, "That wasn't a joke."

"*Sure* it was." She beamed up at him. "You are so funny."

Oh, please. Under my breath, I mumbled, "I thought he was an a-hole."

As a general rule, I didn't curse. Aside from some creative word-smithery, I hadn't truly cursed in years, not since deciding to become a grade-school teacher.

The way *I* saw it, if I gave up those words ahead of time, it would greatly reduce my odds of accidentally cursing in front of the kids – which is why I'd gone with the abbreviated version of what Livia had called Mason earlier.

Even so, she looked at me like I'd just said the F-word in Sunday School. With a little frown, she said, "I can't believe you just said that."

"Me?" I said. "You said it first."

"Yeah, but *I* was only joking."

I knew Livia. *She hadn't been joking.* But I also knew that she'd forgive a guy just about anything if he was hot enough. And Mason was *very* hot. *Rich and famous, too.* He was Livia's dream guy on steroids.

By now, one thing was beyond obvious. A-hole or not, she wanted him, *bad.*

As if to prove my point, she turned back to Mason and said, "Hey, *I* know! You should hire *me.*"

I heard myself gasp. "What?"

She looked to me and said, "Well, *you* can't take it. You already have a job."

"But—"

"Now shush," she said. "Mason and I are talking."

I replied, "You are not."

"Of course we are," she insisted.

"No," I repeated. "You're not. Because *you're* the only one saying anything."

She gave me an annoyed look. "Yeah, because *you're* always interrupting." She looked back to Mason and gave him a winning smile. "So, you were saying…?"

It was then that Mason looked to me and said the most shocking thing yet. "You wanna dance?"

CHAPTER 5

Mason

Her lips parted, and she blinked several times before saying, "Excuse me?"

She was wearing a white V-neck sweater, along with a pale denim mini-skirt. Instead of high heels, she wore white canvas sneakers with white ankle-length socks.

She had nice legs. I'd noticed *this* before I'd ever reached her, just like I *now* noticed the green of her eyes and the fullness of her lips as she stared up at me with obvious confusion.

She looked so cute, I almost smiled. *But I didn't.* I wasn't here on a social call. And hell if I'd be giving her the wrong idea, especially now, when she was going to be living in my house.

I clarified, "So we can talk."

Cami gave her friend a quick sideways glance. "Oh. You mean in private?"

Next to me, the friend said, "Hey! I heard that."

I turned to the friend. "Good. It saves me the trouble."

Yeah, I was being a dick, but I knew her type all too well. She was the kind of girl who'd been playing life on easy mode for far too long. *And it showed.*

The friend gave me a pleading look. "But what about *my* offer? I'd just *love* to be the nanny."

Oh, for fuck's sake. "*You*, I already had. And I'm not interested."

She drew back. "You already had me? What does that mean?" She lowered her voice. "You don't mean sexually, do you? Because I'm sure I would've remembered *that*."

Yeah. She would've.

I might be an asshole in public. But in private, I'd never gotten any complaints, well, not in the bedroom, anyway.

I told her, "That's not what I meant." I looked back to Cami. "You ready?"

She was still staring. "Sorry, what?"

I flicked my head toward the dance floor. As I did, the local band struck up an old love ballad – one I hadn't heard since high school.

I couldn't recall the song's name, but I did recall getting lucky in my old Chevy beater with Tara Johnson in the back seat while that same song had played on my ancient car stereo.

That was twelve years ago.

A lot had changed since then – some for the better, and some for the worse.

I held out my hand to Cami. "Now come on."

She studied the hand for a long moment before giving her friend an apologetic smile. "I'll be back in a few minutes, okay?" And with that, Cami placed her hand in mine and let me lead her out onto the packed dance floor.

As we moved toward its center, the crowd parted, and people turned to stare. By now, I was used to it, but that didn't mean I enjoyed it.

I didn't like the spotlight. But I liked poverty even less, so the way I saw it, the extra attention wasn't worth complaining about, especially now, when there was work to be done.

When we reached the middle of the dance floor, I stopped and took Cami in my arms, holding her like a brother, not a lover. Still, when her eyes softened and her warm fingers grazed the back of my neck, something inside me stirred.

Whatever it was, it wasn't brotherly at all.

Shit. I'd had this reaction the *first* time I'd met her, too. We'd been standing outside on a sidewalk, and I'd been giving Arden – Cami's best friend and my future sister-in-law – a bit of a hard time.

Okay, more than a bit.

At the time, I'd been royally pissed off – and with good reason, too.

Or so I'd thought.

Now, I gave her a look that was all business. "Listen, I'm leaving for California on Tuesday. If you start tomorrow, I'll throw in a signing bonus."

Her eyebrows furrowed. "But I haven't said yes."

With a knowing smile, I replied, "Yeah, but you will."

She didn't smile back. "Well someone's awful sure of himself."

Yeah. I was. Because I knew one thing for damn sure. I wasn't leaving without her. And I *knew* she needed the money.

Before I'd made the initial offer, I'd checked her credit, along with a few other things. She had a flawless history of paying her bills, but she was drowning in student debt. She had a degree in primary education, but had no full-time job. She'd spent the summer tutoring at a local learning center, where she'd earned barely minimum wage, along with rave reviews from her students and their parents.

And speaking of parents, she'd been living with her own parents since May, when she'd graduated with honors from Michigan State.

Was she living in her parent's basement?

Hell if *I* knew. But hey, if I wanted to find out, it would be easy enough.

And I wouldn't hesitate.

When it came to my family, I wasn't above anything, which was why I knew for damned sure that Cami would be taking the job. *One way or another, I'd make it happen.*

First, I'd try the carrot. And if that didn't work, I wasn't above using a stick – speaking metaphorically, that is. During my thirty years on this Earth, I'd never hit a female, and didn't plan to either.

But I *would* be getting what I wanted.

First, the carrot. I looked to Cami and said, "You're taking some classes for your master's degree, right?"

She frowned. "Yeah, how'd you know?"

"Someone in Bayside mentioned it."

Her face relaxed. "Oh, you mean Arden?"

We were still moving in time with the music. The song was slow and sultry, and the local singer was doing a decent job of it. The band wasn't half-bad either.

And then, there was my partner, Camille Josephine O'Neal, soon to be Cami the Nanny, whether she realized it or not.

My hands were her loose at her hips, and I liked the way she moved – sweet and sexy, even if that wasn't her intent. *She wasn't coming on to me.* I knew this, just like I knew she had four younger siblings and an old Ford Fusion in need of new tires.

She didn't like me.

And the way I saw it, that wasn't a bad thing.

In fact, I was counting on it.

In reply to her guess about who'd mentioned the classes, I gave a tight shrug that revealed nothing. I hadn't heard it from Arden, but I'd heard it from *someone*. And that someone was the investigator I'd hired for the background check.

But this, like the credit check, was best left unmentioned.

So I didn't mention it.

Instead, I asked, "So, how many classes are you taking?" I knew the answer, but hey, anything to get her moving in the right direction.

"Only two," she said. "And even *those* I'm doing online."

This was good to hear, even if I'd known it already. Although Willow spent a good chunk of her day in school, the nanny job was still a full-time gig, and I didn't want my little sister getting the short end of the stick.

I gave Cami a knowing smile. "So, how'd you like to have those classes paid for?"

She stopped moving. "What do you mean?"

"That's the signing bonus."

Her brow wrinkled. "The tuition? But it was thousands of dollars."

"I know," I said. "So save us some time and say yes."

The song was still playing, and people around us were still dancing. *But we weren't. Not anymore.* Yeah, we got some looks, but we'd been getting plenty of those already, so hey, what was the difference?

I was still holding her, and she hadn't pulled away.

As I watched, Cami chewed on her bottom lip like she was seriously tempted. It was sexy as hell, and even more so because she had no idea what she was doing to me.

I liked her lips. I liked her eyes. And I liked the way she felt in my arms, even now, when we weren't really dancing.

I decided to enjoy it while it lasted, because there was no way in hell I'd be getting this close again. *She was my employee.*

She just didn't know it yet.

As I watched, she blew out a long, trembling breath. "Honestly, I still don't think I should."

"Why not?" I studied her face. "And don't say it's for Willow's sake, because no matter how long you stay on the job, you'll be better than the last one."

"The last nanny?" Cami frowned. "So what *did* happen with her, anyway?"

It was a fucking nightmare, that's what. As a reply, I repeated what I'd said earlier. "Trust me. You don't want to know."

"But I *do*," Cami insisted. "And I'd *need* to know for Willow's sake."

"Oh yeah? Why's that?"

"Well, for starters, what if Willow was traumatized or something?"

"Don't worry," I said. "*She* wasn't the one traumatized."

Cami hesitated. "So who was?"

If I were the shuddering type, I would've done it now. "Me."

"You? How so?"

"Accept the job, and I'll tell you."

She sighed. "But I can't."

She could. *And she would.* But hey, I'd play along. "Why not?"

"Honestly, I'm not sure you and I would get along."

"We don't *have* to get along," I said.

"Sure we would," she insisted. "You're Willow's guardian. And you'd be my boss. I'm just saying, it wouldn't be good for either one of us."

"And why's that?"

"Well, for one thing, you don't really like me."

She was wrong. I liked her well enough. In truth, I liked her more than I should. But there was no reason to give her the wrong idea, so all I said was, "Hey, I like you more than the *last* nanny."

She gave me a look. "You mean the person that lasted only a month?"

"Yeah. Her."

"Gee, that's so flattering."

"I'm not here to flatter you," I said. "I'm here to offer you a job."

She bristled in my arms. "I'm not looking for flattery. I'm just saying if you don't even like me, why would you want to hire me?"

The answer to this was easy. "Because Willow likes you. And that's more important."

"Oh." Something in her expression softened. "Yeah, I could see that."

"*And* you'd be an improvement."

"You mean over the last nanny?" she laughed. "The one you hated?"

"I never said I hated her."

"You didn't *have* to say it," Cami said. "I could tell by the look on your face. You totally despised her."

"Yeah, well, I had my reasons."

"Which you *still* haven't told me."

"If you want, I'll tell you on the drive."

"What drive?"

"The drive to Bayside."

She made a sound of frustration. "Will you please stop that?"

"Stop what?"

"Stop acting like I'm going to take it. The truth is…" She bit her lip. "Well, honestly, I don't want to be rude or anything, but…well, I don't really like *you* either."

She said this like it was a *bad* thing.

It wasn't.

I replied, "Good."

"Wait, why is that good?"

"Because that means you'll be focused on Willow." I gave her a serious look. "And *not* trying to get into my pants."

Her eyes narrowed. "What?"

"*Or* my bank account."'

From the look on her face, I knew exactly what she was thinking.

And she wasn't wrong.

CHAPTER 6

Cami

What a total prick.

Even though I'd never say such a thing out loud, the point still remained. Instantly, all of Mason's bad qualities – which had *almost* slipped my mind as we'd been dancing – came flooding back with a vengeance.

I told him flat-out, "I don't want to get into your pants."

"I know," he said. "And trust me. That's a plus."

"That's a little arrogant, don't you think?"

"Not if it's true."

"Oh, please. Not *everyone* in the whole world wants you, you know."

The pronouncement had barely left my lips when Livia appeared beside us, dragging behind her one of the first guys who'd bought her a drink earlier. The guy was probably in his late twenties, with dark wavy hair and deep smoldering dark eyes.

Earlier, Livia had called him tall, dark, and handsome. *And he was* – even if he'd been relegated to chopped liver status after the arrival of Mason Blastoviak.

I watched in stunned disbelief as Livia looked to me and said, "So, are you ready to swap?"

I was so thunderstruck, I replied without thinking, "Swap what?"

"Partners," she said, giving Chopped Liver a small shove in my direction.

To the guy's credit, he looked only mildly disappointed at the switch from Livia to me.

But Mason? He wasn't letting go. With a dangerous look, he told the guy, "Forget it. She's mine."

My breath caught. Of course, I knew what he meant. In his mind, I was *already* his employee – because yes, he was that arrogant.

Even so, something inside me stirred. Whatever it was, it was raw and primal. His words warmed me all the way down, like a smooth shot of pricey tequila.

She's mine.

My pulse quickened. *Oh, boy.*

What would it be like to have him say that for real?

I gave a little shake of my head. *It would be totally awful, that's what.* Because Mason Blastoviak – aka Mason Blast – was the least likeable person I'd ever met.

As for the new guy, he held up his hands in mock surrender. With a nervous laugh, he said, "Hey, sorry, not a problem."

Livia made a sound of frustration. "It is, too, a problem." She gave me an accusing look. "You're not even dancing."

Holy cow, she was right.

Of course, on some level I'd already realized this. And yet, I wasn't even sure *when* we'd stopped dancing. I just knew that we weren't dancing anymore – and that Mason *still* wasn't letting go.

Funny, neither was I.

In fact, unless I was mistaken, Mason was holding me tighter *now* than he'd been doing just a moment ago.

And I liked it.

Oh, crud.

This wasn't good.

Maybe I *did* want to get into his pants.

But in my own defense, my self-imposed dry spell had been going on much longer than I'd ever intended. I tried to think. Was Russell the last guy I'd slept with?

Yes. He was.

And now that I thought about it, we'd broken up last November. That was nearly a year ago.

Wow. No wonder a frolic in Mason's pants wasn't sounding so bad.

Reluctantly, I returned my attention to Mason, only to frown in new confusion. He wasn't looking at *me*. He was looking at Chopped Liver. As I watched, Mason gave the guy a look so dangerous, I felt myself swallow.

Wow, he must really hate to be interrupted.

And yet, I found myself captivated by his profile. And the longer I stared, the more I liked it.

By the time I looked back to Livia, she was standing there alone. I squinted through the crowd and saw Chopper Liver pushing his way toward the entrance, jostling people aside like someone had just yelled "fire" in the crowded building.

And speaking of fire, Livia's eyes were flashing with new anger. She looked to me and said, "That was *so* rude. You know that?"

My jaw dropped. "What?"

"He totally wanted to dance with you."

"He did not," I said. "And why am *I* the rude one? *You're* the one who dragged him out here."

"I didn't have to 'drag' him anywhere," she said. "He *wanted* to dance with me."

"Right," I said. "With you. Not me." I was glaring now. "Have you ever considered that maybe *you're* the rude one?"

"Me?" she sputtered. "*I'm* rude? I'll have you know I pulled some serious strings to get you that job interview."

I gave her a look. "You mean with your dad?"

"Yes," she said. "And just so you know, you're totally blowing it."

"Oh yeah?" I shot back. "How can I blow it if you already hired me?"

"What do you mean?"

"A few minutes ago, you told me I was hired."

"Yeah, well…" Her mouth tightened. "If that's true, I can fire you, too, you know."

I almost laughed in her face. "*If* that's true? So you admit I don't have the job?"

"I'm not admitting anything," she said. "I'm just saying, a little gratitude would be nice."

We were still going back and forth when Mason said, "Hey, get me a drink will ya?"

What the heck?

My gaze snapped in his direction. "What?"

But once again, he wasn't looking at *me*. This time, he was looking at Livia.

When I returned my attention to *her*, she was blinking up at Mason, looking like someone had just slapped her silly. After a long moment, she said, "Excuse me?"

"A drink," he told her. "I'm thirsty."

"Oh," she said. "Sorry, I didn't know." She glanced toward the bar. "So, um, what would you like?"

Oh, for God's sake.

When Mason answered, his voice was flatter than a pancake. "Surprise me."

He didn't need to tell her twice. The words had barely left his lips when Livia turned toward the bar and began elbowing her way through the crowd.

I was still staring after her when Mason said, "Huh. Maybe I *should* hire her."

I turned to look at him. "What?"

"I'm just saying, she's got initiative."

"Yeah," I snapped. "Because she – unlike *some* people – would just *love* to get into your pants."

"Well there ya go," he said.

As he said it, the final chords of the song ended, and the band struck up a new tune – this older than the last, but just as slow and romantic.

Embarrassingly, I was still holding onto Mason. Even worse, I wasn't *quite* willing to let go.

Him and his stupid pants.

On the upside, he was still holding onto to *me*, too, which meant that I wasn't making a *total* fool of myself.

It was just that, well, I was reluctant to walk away, that's all – although for the life of me, I couldn't imagine why.

When Mason started moving with the music, I followed suit. *I mean, as long as we were out here on the dance floor, we might as well dance, right?*

And besides, it wasn't for my own benefit. It was for all of the people who were standing around watching. Maybe if *we* started dancing, they'd stop staring and pay more attention to their own partners.

They didn't.

Oh sure, they eventually started going through the motions, but I could still see them watching us with far too much interest. Then again, we had caused quite a scene.

Trying my best to ignore the spectators, I looked to Mason and said, "You wouldn't *really* hire her, would you?"

His lips curved ever so slightly. "If I did, would that be a problem?"

"Of course, it would be a problem," I said. "She doesn't even like kids."

"Yeah, but she likes *me*."

"But so what?" I said. "*You're* not the one who needs a nanny."

He gave something like a shrug. "Well, she couldn't be much worse than the last one."

"Oh, my God," I groaned. "You're not seriously thinking about it?"

He said nothing, but his look said it all.

He *was* thinking about it.
What the heck?
Was the guy off his rocker?

CHAPTER 7

Mason

Cami glared up at me like I'd just suggested hiring Jack the Ripper.

I liked that about her. Already, she was more protective of Willow than the last three nannies combined.

This confirmed what I already knew. *I'd made the right choice.* I just needed to make *her* see it the way *I* did.

It was time for the stick.

"Listen," I said, "I'm hiring *someone* while I'm here. It's either you or your friend." *This wasn't a lie.* That someone would be Cami, whether she realized it or not.

"Oh come on!" Cami said. "You're joking."

"So tell me," I said. "Do you think your friend can start tomorrow?"

"Hah! You don't even know her name."

"Yeah, so?"

"Well, shouldn't you *know* someone's name before you hire them?"

"Eh, names aren't important."

"But what about Willow?" Cami said. "I know *she's* important to you."

Yeah, she was. This explained why I'd driven nearly three hours to see Cami in person – *and* why I was willing to fight dirty to make her say yes.

I replied, "Hey, if you're worried, you can take the job yourself. It's still open."

Her eyes narrowed. "I know what you're doing."

"Do you?"

"Yes. You're trying to manipulate me."

"Am I?"

"Definitely. Because I *know* you wouldn't *really* hire Livia."

"Livia, huh?" I smiled. "See, now I have a name."

"Oh, stop it," she said. "You're just messing with me. I *know* you wouldn't really do it."

"It's better than leaving Willow alone." I gave Cami a no-bullshit look. "Like I said, I leave for California on Tuesday."

Cami was silent for a long moment, and we locked gazes as we continued to move with the music. Her eyes were accusing but gorgeous as hell.

I wanted to pull her closer, to feel her head on my shoulder and inhale the scent of her shampoo. She had nice hair – auburn with a hint of red. Her hair was long and wavy, just the way I liked it.

I was liking a lot of things.

This wasn't good.

It wasn't lost on me that one dance had turned into two – *and* that I hadn't liked it when her friend's lapdog had tried to hone his way in.

One Cami was worth a million of her friend. I knew *this* just as surely as I knew that I wouldn't be leaving town without her.

For Willow.

Not for myself.

I'd be smart to remember that.

Finally, Cami said, "Can I at least have the night to think about it?"

I tried not to smile. *Oh yeah, she was coming with me, alright.*

And from the look on her face, she knew it, too

CHAPTER 8

Cami

I needed a second opinion, and I needed it *now*. Fortunately, I knew just the person to call – my best friend Arden. After all, she was the person who'd gotten me into this mess.

Or, she was the person who'd just saved my bacon. After all, I really did need the money.

As I made my way across the dimly lit parking lot, I was still trying to decide which sentiment was truer.

By now, I was so flustered, I could hardly think. Just ten minutes ago, Mason Blastoviak had strolled out of the club, taking my sanity with him.

He hadn't even waited for the drink he'd ordered from Livia. Instead, he'd left right after the second song had ended, pausing only long enough to give me his business card, along with a reminder to call him by nine o'clock tomorrow morning.

That's when I owed him my answer. It was the time we'd agreed on, but now I was having second thoughts.

It was too soon.

But in my own defense, I'd been finding it hard to think while gazing up into those dark, compelling eyes of his.

As I walked toward my car, Livia's words echoed in my brain. *"He's seen things."*

Of *that*, I had no doubt whatsoever.

Without breaking my stride, I pulled out my cell phone and sent Arden an urgent text. *"Can you talk? It's kind of important."*

I kept on walking, praying like crazy that she was still awake. These days, she was keeping some pretty early hours, so I could never be sure. Already, it was past midnight.

Oh, God. Past midnight?

This meant that "tomorrow" was technically here. I didn't owe Mason an answer *tomorrow*. I owed him an answer *today*.

Goodness gravy.

By the time I climbed into the driver's seat of my car, Arden still hadn't replied. I tried to think. *Should I call her?*

But what if she was sleeping? How rude would *that* be?

Fortunately, I didn't need to wonder, because just as I was about to fire up my car's engine, my cell phone rang.

It was Arden. Thank God.

I answered with an anxious, "Hello?"

Right away, she asked, "What's wrong?"

She sounded so worried that I felt almost guilty. "Nothing."

"Are you sure?" she said. "Because you sound *really* tense."

I *was* really tense. And it wasn't all related to the job offer. It was related to Mason himself. By now, I didn't know what to think of him.

And even stranger, I was no longer sure what he thought of *me*. While we'd been dancing, there'd been moments where I could've sworn he'd looked at me with *real* interest – and not the employer kind either.

To Arden I said, "Well, there *is* something I need to get your opinion on. And I'm really sorry, but it can't wait."

"Oh, stop it," she laughed. "Don't be sorry. What is it?"

Although I was safely inside my own car, I still lowered my voice. "First, are you alone?"

"Yeah." She paused. "I mean, I'm alone with Brody."

I winced. Brody wasn't only her fiancé. He was Mason's youngest brother. "Oh."

"Is that a problem?"

"No." I hesitated. "It's just that, well, it's kind of a girl-talk thing."

"Gotcha. Hang on a sec, okay?" I heard fumbling on the other end, followed by muffled voices and the sounds of a door opening and then shutting. A moment later, Arden said, "Alright. I'm alone on the balcony. What's up?"

Now, this is where it got awkward. "Well, first I should probably apologize, huh?"

"For what?"

"Okay, the thing is, I received Mason's job offer yesterday. And I meant to call you and say thanks, but—"

"Wait. Mason offered you a job? Seriously?"

Now *that* surprised me. "What, you didn't know?"

"No." She sounded genuinely surprised. "I had no idea."

"So you didn't put him up to it?"

"No. Why would you think I did?"

"Because the other day, you said you'd help me find a job."

I hadn't asked for the help. In fact, I'd tried to decline, telling Arden that I didn't want *my* problems to become *her* problems. But she'd been insistent, which had led to my natural assumption that she'd orchestrated the job offer.

On the phone, she said, "Actually, I was planning to hire a head-hunter, you know, someone to find opportunities that aren't publicized."

I smiled. "Awww. But you don't have to do that."

"I know," she laughed. "But I want to, unless…" She paused. "Are you planning to take the job?"

"That's why I called. Do you think I should?"

"I don't know," she replied. "Are you sure you have the stomach for it?"

No. I wasn't. In fact, my stomach had been fluttering like crazy while dancing with my prospective employer. But surely Arden meant something else.

I asked, "What do you mean?"

"Well, he's not very nice," she said. "And if he weren't Brody's brother, I'd be saying a lot worse than *that*."

She paused for only a moment before adding, "Like, I might say that he's one cold S.O.B., or that he's not any nicer in person than he is on the TV show."

Blast was the popular remodeling show that starred all three brothers. And thanks to Arden, I now realized that Brody was the only brother who remodeled the houses full-time.

As for the two older brothers, they showed up only once in a while to look pretty for the cameras – although you'd never know it from watching the show.

It wasn't that the older brothers couldn't do construction, but rather they handled other aspects of the family business, and left Brody to handle the show.

In my car, I listened as Arden rattled off a few more things she "might" say if Mason weren't the brother of her fiancé.

She concluded by saying, "But I won't say any of those things, because he's almost family. Plus, Brody's opinion of him is *a lot* higher than mine." She paused. "Even if Mason *is* a little scary."

A *little* scary?

Oh, I was scared alright. But it wasn't in the traditional sense. Mostly, I was terrified by my reaction to him.

Still, I had to smile at Arden's description. "Good thing he's family or you might've *hinted* that you don't like him."

"He's not family *yet*," she said with a laugh. "But to be fair, I haven't spent a lot of time with him, so he could be nicer than I realize."

I blew out another nervous breath. "Or not."

"Exactly! So, what kind of job was it?"

"You can't guess?"

"No," she said. "I have no clue."

I paused for dramatic effect. "It's the nanny job."

"Ohhhhh," she said. "Yeah, I guess that makes sense. Do you know, the *latest* one lasted only a month?"

"So I heard. But do you know why?"

"No. But I *do* know that she was hustled out of there in the middle of the night."

"Really? How do you know *that*?"

"Okay, get this. It's like three in the morning, right? And Brody gets this urgent phone call from Mason, asking us to come over, like right away."

"You mean to Mason's house?" I felt my brow wrinkle in concern. "Why?"

"Because," Arden said, "he's got to leave for the airport. And apparently, he'd just kicked the nanny to the curb, *literally,* with no notice whatsoever."

"In the middle of the night?" I said. "And he didn't tell you why?"

"No. But it must've been pretty bad, because early the next morning, a locksmith shows up and changes all of the locks – *and* all of the security codes."

"Well that's weird."

"No kidding," Arden said. "And that was two weeks ago."

I frowned. *Two whole weeks?* "So who's watching Willow now?"

"At the moment?" Arden said. "We are."

"Seriously?"

"I don't mean we're watching her full-time or anything," she clarified. "Mason has this house-keeper who's been doing double-duty. And *she's* the one who's been watching Willow after school."

"And what's *she* like?"

"Oh, she's super nice. But she never spends the night, which means that if Mason has to go out of town or something, he's got to find somebody else."

I said, "Like you?"

"Technically, it's Brody," Arden said. "Mason would never call *me* for anything."

Now *this*, I believed. Thanks to something that had happened years ago, Arden's relationship with Mason was shaky at best. *He didn't like her.* And by now, the feeling was more than mutual.

On the phone, Arden continued. "But Brody and I watch her together." With a smile in her voice, she said, "It's like a sleepover. We have loads of fun. Willow's a great kid."

Now I smiled, too. "I know."

I'd met Willow a few months ago when she'd gotten stranded near a construction site. At the time, I'd tried to help walk her home, with less than stellar results.

The whole thing had been a giant misunderstanding, but that didn't mean I appreciated Mason's rude assumptions – as if I'd truly try to kidnap a grade-schooler.

Arden asked, "So, are you gonna take it? The job, I mean?"

"Actually, that's why I called," I said. "I wanted your opinion. Do you think I should?"

"For your sake?" Arden gave a weak laugh. "Not really."

"What do you mean?"

"You *know* what I mean," she said. "The guy's gone through like four nannies in the last year. And you already know what a hard-ass he is."

Once again, a vision of Mason's backside popped into my head. Sure, he was wearing jeans, so the image wasn't terribly indecent. Still, my heart gave a traitorous flutter, even more so when I recalled being held in his arms.

I had to admit, I was insanely attracted to him.

Then again, I was hardly alone in *that*.

Take Livia for example. She'd been ready to pounce on him the moment he'd walked into the club.

The thought had barely crossed my mind when I happened to glance around and spotted Livia walking through the parking lot. She wasn't alone either. She was hanging on the arm of Chopped Liver and laughing at something he'd just said.

The way she was acting now, it would be easy to assume that he was the most fascinating guy she'd met all night.

But he wasn't. And I knew one thing for certain. Even now, if Mason Blastoviak happened to pop out of a nearby car, Livia would ditch Chopped Liver like stale leftovers.

On the phone, Arden was saying, "But can I confess something?"

"Sure, what?"

"If I were being totally selfish, I'd beg you to take the job."

I smiled. "Oh yeah?"

"Definitely. We'd be living in the same town. And I *know* you'd be great for Willow." She hesitated. "But tell me, was it a good offer? Meaning financially?"

Was it ever.

After I gave Arden the highlights, she said, "Seriously?"

"Yeah. But you realize what *that* means, don't you?"

"What?"

"It means it's too good to be true."

"It's not *that* good," she said. "You'd still have to put up with Mason."

Silently, I considered what it would be like to live in the same home as Mason Blastoviak, to eat at the same breakfast table, to see him in the mornings or at night.

It would be terrible for all kinds of reasons, including my stupid attraction to him. I murmured, "Well, there's that."

"And," Arden continued, "I'm sure he'd want you to start right away. He's leaving for California in just a few days. We *all* are."

"You mean for the show?"

"Yup. We're finishing this house in wine country. The house is practically done, so all of the brothers need to be on site for some final footage."

Arden would definitely know. Earlier this year, by some twist of fate, she'd ended up playing a role of her own on the TV show. It had all started when she and Brody were hot for the same property – a Victorian beach house that had belonged to Arden's grandparents.

In the beginning, she and Brody had totally hated each other. Now, they were so obnoxiously in love, I might've been jealous if I weren't so happy for her.

Thinking of Brody's older brother, I said, "Actually, Mason wants me to start tomorrow."

"Wow. That soon?"

"Oh yeah. And I forgot to mention, if I *do* start tomorrow, he said he'd pay my tuition for *both* of my summer classes."

"No kidding?"

I considered the dollar-amount in question. To Mason, it was probably chump change. But to me, it was *a lot* of money. "That's what he said."

Across the parking lot, Livia and Chopped Liver stopped beside a white Mercedes. He pulled her into his arms and kissed her, hot and heavy. Livia sagged against him and kissed him back with a vengeance.

When he grabbed her ass, she grabbed *his* in return.

As I watched from my darkened car, I felt just a little bit icky, and not only because I was watching them in secret.

It was because the guy was Livia's second choice. And surely, he knew it. Earlier on the dance floor, *anyone* could've seen that she'd been ten times more interested in Mason.

Didn't the guy care?

Didn't *Livia* care?

And why did *I* care?

I *shouldn't* care. But the fact I did, well, it went a long way in explaining why my sexual dry spell had lasted so long.

I wasn't the casual type. In my whole life, I'd been with only four guys total, and all of them had been long-term boyfriends. It was true that the relationships had ended eventually. But with all four, I *had* been in love. Or at least I'd been in something that felt like love.

Even so, none of them had jump-started my heart quite like Mason Blastoviak.

And with *him*, all we'd done was dance.

It wasn't even dirty dancing.

From start to finish, it had been perfectly chaste.

God, he was sexy.

I was so lost in my own thoughts that I didn't quite catch what Arden had just said

Feeling like a total clod, I said, "Sorry, could you repeat that?"

"I was just saying, we don't even know where he went tonight."

"You mean Mason?"

"Right," she said. "All I know is that he's not coming back until tomorrow. And he left straight from the office."

Well, that explained the business suit.

Still, I had to laugh. "And he seriously didn't tell you where he was going?"

"No. And before you ask, I can't even guess."

"You don't need to guess," I said. "Because I'll tell you exactly where he was."

And then, as she listened, I explained how Mason had showed up in Petoskey, in a nightclub no less, looking to hire me on the spot.

When I finished, she said with obvious surprise, "Oh, shut up. You're joking, right?"

"Nope."

"Huh. Well, that's something."

Yes. It was.

And what that something was, I didn't quite know. But I did know one thing by now. For better or worse, I'd be taking the job.

And why? It was because the offer was so terrific, I'd be an idiot to turn it down, especially after realizing that it would be good for Willow after all.

But would it be good for *me*?

The way it looked, I'd soon be finding out.

CHAPTER 9

Cami

Turns out, Mason wasn't kidding about giving me a ride to Bayside.

After I called him at nine o'clock the next morning and told him that I was accepting his offer, he informed me that he would be swinging by my parent's place at noon to pick me up.

"Why noon?" I asked.

"Because I figured you'd want some time to pack your things. But hey, if you're ready now—"

"I'm not."

"Alright, noon it is."

True to his word, he'd shown up exactly at noon, driving a bright orange SUV, which happened to be the same exact color of his tool company's logo.

No coincidence there, huh?

The vehicle wasn't the only thing that caught me off-guard. It was Mason's clothes. The tailored business suit was long gone, and in its place were jeans and a black T-shirt, along with black high-top sneakers.

He looked ten years younger than he had last night, and *almost* human, as he opened the rear hatch of the orange SUV and helped me load up my two battered suitcases, along with a few boxes containing extra clothes, some of my favorite books, and other basic necessities.

Today was Sunday, which meant my youngest siblings – Carrie and Tanya, who were still in high school – were home today, and thus, able to gawk at Mason to their heart's content.

I couldn't exactly blame them. *Blast* was the Home Network's number-one hit show of all time. With its killer ratings and wide appeal, it had made all three brothers famous.

My whole family loved the show, even my parents, who were not only supportive of my sudden career move, but viewed it as an excellent opportunity to bulk up my resume for next year's job search.

I saw what they meant. And yet, as I loaded up my things, next year seemed so very far away. At the moment, it was *this* year that was scaring the pants off me.

After a final round of hugs and goodbyes between me and my family, Mason and I were officially on the road.

I could hardly believe I was doing this.

But from the look on Mason's face, it was exactly what he'd expected all along. Ten minutes later, as we pulled out onto the highway, I gave Mason a long, sideways look.

He looked too smug by half.

In fact, he looked *so* smug that I couldn't stop myself from saying, "Good thing I said yes, huh?"

With his gaze trained on the highway, he replied, "Meaning?"

"Well, if I *didn't* say yes, you'd have *Livia* in your passenger's seat. And *she* has a lot more luggage."

Sounding only mildly interested, he replied, "Does she?"

"Oh yeah. You'd probably need to rent a trailer or something."

I wasn't even lying. Livia and I had both gone to Michigan State. I'd roomed with her during my freshman year. *She had a ton of stuff.*

In the driver's seat, Mason said nothing in reply. But I swear, I saw the hint of a smile play across his lips. What that smile meant, I had no idea.

I decided to push the issue. "So you must be pretty relieved, huh?"

"No. Because I knew you'd say yes."

"Oh, so you think I'm *that* predictable, huh?"

"No. I think I'm that persuasive."

I almost rolled my eyes. "Well, someone's awful sure of himself." Even as the words left my mouth, I recalled the first time I'd said this to him. It had been just last night, when he'd told me flat-out that I'd be saying yes to his offer.

And I had.

How embarrassing was that?

When I gave Mason another glance, he looked *doubly* smug.

Well, this was just terrific.

I sank lower in my seat. "That doesn't prove anything, you know."

"It proves *something*," he said.

"Oh yeah? What's that?"

"That you know a good thing when you see it."

I studied him from the corner of my eye. I *did* know a good thing when I saw it, but not the way he meant.

His hand was draped loose over the steering wheel, and he was leaning back in the driver's seat. Even so, the muscles in his forearms were a sight to behold as he navigated the next curve of the highway.

And now I was all distracted.

Desperate for a change of topic, I said, "So you stayed in town last night?"

"Well, I didn't drive back to Bayside if that's your other guess."

His sarcasm grated. Still, I pressed on. "I know. I talked to Arden. And I'm just curious. Why didn't you tell her – or even Brody – that you were coming to Petoskey to see me?"

"Because I didn't want you to know."

"Oh," I laughed. "So you didn't want her to warn me? Is that it?"

"Pretty much."

"But why?"

With a half shrug, he replied, "Call it the element of surprise."

"Or," I said, "we *could* call it an ambush."

"Call it whatever you want," he said. "You're here, aren't you?"

Terrific. Now his *smugness* grated. It was definitely time to turn the tables. "Oh, I'm here, alright, which means you owe me. Remember?"

"If you mean the bonus," he said, "it's already done."

I blinked. "You mean the tuition money?"

He flicked his head toward the passenger's side dashboard. "The check's in the glove compartment."

I glanced at the nearby compartment. "Seriously?"

"Look for yourself."

Feeling only slightly foolish, I did what he suggested. Sure enough, inside the glove compartment, I found a business check made out to me from Mason Blastoviak.

On the check, he'd used my full name – Camille Josephine O'Neal. But as far as the dollar amount, it wasn't quite accurate. I'd charged my tuition to my credit card. The amount had put me scarily close to my limit – so I knew the exact total by heart.

The check from Mason exceeded that amount by nearly two hundred dollars. *But why?* And then it hit me. Unless I was mistaken, the extra money was the precise amount I'd spent on books for both classes.

As I stared at the check, I asked, "How'd you know the amount?"

"Two classes, four credits each. I did the math."

I was still looking down. "But this includes money for books, too."

"Yeah, so?"

"So how'd you know which classes I was taking?" I lowered the check and turned my head to look at him. "Or how much the books cost?"

He kept his gaze firmly on the road. "Because I made it my business to know."

I felt my eyes narrow. "Wait a minute. You didn't run a background check on me, did you?"

"What do *you* think?"

I studied his profile. "Actually, I'm thinking you did." When he said nothing in reply, I persisted. "So…do you admit it?"

Looking utterly shameless, he said, "Well, I'm sure as hell not denying it."

My jaw dropped. "But I wasn't even your employee at the time."

"Right. And you *wouldn't* have been if you hadn't passed."

Now I didn't know what to say.

I hated the idea of anyone prying into my business. But I also understood that Mason Blastoviak was beyond rich and famous, which would make Willow a target for all kinds of potential trouble.

I didn't want her in trouble.

I wanted her safe and happy.

This was, after all, part of the reason I'd accepted the job. Finally, when no words came to mind, I tucked the check into my purse and decided to think about this later, when I didn't feel like throttling him.

And besides, he'd totally missed my original point. I tried again. "When I said you owed me, I wasn't talking about the bonus."

He didn't even glance in my direction. "Oh yeah?"

"Yeah. What I *meant* was that you owed me the story of why the last nanny was fired. You promised to tell me during the drive. You remember, right?"

Judging from his face, he remembered just fine. And he wasn't happy with the reminder.

CHAPTER 10

Mason

Shit.

Yeah, I remembered. And I'd known what she'd meant the first time. But I'd been hoping the bonus would distract her.

Hell, it was the reason I'd confessed to the background check. If I'd been lucky, she would've been pissed-off enough to forget about the fired nanny, along with my ill-advised promise from last night.

Why in the hell had I promised to tell her?

The last thing I wanted now was to give her ideas – ways to make a quick buck at Willow's expense.

Maybe Cami wasn't like that. Or more likely, I'd let down my guard too much already. *What was it about her, anyway?*

In the passenger's seat, she said, "You *are* gonna tell me, aren't you? That was the deal, remember?"

I never welched on a deal, but that didn't mean I was happy about it. "Fair enough," I said. "But the drive's not over."

"Oh, so you're stalling?" she laughed.

She had a nice laugh. It was warm and happy, not like the fake laughter I'd heard from her friend *or* countless girls like her.

But that was no reason for me to go soft. "First," I said, "you tell *me* something."

"What?"

"Do you always text in dark parking lots?"

She stiffened in the passenger's seat. "Excuse me?"

"Last night," I said. "You were texting as you walked to your car." I paused to let that sink in before asking, "Did you see the guy coming up behind you?"

With no trace of laughter, she said, "You were watching me?"

"I wasn't the only one."

"What's that supposed to mean?"

"Some guy, maybe six-foot tall, dark coat, receding hair – he was maybe ten paces behind you."

She hesitated a long moment before saying, "So?"

"So that's a problem."

"Wanna know what *I* think's a problem?"

"What?"

"Somebody watching me when I don't know it."

My fingers flexed around the steering wheel. "Yeah. He was." *And that guy – he'd been watching Cami with far too much interest.*

She said, "I wasn't talking about *him*. I was talking about you. Where were you, anyway?"

"In the same lot," I said. "Three rows back."

She pointed vaguely toward the dashboard. "You mean in *this* vehicle?"

"It's the one I drove, isn't it?"

"I don't know," she said, "because I didn't see it last night."

"Right. Because you weren't looking."

She turned sideways in her seat to face me. "What is this, anyway?"

"What do you think it is?"

"You know, I *really* don't like that."

"You don't like what?"

With obvious annoyance, she said, "When you answer a question with a question."

She could be annoyed all she wanted. I wasn't letting her off the hook. "Wanna know what *I* don't like?"

"No. I don't actually."

I told her anyway. "I don't like the idea of you not being careful."

"Oh yeah?" she said. "And *I* don't see where that's any of your business."

I gave her a long sideways look. "Isn't it?"

Her mouth opened, and then quickly shut again. Abruptly, she turned forward in the seat and said nothing more.

That was fine by me. Because *I* had something to say. And whether she wanted to hear it or not, I was going to tell her.

CHAPTER 11

Cami

Dang it.

I knew exactly what he was getting at. But I still didn't appreciate it.

Last night, I hadn't been his employee. I'd been a girl in my hometown, walking through a parking lot that I'd walked through at least fifty times already.

And yet, I couldn't disagree with the gist of what he was saying. The truth was, I usually paid more attention to my surroundings, especially when I was on my own.

At night.

In a dimly lit parking lot.

With a stranger following after me.

I bit my lip. *I hadn't even seen the guy.*

I hadn't *heard* him either.

Now, I heard myself say, "The guy was probably just walking to his car."

"Probably," Mason agreed. "But that doesn't change the fact that you didn't notice him." A new edge crept into his voice. "And I'll tell you this. *He* noticed *you.*"

I didn't like the way that sounded. But I refused to give Mason the satisfaction. "So?"

"Listen," he said, "we both know you get it, so don't pretend otherwise."

"I'm not pretending anything," I said. "I just think it's none of your business, that's all."

"So I'm hassling you for no reason."

"Oh, so you admit you're hassling me?"

"Hell yeah, I'm hassling you." His voice hardened. "And when you're with Willow, I'll do *more* than hassle you if you're not careful."

Now *that* did it.

Once again, I whirled in the seat to face him. "Was that a threat?"

"No. It's a promise. You mess up with her safety, and you'll be out faster than the last one."

"The last nanny?" I gave a bark of laughter. "So you'll kick me to the curb at three in the morning, huh?"

His voice was deadly calm as he replied, "If it comes to that."

"Oh, please," I said. "What do *you* think? That I'll be taking a grade-schooler to a nightclub? And then, I'll text up a storm in some dark parking lot while Willow's left to fend for herself? Because if that's what you think, you probably shouldn't have hired me in the first place."

In the driver's seat, Mason looked way too composed in the face of my anger. Without so much as a glance in my direction, he said, "You can get pissed all you want, but here's the deal. Starting today, you're gonna be looking after someone who's important to me, which means you'll need to be more vigilant."

I made a sound of annoyance. "Which I *will* be when I'm with her."

"That's all I'm asking." He gave a tight shrug. "What you do on your own time is your own business."

At that moment, I wasn't sure what bothered me more – that he thought so little of my judgment *or* the fact that apparently, I was expendable.

I said, "Oh, really?"

"You're not family, so do what you want." Again, his voice hardened. "On your own time."

Lovely.

It didn't help that his original point was valid.

Yes, I realized that in a small town like Petoskey, the odds of something bad happening were pretty darn low, but I also realized that any expert on self-defense would've agreed with Mason ten times over.

And speaking of defense, I was tired of fending off his attacks.

Without preamble, I launched into my counter-attack. "So tell me. Do *you* ever text in parking lots? Or do you always wait until you're nice and safe inside your vehicle?"

"What *I* do is irrelevant."

"Oh yeah? Why's that?"

"Because if I'm followed, I can handle it."

Dang it.

He was probably right.

Everyone knew that Mason Blastoviak was the kind of person who could handle just about anything.

I knew this from watching the show – and from Arden, who'd told me a little more about his family history.

His parents – first his dad and then his mom – had taken off when Willow hadn't been much older than a baby. And Mason? He'd stepped in to take up the slack.

Under his guidance, his siblings had not only survived, but thrived. Together, the three brothers had built a global tool empire while Willow appeared to be surprisingly well adjusted, all things considered.

Then again, I'd only met her the one time.

Thinking of Willow, I said, "So, about the last nanny, are you going to tell me what happened? Or are you planning to wait until we're actually pulling into the driveway?"

Just then, my cell phone chimed in my pocket. The ringtone was the one I'd assigned to Livia. I could only imagine why she was calling me now.

Last night, I'd left the club without saying goodbye. Then again, so had she. Of course, we'd driven there separately, so it's not like either one of us had ended up stranded or anything.

As far as Livia, she hadn't ended up lonely, that's for sure. After that impromptu make-out session near the Mercedes, she and Chopped Liver had gotten into that same car and driven off to wherever.

Her place?
His place?
Some hotel?

I didn't know, and I tried not to care. Livia wasn't one to play it safe, and besides, she didn't like me nagging *her* any more than I liked Mason nagging *me*.

From the driver's seat, Mason said, "If you want to get that, go ahead."

Nice try, Bucko. "I can't," I replied, "because you were just about to tell me what happened with the nanny."

At the reminder, Mason looked just as thrilled as *I'd* felt about his lecture on parking lot safety. And yet, to his credit, he actually lived up to his end of the bargain and told me what I wanted to know.

CHAPTER 12

Cami

As I listened, Mason explained that he'd caught the last nanny trying to sell pictures of Willow to the media. Apparently, the nanny's treachery was discovered not by Mason himself, but by his brother Chase, who learned of it from one of his media contacts.

Mason's story took only a minute to tell, but when he finished, I was so horrified I could hardly speak.

Bracing myself, I asked, "What kind of pictures?"

"Nothing obscene," he said. "Thank God. But it was bad enough." He went on to explain that the nanny had been offering candid shots of Willow around the house, along with images of Mason himself – shots she'd apparently taken with her cell phone.

"Oh, my God," I said. "That's awful."

"Awful *and* stupid," he said. "She signed a nondisclosure." With a hard look in my direction, he added, "And you'd be smart to remember that."

My jaw dropped. "So you think *I'd* do something like that?"

"Not if you're smart," he said. "You signed the agreement, too. Remember?"

Of course I remembered. Earlier, just before leaving my parent's place, he'd had me sign a document where I agreed to not blab about him or his family. Or at least that was the gist of it, even if the agreement hadn't been worded quite so casually.

Instead, it had been filled with all kinds of legal mumbo-jumbo, warning me of financial and legal retribution if I gave media interviews or shared any private information with the public – including pictures.

From the passenger's seat, I said, "Just so you know, I wouldn't violate your privacy regardless. *Or* Willow's."

"Good. Because if you do, you'll regret it."

"You don't need to warn me," I said. "I'm not that type of person."

"We'll see."

I bristled, "Yeah. You will – and not because I'm afraid of a lawsuit *or* of being kicked out at three in the morning. I won't do it because it's a cruddy thing to do."

In the driver's seat, he said nothing.

"And here's a question," I said. "You said you learned all of this in the middle of the night?"

"That's what I said."

"But why *then?*"

"Because that's when Chase found out."

"But why so late?"

Mason made a sound of disgust. "Because he was banging the reporter."

"Oh." *Pillow talk.* I was embarrassed, but not terribly surprised.

Chase was a notorious womanizer. I knew this from watching the show and from snippets I'd heard from Arden.

But Mason? He was something different entirely. Unlike Chase, he was very private. And yet, Mason *had* been linked with at least two women that I knew of. There was that dance instructor from Chicago and an East Coast fashion model who'd gone off the deep end when Mason had dumped her on New Year's Eve – or at least that was the internet rumor at the time.

In the driver's seat, Mason added, "And as long as we're laying it all on the line, my bedroom's off-limits."

I stiffened. "What?"

"So don't be knocking on my door."

I stared in horrified disbelief. "Your bedroom door? Seriously?"

"Dead serious."

"Just curious," I said with forced civility. "Are you *trying* to insult me?"

"No. I'm trying to save both of us some trouble." He gave me a quick sideways glance. "The knocking – it's happened before."

"Wait, you mean from a nanny?"

"No."

"But—"

"More than one."

"Oh." On one hand, this wasn't surprising. *I mean, just look at the guy.* He was hot as sin, with a gorgeous face and a body to match. On top of *that*, he was rich and famous.

All things considered, was it any wonder that women were beating down his bedroom door?

Still, I heard myself say, "So this happens a lot?"

"You might say that."

By now, I felt so awkward, I hardly knew what to say. *And why was he telling me this at all?*

He didn't think *I* was going to do that, did he?

Going for a joke, I said, "Well, just so you know, I'm allergic to door-knocking."

Mason didn't laugh. He didn't even smile as he said, "Good."

When I said nothing in reply, he turned his head and gave me a look so cold, I almost froze in my seat. "Because I'm telling you in advance, I don't bang the help."

CHAPTER 13

Mason

I felt like a prick for saying it. But it needed to be said – not just to Cami, but to myself.

I liked her. I liked her more than I'd liked anyone in a long time. And, as if that weren't bad enough, I was more attracted to her than was safe.

On the upside, she was looking at me now like she'd rather sleep with a rattlesnake than me.

Good.

Mission accomplished.

From the passenger's seat, she said with slow precision, "The help?"

"Is there a problem?"

She was glaring now. "I can't believe you just called me that."

"Eh, don't worry," I said. "*I've* been called worse."

"Wow, that's a shocker."

I kept my gaze on the road. "Not really."

She made a sound of annoyance. "I was being sarcastic, as you darn well know."

I refused to get riled. "Nice of you to spell it out."

"Hey, *I* thought so," she said. "And let's get one thing straight. If you *ever* plan to call me 'the help' in front of Willow, you might as well turn this car around, *right now.*"

"It's not a car."

"What?"

"It's an SUV."

"I don't care if it's a flying magical bus," she said. "I mean it."

I gave her a sideways glance. *She wasn't bluffing.* Maybe it was time to throw her a bone. "Fair enough."

"I mean it," she said again.

"Yeah. I heard you the first time."

"Well, maybe it bears repeating," she said. "Because if you *ever* treat me with that kind of contempt in front of Willow – *and* if I take it, which I won't – *she'll* have contempt for me too."

"I doubt it."

"And why do you say that?"

"Because she's nicer than I am."

"Yeah," Cami scoffed, "Tell me something I *don't* know."

There was a lot she didn't know. For one thing, she didn't know how beautiful she was, even now, when she looked like she wanted to slap the shit out of me. *Maybe I deserved it.* But I needed her to stick around for the full year, or eleven months, or whatever it was.

I'd been through five nannies in the past two years – four in the past year alone. This wasn't good for anyone, especially my little sister.

And the way *I* saw it, the odds of Cami sticking would be a lot higher if there were no complications between us. *No knocking on my door. No lingering looks over breakfast. No subtle hints or sly innuendos.*

Maybe she wasn't the type. But I'd been surprised before, and never in a good way.

When I replied with only a shrug, Cami said, "And you *do* realize what will happen if you *don't* treat me with respect?"

"What?"

She turned sideways in the seat and gave me a slow, evil smile. "You'll be stuck with Livia."

"The hell I will."

"*Or* someone equally willing to take your crap." Her hands flew to her mouth. "Oh, fudge!"

"What?"

"I don't swear."

I didn't get it. "What do you mean?"

"I mean, I don't curse."

"Yeah, so?"

"So I just did."

I frowned. "Fudge?"

"No." She lowered her voice. "The c-word."

I gave her a long sideways look. "You sure about that? Because if you did, I must've missed it."

She sighed. "I didn't mean the *big* c-word. I meant the *little* c-word."

My eyebrows lifted. "So crap's a swearword now?"

"Well, it *is* on my list."

"Your list of what?"

"Banned words."

For some messed up reason, I wanted to smile. "So who banned them?"

"Me."

"Oh yeah? When?"

"When I decided to become a grade-school teacher."

I made a show of looking toward the back seat. "You see any kids in the back?"

"No. But there *will* be. And that kid'll be *your* sister. Oh sure, she'll say those words eventually. Maybe she already does. But she won't be hearing them from me."

Man, I liked this girl.

Too fucking much.

In Cami's pocket, her cell phone chimed again, interrupting our conversation. This wasn't a bad thing, because the more she talked, the more I liked her – and not as a nanny either.

Shit. Maybe I *should* turn the car around.

Instead, I glanced toward her pocket. "You gonna get that?"

"No. It's just Livia. I'll call her back later."

"Livia – the friend from last night?"

"Yup." Cami blew out a long, shaky breath. "And I know why she's calling."

"Oh yeah? Why?"

"To chew me out."

If that was true, I didn't like it. In a careful voice, I said, "For what?"

"For you, actually."

"Me?"

"Yeah. She was really insulted, I could tell."

"Good," I said.

"But why is that good?"

"Because I meant to insult her."

"Why?"

"Because she had it coming. And you damn well know it."

Cami sank lower in her seat. "Maybe."

I reached toward her and held out my hand, palm up. "If you want, I'll answer."

She glanced down at my hand. "Oh, stop it. You wouldn't."

I kept my hand in place. "Wanna bet?"

"Alright, scratch that," she said. "You probably would. And that's not a good thing."

"Why not?"

"Because you'd probably say something totally rude."

"Got *that* right."

Cami shook her head. "You're not getting it."

I returned my hand to the steering wheel. "Hey, don't say I didn't offer."

"I wasn't talking about the phone," she said. "I *mean* you're not getting the gist of what I'm saying."

"Which is…?"

"That Livia and I have been friends for a long time. Yeah, we don't always see eye to eye. And I know she can be a bit…well, difficult, I guess. But there's a lot of *good* history there, too."

Now *this* I had to hear. "Like what?"

"Well…in grade school, we were best friends." Cami lifted her hands and made little air quotes. "BFF's and all that."

"Best friends forever, huh? How'd *that* work out?"

"Fine. Mostly. And maybe she didn't stay my *very* best friend. But in college, we roomed together my freshman year."

I recalled what I'd seen on the background check. "At Michigan State, right?"

"Right," Cami said. "And she was a good roommate. *And* a good friend. Well, most of the time, anyway."

"She couldn't have been *too* good," I said, "if you only roomed with her the one year."

"Yeah, but that wasn't her fault," Cami said. "I didn't go back after my freshman year." She hesitated. "Well, not until a whole year later."

"Why the gap?" I asked.

"Well…Mom got sick, and I'm one of five kids. Three of them are younger, so I figured I'd take a year off, to help out at home, you know?"

Silently, I considered what she was telling me. I'd met the mom earlier today. She seemed like a nice lady – and perfectly healthy, too. I asked, "How sick was she?"

"At the time, we didn't quite know." Cami bit her lip. "Breast cancer." A note of worry crept into her voice. "Now *that's* a c-word."

I didn't like to see her worried. More softly, I said, "But she's okay now?"

"Oh yeah," Cami said. "But we didn't know it at the time, so…" She shrugged. "Anyway, it all turned out in the end."

"Good." *And I meant it, too.* From what I'd gathered, Cami had come from a decent family, the kind where the parents actually gave a rat's ass about their kids.

It was a long way from my own family history.

But if things worked out, the better dynamics of *Cami's* family just might rub off on my own household.

And soon, they did.

This should've have been a good thing. And it was, especially for Willow. But the longer Cami stayed at my house, the more I wasn't so sure about the rest of it.

Cami might be good for Willow. But as the days turned into weeks, one thing became pretty damn obvious.

She *wasn't* good for *me*.

CHAPTER 14

Cami

I was there for only a month when I started to seriously wonder if I'd made the right decision.

Things were going well. *Almost too well.*

I absolutely adored Willow. She was eight years old and had just started the second grade. She'd spent much of the summer going to a local day-school, where she'd gotten a good head start for the regular school year.

Or more likely, she was simply *that* smart – much like her older brother.

My boss.

My nemesis.

My growing obsession.

I didn't *want* to be obsessed. But the longer I lived there, the more difficult he was to figure out. He was a total hard-ass with everyone but Willow.

When dealing with *her*, he seemed almost human. But when dealing with me, I wasn't sure what he was, except so cold and distant, I might've felt unwelcome, if only he weren't literally paying me to stay.

As far as Willow herself, she had long brown hair and big brown eyes, along with a smattering of freckles across her nose. She loved books, knock-knock jokes, and puzzles of all things.

At night, she devoured books the way some kids devour candy.

She was loads of fun and so eager for someone to love her, it nearly broke my heart.

Sure, she had three older brothers she obviously adored, Mason in particular. But from the first moment I'd walked into his house, it became painfully apparent that Willow had been starved for a mom – or maybe a sister, an aunt, a grandma, or even a female cousin.

She had none of these things.

Now, she had me, but that was hardly the same. I wasn't going to be here forever. *Willow knew this.* And why? It was because I refused to lie to her, that's why. And Mason, to his credit, didn't ask me to.

We didn't dwell on it, but we didn't hide it either. Next year, I'd surely find a teaching job, and Mason would need to find another nanny.

But for now, I was living the kind of life I never would've anticipated.

Mason's home – or more accurately, his mansion – was located on two manicured acres near the mouth of the Saginaw River, within sight of the Saginaw Bay. The house was two stories high and beyond spectacular, with beautiful views from nearly every room.

My own room, complete with its own private bathroom, was located on the second floor right next to Willow's. And even though my room didn't have a view – unless I counted a view of the long, winding driveway – it was nicer than any bedroom I'd ever had before.

On weekdays, Willow was in school until nearly three o'clock, which meant that I had a surprising amount of free time. In fact, I had so much free time, I felt almost guilty.

Watching Willow was no hardship, and I wasn't expected to do much else.

Mason had a housekeeper who did most of the cleaning, a part-time cook who did most of the cooking, and a lawn service that did everything in the yard that needed doing.

Mason paid for everything – the groceries, the utilities, and even gas for my vehicle – okay, not *my* vehicle officially, but rather the one I drove as part of the job.

Turns out, it was the orange SUV he'd driven up to Petoskey, and the vehicle was actually growing on me. It had tons of safety features, and was perfect for shuttling Willow to and from school and to wherever else she needed to go.

In so many ways, I was living the dream.

Except for one thing.

Mason.

The longer I stayed here, the more I couldn't stop thinking about my boss.

Although we never spent time alone, I saw Mason quite a bit while spending time with Willow.

When he was in town, the three of us ate breakfast together – well, whenever Mason didn't go into the office early, that is. We ate dinner together, too, except for all those times when Mason decided to work late.

And then, there were the weekends. Even though Mason was home more frequently on Saturdays and Sundays, he still spent long hours inside his home office while Willow and I did whatever around the house.

We played board games. We baked cookies. We put together lots of puzzles, and read a ton of books. Sometimes, they were the *same* books – kids' books that we'd take turns reading to each other.

Or sometimes, Willow and I would each have our own book, and we'd lounge side-by-side on the couch or, weather-permitting, out on the back patio, reading in easy silence.

But when it came to Mason, there was nothing easy about *him*.

He made me think of things I shouldn't, *dangerous* things that only fueled my fascination, especially one Saturday night, when I happened to catch him alone for the first time since my arrival.

CHAPTER 15

Mason

With a quiet curse, I stopped in the kitchen doorway.

Cami looked up. At the sight of me, she froze like I'd just caught her stealing the silverware. She was standing in front of the fridge, holding a pint of ice cream in one hand and a spoon in the other. "Oh, hi." She winced. "I didn't wake you, did I?"

She had, but not in the way she thought. Choosing to keep it simple, I replied to the gist of her question. "No."

My bedroom was located a long way from the kitchen *and* insulated for sound. But it didn't matter. Lately I hadn't been sleeping so great, tossing and turning in my oversized bed. And the reason for *this* was standing a few strides away.

The time was just past midnight, and Cami was wearing little white shorts and a thin pink T-shirt. Her hair was tousled, and her face was scrubbed clean of all makeup.

The lack of makeup wasn't a surprise, and her face didn't look much different than it had over dinner with me and Willow.

Unlike the last few nannies, Cami favored a more natural look.

I liked it.

In more bad news, it wasn't the only thing I liked, especially now as I eyed her from across the kitchen. Her clothes – they were skimpy enough to sleep in.

Hell, maybe she *did* sleep in them.

In her bed.

Just down the hall from my own.

Fuck.

Now *that* was a thought I didn't need.

From the open doorway, I told her, "I came down for water."

She glanced down at the pint of ice cream of her hand. The pint wasn't yet open, and she'd wrapped a paper towel around its exterior, as if to protect her hands from the cold, or maybe to catch any condensation.

Either way, she looked cute as hell.

With a sheepish smile, she said, "Yeah, me too." She lifted the pint of ice cream in a mock toast. "Honest."

I was so distracted by the sight of her, I'd lost track of the conversation. But hell if I'd let *her* see it. With a tight shrug, I replied, "Oh yeah?"

She gave a solemn nod. "Sure, but here's the crazy thing. When I reached for the water, the pint of ice cream jumped right into my hand." In a stage whisper, she added, "I think it might've bit me."

I wanted to smile. But it wouldn't be smart, so I didn't. "Is that so?"

Her own smile faded. "Maybe."

And now I felt like a dick for not giving in to the joke. But Cami was dangerous even if she didn't know it.

I'd brought her here for Willow, not for myself. The only problem was, I was having a hard time remembering that.

I was wearing dark running pants and a basic white T-shirt. This wasn't what I slept in, but it *was* what I wore when I ventured out of my bedroom at night.

The truth was, I slept naked. Lately, that was a problem, too, because being naked in the house, even behind a locked door, was a troublesome reminder that Cami the Nanny might be naked, too.

And just down the hall.

As the thought crossed my brain, I felt the brain down below begin to stir. *Shit.*

I shifted my stance. *It was time to get out of here, and fast.*

Deliberately, I moved toward the fridge. As I did, Cami stepped aside, clearing my path to claim what I wanted.

Water.

And only water.

Striding past her, I opened the fridge and reached inside. I grabbed a bottle of water and made a mental note to begin storing some in my bedroom.

I didn't care if they were cold. Better to drink it at room temperature than to risk being alone with Cami.

The habit wasn't a new one. I'd done similar things with the other nannies, too.

I'd avoided them when I could, and kept a safe distance when I couldn't. But with them, the dynamics had been the polar opposite.

With them, the goal had been to keep their focus elsewhere – on Willow and not on me.

But with Cami, the problem was on my end, not hers.

And it *was* a problem. The biggest kick was, it wasn't going away. *It was only growing larger.*

She wasn't going away either, not if *I* could help it.

She was great with Willow and no slacker in the nanny department. During the last month, I'd noticed more than she realized – the laughter coming from the kitchen, the sounds of their voices as they read to each other on the sofa, the giggles on both sides as they told each other the dumbest jokes.

Willow was happier than I'd seen her in years. *But me?*

I didn't know what I felt. But it wasn't happiness.

I opened the bottle of water and turned to go. As I did, Cami said, "Wait."

I stopped to give her a look. "Yeah?"

She lifted the pint of ice cream in her hand. "I think I owe you for this."

I wasn't following. "How so?"

"Well, the first couple of pints I bought on my own when I hit the grocery store. But ever since then, it's been showing up in the freezer." She gave the pint a worried glance. "And I know I'm the only one who eats this, so I'm wondering if I should start keeping track or something."

"Why?"

"*You* know, so you're not stuck paying for my extras."

I wasn't stuck. And I wasn't worried. During Cami's first week, I'd asked the cook and the housekeeper to make a note of anything new in need of stocking, and to add it to the list. Apparently, they'd noticed the ice cream and acted accordingly.

It was good to know they were doing their jobs, but I still didn't see the problem.

I told Cami, "Trust me, I can afford it." *And I could.* Hell, with as much money as I was making now, I could buy the whole damn ice cream factory and call it good.

But here in the kitchen, Cami said, "I know you can afford it. I'm just saying, I don't want to take advantage, that's all."

Now, I couldn't decide if I was pissed off or touched. It had been a long time since anyone had worried about, in Cami's words, "taking advantage."

It didn't matter. I was perfectly capable of looking after my own interests. No one – and I mean, *no one* – took advantage of me *or* my family, not if I could help it.

I replied, "Wanna know what I want?"

"What?"

"For you to stop worrying about it." And with that, I turned to go.

I'd taken maybe two steps when Cami said, "Sorry, but I've got another question."

I stopped and gave her another look. I had questions, too. Like right now, I was questioning whether she realized that either her T-shirt was too thin or the temperature was too cold.

Through the pale pink cotton, I could see the faint outlines of her nipples, straining against the thin fabric. I wouldn't call it obscene, not here in private where she probably hadn't counted on company. But it was a distraction – one that I tried like hell not to notice.

But I *was* noticing.

She wasn't wearing a bra.

Huh. Maybe she *was* dressed for bed.

Silently, I compared Cami's appearance with that of the last nanny. That one had tried to get sexy. But Cami – she was sexy without even trying.

The real kicker was, it wasn't just her looks. It was the sound of her voice, the intelligence in her eyes, and the way her lips twitched when she tried not to laugh.

But she wasn't laughing now. With a little frown, she said, "So…should I ask it?"

I stiffened. *Shit.*

I'd gotten lost in my thoughts again. It was becoming a bad habit – one I thought I'd given up as a kid. And I hadn't been one of *those* since I'd been maybe ten years old.

In the kitchen, I made a forwarding motion with my hand. "Go ahead. Ask."

"Well…I'm just wondering, what's your policy on guests?"

My shoulders tightened. "My policy?"

"Yeah, I mean it's your house and all, but I was wondering if I could have someone over."

My jaw clenched. *Who? Some guy?*

In a careful voice, I replied, "It depends."

"On what?"

I gave her a hard look. "Who the guest is." As I said it, I envisioned Cami in her bedroom, looking like she looked now, all tousled and sexy – *and* with a guy who wasn't me.

I didn't like it.

Before she could get any ideas, I added, "But if you're looking to have a sleepover, forget it."

She frowned. "A sleepover? You mean like in high school, or…" Her words trailed off, and a slow blush crept up her cheeks. "Wait, you think I was asking to bring a *date* home? Like overnight?"

Home.

From *her*, the word sounded nice. But her expression wasn't as she continued, "Just what do you think I'm asking, anyway?"

"You tell me."

Her eyes narrowed. "I was *asking* if I could invite Arden over for coffee."

Something in my shoulders eased, and that, too, pissed me off. "She's a relative," I said. "You don't need to ask."

Cami's chin lifted. "But a few weeks ago, you reminded me that she wasn't a relative yet, so *maybe* I wanted to make sure."

"And you did. Anything else?"

She was glaring now. "No."

"Good," I said. "Because I leave tomorrow for Columbus. And when I'm gone, remember, no overnight guests."

She made a sound of annoyance. "Just what do you think I'm gonna do, anyway?"

"Don't know, don't care." I gave her a final hard look. "So long as you do it somewhere else."

CHAPTER 16

Cami

I gave Arden an exasperated look. "I think he hates me."

Arden was petite with long, dark hair and eyes that hid nothing. Those eyes filled with sympathy as she said, "Don't worry. He hates everyone."

I saw what she meant. Still, I had to say, "Not *absolutely* everyone."

"Okay, he hates everyone but his siblings."

Now this, I believed.

After he'd given me that unexpected warning about having overnight guests, he'd turned and left the kitchen without so much as a goodnight. And now, he was out of state on business – something to do with their newest factory in Ohio.

I hadn't seen him since that unsettling encounter, which was probably a good thing, considering how distracted he made me feel, even now while I was having coffee with my best friend.

We were sitting at the small table in Mason's breakfast nook, and I'd just poured each of us another cup of coffee. With a sigh, I said, "And sometimes, I swear, I hate him right back."

It was just past noon, and I still had nearly three hours until I needed to pick up Willow from school. Until then, I had the whole house to myself.

During the past month, Arden and I had been meeting for coffee at least a couple of times a week whenever she wasn't traveling, but this was the first time I'd actually invited her over to Mason's place.

From the other side of the table, she gave me a long, penetrating look. "Are you sure?"

"What do you mean?"

"Well, sometimes, it almost seems like you like him." She winced. "I mean, romantically."

I drew back. "Me? No. Definitely not." I hesitated. "I mean, sure, he's attractive, and really interesting. And smart, too, but…well, that doesn't mean I like him."

Arden groaned, "Oh, my God. You have a crush on him."

"Oh, please. I do not." Of this, I was absolutely certain – or at least mostly certain. *Okay, somewhat certain.*

Sounding less than convinced, Arden said, "Are you sure?"

"Mostly." I tried to laugh. "To have a crush, you're supposed to like someone, remember?"

"Yeah, so?"

"So he's not exactly likeable." I paused to think. "I mean, he's great to Willow, and he's been a really generous employer."

I glanced around, taking in my luxurious surroundings. Even the breakfast nook, as cozy as it was, took up twice the space of my last kitchen and was ten times nicer. "And really, the job's not even hard."

Arden stared across the table. "You can't be serious."

"Why not?"

"Because the job *must* be hard if the nannies keep getting fired."

I saw her point. But unlike me, she didn't have the full story. In at least two cases, the nannies had been fired because they'd been, well, naughty I guess.

But was it any wonder?

Mason had it all – looks, money, and more fame than he obviously wanted. On top of that, he was quite simply the most intriguing person I'd ever met.

If it weren't for Willow, I might've said he had no heart. But sometimes, like when I saw him smile at his little sister, I couldn't help but wonder if there was a softer side buried somewhere deep inside him.

Across from me, Arden continued. "And he's been through four nannies in the past year alone. Do you realize, that's a new nanny every three months?"

It was a sobering reminder. If I followed the trend, this meant I had only two months before I, too, was kicked to the curb.

But that wasn't going to happen, because for one thing, I wasn't going to get naughty with anyone, especially Mason Blastoviak – even if the thought was stupidly appealing.

Absently, I replied, "Yeah, well…maybe he's had bad luck."

"But it's not just the nannies he has trouble with. Everybody's scared of him. When he walks into the office, people literally tremble."

Sometimes, I almost trembled, too, but in a totally different way. Regardless, I wasn't scared, not unless I counted my primal reaction to him, which was only *slightly* terrifying.

Across from me, Arden added, "But he *is* great with Willow, so that's something, I guess."

"Which reminds me," I said. "I've got a question. When you and I first met Willow, before we even realized who she was, she told us that Mason was her dad. But she doesn't call him Dad. She calls him Mason."

"Yeah, I know."

I felt my brow wrinkle in confusion. "But a while back, you told me that she begged Mason to let her call him Dad, and that he agreed."

"Oh, *that*." Arden, leaned forward. "It was when Willow was in pre-school. They were doing this Father's Day thing, and of course, Willow *has* no father."

"Right. Because he died."

"He didn't just die," Arden said. "He took off for good while their mom was still pregnant."

I'd known this, but it still made me angry. And yet, there was something I didn't quite get. "For good? What do you mean?"

"Apparently, he was always leaving and coming back. But the way Brody talks, he was gone a lot more than he was around."

I frowned. "What a lunk-blaster."

"Yeah. No kidding," she said. "And then, he dies in a car crash when Willow's barely a year old, right after the mom takes off, too."

Even though I knew the story, it still made me sad to think of everything those kids had gone through – and yes, even Mason.

At the table, Arden continued. "So the way Brody tells it, Willow came home crying in preschool, saying that *she* wanted a dad, too. And she asked Mason if *he'd* be her dad."

The thought nearly broke my heart. "And what'd he tell her?"

"What he tells her is that he's her brother, not her dad, but he loves her like his own daughter, and if she ever wants to call him Dad, that's fine by him."

Hearing this, my heart warmed for both of them. Still, I had to say, "But she doesn't – call him Dad, I mean."

"Well not to him directly," Arden said. "But when she's talking to other people, especially people she doesn't know very well, she calls him that as sort of a shortcut."

I saw what she meant. "Oh. So she doesn't have to explain her family history?"

"That's *my* guess," Arden said.

The theory made sense. And later that night, when I'd almost decided that I had their family dynamics all figured out, Willow herself told me something that opened up a whole new line of thought.

And I wasn't quite sure how I felt about it.

CHAPTER 17

Cami

Willow gave me a crooked grin. "Guess what I got for my *last* birthday."

We'd finished dinner maybe an hour ago, and the two of us were lounging side-by-side out on the back patio, overlooking the river.

It was almost November, and the air was cool and brisk. But the patio had become one of our favorite spots, so here we were, bundled up in sweaters and blankets, drinking hot cocoa and enjoying the view.

We'd been talking about our favorite holidays, which had led to the subject of birthdays and favorite presents.

Before I had the chance to guess Willow's latest birthday gift, she added, "And just so you know, it was one of my favorites."

"A favorite gift, huh?" I pretended to think. "Was it a…. giant squid?"

She giggled. "No. I don't want a squid, Silly."

I smiled. "Can you give me a hint?"

"What kind of hint?" she asked.

"Okay, how about this?" I pulled out my best horror-show voice. "Is it alive?"

She nodded. "Yup."

Huh. Now that was unexpected. She had no pets, so I couldn't imagine what she meant. But we both loved guessing games, especially when they turned ridiculous, so I asked, "Was it a dinosaur?"

She giggled again. "Dinosaurs aren't real."

I furrowed my eyebrows in mock concentration. "Hmmm…Then I guess a unicorn is out of the question."

With a little frown, she said, "You never know. Those *might* be real."

If only.

I said, "Okay, give me another hint. Like…how many legs does it have?"

She glanced down toward my feet. "Two."

I froze. *She couldn't mean me?* But then, realizing how ridiculous the mere thought was, I silently classified it in the same category as the unicorn and teased, "Was it…*meeeeeee?*"

She nodded. "Yup!"

I blinked. "Seriously?"

She flashed me another grin. "Oh yeah. And you were the only thing I asked for. Ask Mason. *He'll* tell you."

Now, I hardly knew what to say. I was so touched, my eyes grew misty even as I marveled at the new information. *So that's why Mason had recruited me?*

No wonder he wouldn't take no for an answer.

Next to me, Willow said, "I got other presents, too. But you were still my favorite, even if you got here late."

Her birthday was September 17th. I considered the timing of Mason's trip to Petoskey. Now that I thought about it, he *had* shown up only a few days after Willow's birthday.

Absently, I murmured, "So, I was a week late, huh?"

"Oh yeah," she said. "But I didn't mind. Honest."

"Awwww…" With a smile, I reached out and gave Willow's hand a gentle squeeze. "I'm really honored. I've never been anyone's birthday present before."

Even though I was truly touched, this new information made me feel just a little bit funny. Why, I wasn't even sure.

Was it because I'd be leaving someday, and I was worried how Willow would take it?

Or maybe it was because this meant that Mason had hired me *not* because he thought I'd do a good job, but rather because Willow had requested me personally.

I mean, seriously, how could he say no?

I was still mulling all of this over when the sounds of yelling erupted from the other side of the river.

I couldn't tell *who* was yelling, but it sounded like a family argument. And it was coming from the big, glorious mansion directly across from us. The home was ultra-stylish, with lots of balconies, elaborate landscaping, and a huge back patio.

Next to me, Willow said, "You just wait. They'll come outside in a minute."

"Who?" I asked.

"The people across the street."

I shook my head. "The street?"

She pointed toward the river. "The river street. Where the boats go."

"Oh."

"On the *regular* street," she continued, "we don't have anyone living across from us." She grimaced. "But on the river street, we've got *them.*"

She said "them" like it was a pack of child-eating monsters.

True to her prediction, less than thirty seconds passed before a couple of teenagers – a girl and a boy – erupted from the patio door. As they did, the girl – a spiky-haired brunette who appeared to be about seventeen – turned and hollered back toward the house, "You're not the boss of me!"

I winced. *Talk about a cliché.*

The boy, a stocky kid with longish brown hair, chimed in, "Yeah! Up yours, loser!"

Next to me, Willow said, "They're yelling at the nanny."

"How do you know?"

Her voice grew solemn. "Because they *always* yell at the nanny."

I frowned. "Aren't they a little old to have a nanny?"

"Well, yeah," Willow said. "But I'm a little old, too. So I guess it's okay."

At this, I had to smile. "Well, you *are* eight now."

"Oh, I know," she said. "That's why I asked for you. I didn't want to be treated like a baby anymore."

I was just about to reply when a third person erupted from the same mansion. It was a young woman around my own age. She was very pretty with ice blonde hair pulled back into a tight bun. She was wearing a black dress that looked almost like a maid's uniform. Her face was flushed, and the front of her dress was covered in what looked like…? I frowned. "Is that breakfast cereal?"

Willow said, "Yup."

I shook my head. "But, it's not even breakfast time."

"I know," Willow said. "That's what makes it so interesting."

That was *one* way to put it. "Oh?"

Willow nodded. "But sometimes, they hit her with oatmeal."

"Seriously?" I was so stunned, I didn't know what to say. "And she puts up with it?"

"It's not always *her*," Willow said.

I frowned in confusion. "You mean, like, they have more than one nanny?"

"No. I mean the nannies keep changing."

"Oh. I can see why." I bit my lip. "You know what? I think we should go inside."

"But why?" Willow said. "If it's because of them, don't worry. They'll go back in a minute."

Again, I asked, "How do you know?"

"Because it's just a trick to lock her out."

"You mean the nanny?"

"Oh yeah," Willow said. "You just watch."

Sure enough, the two teenagers dodged around the nanny, raced back into the house, and slammed the patio door shut behind them.

When the nanny marched to the same door and yanked at the doorknob, nothing happened.

She pounded on the door and called out, "Hey! You didn't lock me out, did you?" She gave another frantic tug at the knob. "Open up! I mean it!"

I looked to Willow. "Do you think we should call someone?"

Yes, I realized I was asking an eight-year-old for advice, but the truth was, she seemed far better informed than I'd ever be.

With a little shrug, she replied, "Nah. She'll just go through the window."

"What window?"

Willow pointed toward a low window near the back corner of the house. "That one."

"How do you know?" I asked.

"Because that's what they always do. You just wait."

In morbid fascination, I watched as the nanny checked several windows one after another. Finding them all locked, she kept on going until she reached the same window that Willow had indicated earlier.

When the nanny tried *this* window, it opened up on the first try. With obvious relief, she yanked it all the way up and shimmied back into the house, leaving us staring after her.

As she turned and shut the window behind her, I blew out a long, shaky breath. *The poor nanny.*

I turned to look at Willow. With an awkward laugh, I said, "Hey, guess what *I'm* thankful for."

"What?" Willow asked.

I reached out and gave her a playful tap to the tip of her nose. "You."

She grinned. "Really?"

"Oh, yeah." And I meant it, too. I *really* liked her, and not only because she had never locked me out of the house. For some reason, she and I just clicked.

The truth was, this wasn't feeling like a job at all, even if the guy who employed me was a different matter entirely – as I soon learned when I asked him about the birthday thing.

CHAPTER 18

Cami

Mason gave me a hard look. "Was that a serious question?"

It was nine o'clock in the morning, and I'd just returned from taking Willow to school. I'd parked in the attached garage like I always did, and had entered the house expecting to find myself alone.

I couldn't have been more wrong.

When I entered the kitchen, I'd spotted Mason near the fridge, dressed in tailored slacks and a thin white T-shirt. At the sight of me, he'd frowned like I'd just barged into his bedroom uninvited.

And me? I'd blurted out the first thing that had popped into my head, or rather the *second* thing, considering that the *first* thing was a totally inappropriate observation that he looked way too fine standing there only semi-dressed.

I replied, "Of course it was a serious question. So…Was I? Her birthday present, I mean?"

His mouth tightened. "No."

I waited, wondering what he'd say next. And when he said nothing, I refused to let it drop. "Just so you know, she told me to ask you, so I'm not breaking her confidence, if that's what you're worried about."

His eyebrows lifted. "Do I look worried?"

No. He looked like the kind of guy who made girls swoon, even while standing in the kitchen.

How unfair was that?

From what I could tell, he was wearing the lower half of a business suit, along with the T-shirt that would go underneath his dress shirt, and then eventually his jacket and tie.

What did this mean?

Was he halfway dressed? Or halfway undressed?

According to his schedule, he was supposed to be returning from Ohio later on tonight. But instead, here he was, looking good enough to eat.

From watching him on TV, I'd seen him wearing clothes that weren't terribly different – meaning jeans and a thin T-shirt.

On the show, he'd looked spectacular, whether he was swinging a hammer or glowering at whatever poor slob happened to cross his path.

And now, he was glowering at me.

The only problem was, he was the kind of guy who made glowering look sexy. His hair was tousled, and his eyes were dark and brooding, the kind of eyes a girl couldn't get lost in, if she wasn't careful.

His gaze locked on mine as he said, "Do I?"

I blinked. "Do you what?"

"Look worried."

Oh, crud. Once again, I'd lost track of the conversation. With renewed focus, I replied, "No. But you *do* look irritated."

"Good call." As he said it, he crossed his arms, making his biceps bulge in a way that didn't help my concentration.

Still, I tried again. "At least tell me this. Did she *ask* for me as a birthday present?"

"She did."

I almost sighed in relief. At last, we were getting somewhere. "So, *that's* why you hired me?"

"No. Just like I said."

Oh. I guess he did. And yet, I remained oddly unsatisfied. Or maybe my dissatisfaction stemmed from something else entirely, like his T-shirt. It was definitely a problem.

The thin cotton clung too perfectly to his pecs, showing off muscles so fine, I was trying hard not to stare. On top of that, his biceps were pumped, and his six-pack was so perfect, the thin fabric of his shirt did little to disguise all of those interesting lines and ridges.

And now I was pretty sure I was staring.

With a start, I yanked my gaze upward. "Yeah, I know you said that, but I feel like I'm missing something." I gave him a pleading look. "I know you probably think I'm just being nosy, but I'm trying to understand the family dynamics here."

When his only reply was a cold look, I summoned up an encouraging smile. "I *like* Willow. I like her a lot. But I need to know who hired me. Was it her? Or you?"

"And here's *my* question," he said. "Who signs your check?"

My chin lifted. "No one. Your bookkeeper set up direct deposit." I tried for a smirk. "Remember?"

"And the bonus check?"

My smirk faded as I recalled the check he'd given me during the drive from Petoskey. "Well, yeah. I guess you signed *that* one."

"Right."

"Okay, fine," I sighed. "If you don't want to tell me, that's your decision, but I really *do* care about Willow. And I *know* you do, too, so I figured we could have a reasonable discussion about it. That's all."

He gave me a look. "Reasonable? Or intrusive?"

"Oh, please. What's so intrusive about it? Nothing. That's what."

"Not the way *I* see it." And with that, he turned away, heading out of the kitchen.

He'd barely reached the doorway when a horrible thought occurred to me. As the blood drained from my face, I called out, "Wait!"

Slowly, he turned back. With an obvious lack of enthusiasm, he said, "What now?"

"I need to know something."

"Again?"

I almost rolled my eyes. "Yes. *Again*. Even though you barely answered my first question." I strode forward until we were standing within arm's reach. "Is Willow in trouble?"

"What?" He stiffened. "What happened?"

"Nothing happened," I said. "I just want to make sure that I didn't get her in hot water by asking about the birthday thing." I winced. "I mean, you're not going to yell at her or anything, are you?"

He visibly relaxed. "I don't yell."

"Alright, fine," I said. "You're not gonna give *her* that look, are you?"

"What look?"

"The one you're giving me now." I crossed my arms. "Because I've got to tell you, it's a little scary."

He was silent for a long moment as our gazes locked and held. And even though I had to crane my neck to stare up at him, I refused to look away. *Who knows?* Maybe I didn't *want* to look away.

In the light of the kitchen, I could see the flecks of brown in his dark, compelling eyes. *Oh yeah. A girl could definitely get lost in them.*

And then, he did the strangest thing. He *almost* smiled. "You can't be too scared," he said. "You're still here."

I was so startled by the near-smile, I blinked in sudden confusion. "Well, yeah," I stammered, "because I'd rather have you glaring at *me* than at her."

Slowly, his gaze dipped to my lips, and I felt my knees go wobbly for reasons I couldn't quite decipher.

In a quieter voice, he said, "I'm not glaring."

It was true. He wasn't. Not anymore. As far as my own face, I had no idea what it was doing, because my emotions were swinging so wildly from irritation to something I didn't dare consider.

How could one guy make me feel so many conflicting emotions?

And now, I didn't know what to say. So I said nothing as my pulse quickened and my skin grew warm.

In the end, it was Mason who broke the silence. "Don't worry," he said. "*She's* not the one in trouble."

Somehow, I managed to ask, "Then who is?"

With a low scoff, he replied, "Me." And with that, he turned and walked away, leaving me staring after him, wondering what on Earth had just happened – and whether it would happen again.

CHAPTER 19

Mason

I walked into my office to find my brother Chase sitting behind my desk. He was leaning back in my chair, with his hands clasped behind his head and his heels resting on the mahogany desktop.

I stopped just inside the open doorway and gave him a look. "What?"

He didn't move an inch. "What do you mean, what?"

"What are you doing here?"

He grinned. "I work here."

Yes. He did. Chase was the company's driving force when it came to marketing and publicity. If I were in the mood to give him credit – which I wasn't – I might've acknowledged the fact that he was the reason our sales had exploded during the last few years.

Among other stunts, he was the one who'd come up with the idea for *Blast*, the surprisingly popular reality show that aired weekly on the Home Network. The show starred my youngest brother, Brody, along with me and Chase, as we used our own brand of tools to restore old houses or sometimes build new ones.

I fucking hated it.

It's not that I minded getting dirty or working with my hands. That part, I liked. But the personal publicity? *It wasn't my thing.*

Fame was a pain in the ass – one I didn't want or need. Me, I liked to fly under the radar, to see rather than be observed, to listen rather than be overheard, and to associate with whoever I wanted without wondering what the hell they were after.

But Chase? He didn't mind the spotlight – or the abundance of star-fuckers, providing they had the looks to match.

Chase was the face of the company.

Much like myself, he was six foot two, with dark hair and a muscular build. But *unlike* me, he was what you'd call a people person – the kind of guy who shook hands and smiled for the cameras. He dressed sharp, talked smooth, and made people feel like they really knew him.

They didn't.

But *I* did, which is how I knew he was here for a reason – and it wasn't to warm his ass in my seat.

I got straight to the point. "Whatever it is, spit it out."

"What do you mean?"

"You've got news," I said. "So go ahead, tell me."

"Don't you wanna sit down?"

I gave him a pointed look. "Yeah. As soon as you get out of my chair."

Finally, he removed his feet from my desktop and stood. With a shit-eating grin, he circled my desk and claimed one of the visitor's chairs, where he promptly leaned back and returned his feet to the desktop.

It was vintage Chase. He'd been goading me since he was eight – the same age as Willow, but with a lot more attitude.

As I reclaimed my seat, I made a forwarding motion with my hand. "Whatever it is, just say it."

"Alright," he said. "Guess who just left."

"You mean the building?"

"The building *and* my office."

Chase's office was just down the hall, here at the company headquarters, which was located on the top floor of our largest factory. On any given day, hundreds of people might be coming or going.

I replied, "I have no idea."

"I'll give you a hint," Chase said. "You fired her this past summer."

I frowned. "You don't mean Veronica?"

Veronica had been the nanny for three months until she'd been fired for losing track of Willow. On the upside, she'd been one of the few nannies who hadn't tried to get into my pants. I'd been suitably impressed until I discovered the reason for her prim and proper attitude.

Turns out, she'd been getting naked with my brother – the one now sitting in my visitor's chair.

The reminder didn't make me happy. "So, did you fuck her?"

He grinned. "You mean today, or…?"

"Yeah. Today."

He gave it some thought. "I could've. Trust me, she was more than willing." He chuckled. "And get this. She wasn't wearing panties."

Veronica was a leggy brunette with a pretty face and a body to match. But that didn't mean I wanted her flashing her privates in *my* building.

In a tight voice, I said, "And you know this, how?"

"Eh, she dropped her purse, bent over to get it…" He shrugged. "You know, the usual."

Not in *my* world, it wasn't. Yeah, I had plenty of offers, but the day *anyone* felt comfortable enough to flash their ass in my office would be the day I knew I was losing my touch.

At work, I was all business, as everyone damn well knew – or rather everyone except for Chase, who seemed determined to make me lose it.

It hadn't happened yet, and it wasn't going to happen today.

I listened in silent resignation as he detailed the shape of her ass and the rose tattoo on her right butt cheek.

When he finished, I said, "And you're telling me this, why?"

"Because I figured you'd want to know."

"Yeah, well I *don't*."

"But you'll want to know *this*." He removed his feet from my desk and leaned forward in the chair. "I wasn't her first stop."

"Meaning?"

"Before she came to see *me*, she went to see Willow."

I stiffened. "What? Where?"

"At the school, a few hours ago, when Willow was just getting out."

"Shit." I got to my feet. "I've gotta go."

Chase laughed. "Why?"

"To check on Willow."

"Relax, she's fine." Chase pointed toward my now-empty seat. "Sit. I'll tell you the rest."

I remained standing. "There's more?"

"Oh yeah. And let's just say, it wasn't *Willow* who cried in my office."

"What?"

"It was Veronica."

"Yeah, so?" *Veronica wasn't family.* She could cry all she wanted. She'd be getting no sympathy from me. Looking to make a point, I said, "Was that *before* or *after* she flashed you?"

"After." Chase paused. "No, wait. Before."

Oh, for fuck's sake. "So let me get this straight," I said. "She cried first and flashed you second?"

"Pretty much."

"She was playing you," I said. "You know that, right?"

"No. She was *trying* to play me. Big difference."

"Not if you're in here, pleading her case."

Chase laughed. "That's not why I'm here."

Yeah, right. "It's not?"

"For your information," he said, "I'm here to tell you what the *new* nanny did."

Suddenly, I was all ears. "Cami? What'd she do?"

"The way I hear it, she gave Veronica a good ass-chewing. And more."

I sank back into my chair and stared across the desk. "You're joking."

"No joke," Chase said. "Just listen. Veronica goes to Willow's school, thinking she'll wander up and say hi—"

"Wait. Why would she do that?"

"Because," Chase said, "she wants her old job back."

That wasn't gonna happen. "Is she nuts?"

Chase smiled. "Hell yeah, she's nuts."

"In case you don't know," I said, "that's not a mark in her favor."

"Yeah, well...I guess it depends on what you're doing."

Knowing Chase, he'd done plenty. I replied, "So I hear."

Chase reached up to tug at his collar. "Anyway, the way Veronica sees it, it's been a few months, so she figures you're due to fire the next nanny."

Nope.

Not a chance.

It had been only a week since Cami and I had talked in the kitchen. And yeah, she was still making me crazy, but that didn't mean she was going anywhere, not if I could help it.

To Chase, I replied, "Is that so?"

"Sure," he said. "Personally, I thought she showed initiative."

"Veronica?" I gave him a hard look. "No. She showed you her ass. Big difference."

"Not *just* her ass," Chase said. "Did I mention she wasn't wearing a bra?"

"No."

"Well, the thing is—"

"I don't wanna hear it," I said. "Tell me what happened at the school."

"Alright," Chase said looking decidedly disgruntled. "So, you know how the parents walk up and get the kids, right?"

"Yeah?"

"Well, when the new nanny –"

"Cami."

Chase brightened. "Yeah. Cami the Nanny. It has a nice ring, doesn't it?"

It did. But hell if I'd admit it. "Go on," I said.

"So they're at the nanny-mobile, and–"

"The what?"

"The thing the nanny drives – that orange SUV."

It wasn't a "nanny-mobile." It was the vehicle Cami drove to make sure Willow safely arrived wherever she needed to go. It was also what Cami drove whenever she had an errand of her own.

It was a basic company vehicle, not too fast and exceptionally safe. I'd had it painted orange so it would be easy to spot in a pinch.

The funny thing was, Cami looked cute as hell driving it.

She didn't look like a nanny. She looked like a college co-ed or the girl next door, the one you couldn't stop thinking about, no matter how hard you tried.

Lately, I'd been thinking about her a lot. *It was a problem.* Even worse, she wasn't living next door. She was living in my house.

It was making me nuts.

Chase was still talking. "So Veronica catches up with Willow and Cami as they're getting into the nanny-mobile. And she explains to Cami that she's living nearby and wanted to say 'hi' to Willow, you know for old time's sake."

I didn't like where this was going. "And Cami *let* her?"

"Yeah, for maybe two minutes."

"What do you mean?"

"This is where it gets good," Chase said. "So, after a minute or two, Cami tells Veronica that they're running late, and she cuts the visit short."

I frowned. "Not short enough."

"Not the way Veronica tells it," Chase said. "Anyway, Cami gets Willow settled in the back seat, all calm and friendly like the three of them are best buddies. But as soon the door shuts behind her—"

"You mean Willow."

"Right. Cami and Veronica are still outside."

I could almost see it. "Go on."

"So Cami pulls Veronica aside – *behind* the vehicle, where Willow can't see – and she tells Veronica that if she ever bothers Willow again, she'll have her hiney hauled away, pronto."

I paused. "Hiney?"

"It's another word for 'ass.'"

"I *know* what 'hiney' means."

"Are you sure?" Chase said. "Because you look confused."

I wasn't confused. I was unsettled, even more so when Chase went on to tell me that somewhere along the way, Cami called Veronica a "lunk-blaster" and kicked her in the shin.

I waited several beats before asking, "Why the shin?"

"Hell if *I* know," Chase said. "Why the lunk-blaster? What the fuck *is* that, anyway?"

Now it was *my* turn to say it. "Hell if *I* know."

"Well, it wasn't a compliment."

No shit, Sherlock. "What gave it away?" I said. "The kick?"

"According to Veronica, there wasn't just kicking." Chase grinned. "There was slapping, too."

What the hell? "Who slapped who?"

"Does it matter?" He was still grinning. "Man, I would've loved to see *that*."

Not me.

Not with Cami involved.

Under my breath, I said, "That makes *one* of us."

Chase reached up to stroke his chin. "That Cami, she's pretty hot, huh?"

I felt my body go rigid. "What?"

"I'm just saying, she's got that girl-next-door look."

I'd noticed. But the fact that Chase had noticed, too, well, I didn't like it. I said, "How would *you* know?"

"I met her at the coffee shop."

I stared across the desk. *So she'd had coffee with my brother?*
And no one had thought to mention it?

In a tight voice, I asked, "And when was this?"

"A couple days ago." Again, Chase leaned forward. "So, she's a real spitfire, huh?"

Cami the Nanny? She was *something*. I just didn't know what.

I told Chase, "She's the nanny, not a notch in your bedpost."

"Well, not yet."

I felt my fingers tighten into fists. "Look, you've fucked two already. Isn't that enough?"

"Hey, don't blame *me*," he laughed. "*They* offered."

Cami wouldn't offer.

Would she?

No.

And yet, I silently asked myself, "*What if she did?*"

The thought bothered me more than it should've. And *that* bothered me, too.

Fuck. These days, everything bothered me. And the lack of sleep wasn't helping.

I stood. "Are we done?"

Chase remained sitting. "Why? You in a hurry?"

Oh, yeah.

I was *now*.

I needed answers, and I knew just where to get them. And it wasn't here at the office.

CHAPTER 20

Cami

I knew something was up the moment he walked into the kitchen. Willow was sitting at the kitchen table doing her homework, and I was sitting across from her, doing homework of my own.

Even though I could've done all of mine during the day when Willow was at school, I'd saved a portion of it for the evening, so she and I could finish our schoolwork at the same time.

Mason, who was obviously returning from the office, had just walked in from the attached garage, which was near the kitchen.

All in all, this was fairly normal, except for one thing.

Mason looked royally ticked.

Okay, even on the best of days, he wasn't all sunshine and roses. Still, there was something about the look in his eyes today that made me want to gather up my things and bolt for the privacy of my bedroom.

But I'd never do that. I was no coward. And besides, there was no way on Earth I'd leave Willow on her own, not with Mason looking so ominous.

His gaze was dark, and his mouth was set in a thin, angry line as he stalked toward the table.

Still, I tried to smile. "Oh, hi. How was your day?"

His jaw clenched. "I might ask the same."

I winced. *Oh, crud.*

So he'd heard?

But of course, he had. Although that little tiff in the parking lot hadn't been a *giant* spectacle, it had definitely turned a few heads. Obviously, one of those heads had belonged to someone who'd called Mason to tell him what had happened.

Bad luck for me.

But in my own defense, I'd been planning to tell him tonight, as soon as we had a moment alone. Until then, I saw no reason to drag Willow into our discussion, especially since I'd managed to shield her from the worst of it.

Hoping Mason would take the hint, I gave Willow a meaningful glance before saying, "My day? Well, it was definitely interesting. I'll fill in you later, alright?"

His expression only darkened. "No. Not later. *Now.*"

Jeez, could he not take a hint? With another meaningful look, I replied, "Then maybe you want to talk outside?"

So far, he'd said nothing at all to Willow, and she was eyeing him with obvious concern.

I knew why. It was Mason's demeanor. Normally, regardless of whatever else was going on in his life, he managed to summon up at least a smile or two for his little sister whenever he walked in the door.

Not today.

And why? It was because he was too busy giving me a cold, silent stare. And he never *did* respond to my suggestion of talking outside.

With a stiff smile, I tried again. "Like, maybe we could discuss it out on the back patio while Willow finishes her homework? You know, so we're not distracting her."

"Fine. I'll see you in five." And with that, he finally turned his attention to his little sister. With a pale imitation of a smile, he said, "And how was *your* day?"

At the table, Willow visibly relaxed. "You really wanna know?"

His gaze softened. "I always wanna know."

Watching, my heart went out to both of them, even Mason, who was surely about to read me the riot act. I bit my lip. *Was I about to be fired?*

At the table, Willow beamed up at Mason and announced, "It was the best day, ever."

I did a double-take. *It hadn't seemed so great to me.* Other than the tense encounter with Veronica, Willow's day had been pretty standard. Or at least, she'd said nothing to indicate otherwise.

With a dubious look, Mason said, "That good, huh?"

Willow's smile only widened. "Oh, yeah. We saw Veronica."

Mason didn't smile back. "Is that so?"

"Oh, yeah." Willow's eyes brightened. "Cami slapped her. It was awesome!"

I stifled a gasp. "What? You saw that?"

Willow beamed over at me. "Oh, yeah. I was super glad."

Oh. My. God.

I wasn't glad. Far from it. And, now I felt like crawling into a hole and hiding. "I, um, didn't realize you saw that. I mean, I thought you were facing the other way." I swallowed. "Weren't you?"

"Oh, yeah," Willow repeated. "But I saw the whole thing in the mirror."

Double crud.

Obviously, she meant the rear-view mirror, which only confirmed that she'd seen the whole sorry spectacle. And now, I was so flabbergasted, I could hardly speak. Somehow, I managed to stammer, "And, um, you didn't say anything?"

Her smile faded. "You looked sad. But I wasn't sad. I was happy. I just didn't want you to cry, that's all."

Funny, I *had* felt like crying, even if I'd been working hard not to show it.

It suddenly struck me that during the drive home from school, Willow had told me knock-knock jokes non-stop, including all of my favorites. At the time, I'd been beyond relieved, thinking it meant that she'd seen nothing of the ugly encounter.

Turns out, it meant just the opposite.

Now, I felt like crying all over again, but not because I was in trouble. "Awww…that was so nice of you." *And I meant it, too.* Still, I had to tell her, "But you don't need to worry about me. I'm supposed to be looking out for *you*. Remember?"

She smiled. "We can look out for each other. You know, like sisters."

As I smiled back, something squeezed at my heart. *God, I loved this kid.* But I needed to set a better example. "Just so you know," I said, "I never should've slapped her."

"But why?" Willow said. "She slapped you first."

Well, there was that. "Yeah, well…" My words trailed off as I considered the truth. In reality, I wasn't sorry that I'd returned Veronica's slap. I was only sorry that Willow had seen it.

Still, I had to wonder, what would've been worse? For her to see me shrink away and not give as good as I got?

Even though I wasn't the type to start fights, I'd grown up in a big, noisy family. We never hit each other, but we didn't let ourselves be bullied either.

Willow said, "You're a really good slapper."

Oh, boy. I reached up to rub the back of my neck. "Um…thanks?"

From beside the table, Mason's voice cut through our conversation. "Tell me," he said, looking to Willow. "Did she *ever* slap *you?*"

My gaze snapped in his direction. "Hey! I would never slap a child."

This was the unvarnished truth. And I wasn't saying this only for *his* benefit. I was saying it for Willow's benefit, too. The last thing I wanted was for her to worry that I'd get all slappy with her.

In reality, Veronica had been the first person I'd ever slapped in my whole life. If I had *my* way, I'd never slap anyone again.

From beside the table, Mason turned and gave me a good, long look. Speaking very slowly and clearly, he said, "I wasn't talking about *you.*"

Heat flooded my face. "Oh."

And now I felt stupid. *Dang it.* I should've realized that. But as usual, Mason was making it hard for me to think. His anger was supremely unsettling, even more so because he was doing a surprisingly good job of containing it.

And yet, I could still see the signs – the set of his jaw, the look in his eyes, and his unnatural stillness that for some reason, seemed more dangerous than a full-blown tantrum.

I felt myself swallow. He might look reasonably calm on the outside, but inside? A storm was definitely brewing.

Our gazes locked for a long, tense moment until he looked back to Willow and said, "So tell me. Did she ever lay a hand on you?"

Willow frowned in obvious confusion. "I don't know."

Mason practically growled, "What?"

Across from me, Willow was looking not only confused, but nervous.

I could totally relate. I spoke up. "What he means is, did anyone ever hit you? Or slap you? Or pinch you or anything?"

Willow's confusion cleared. "Oh." She gave a decisive shake of her head. "No."

In a soothing voice, I said, "Never? Not even once? Are you sure, Sweet Pea?"

Willow nodded. "If anyone did *that*, I would've told on them for sure."

From beside the table, Mason gave a curt nod. "Good girl." And then, he turned his dark gaze on me. "You and me – we need to talk."

CHAPTER 21

Cami

After he closed the patio door behind us, he didn't waste any time. "So, tell me. What happened."

Night had already fallen, and the air was too cold to be comfortable. But I didn't feel like I could complain, considering that I was the one who'd suggested talking out here in the first place.

Already, I was regretting it. Even though I was wearing a sweater, the cold breeze made me want to kick myself for not also grabbing a jacket on the way out.

On the upside, my story wouldn't take long to tell.

Sticking with the basics, I replied, "After school, Veronica showed up in the parking lot and tried to talk to Willow. I didn't want to upset her – meaning Willow, not Veronica – so I let them talk for a minute or two, and then I said we had to leave. The whole thing lasted barely ten minutes."

Tonight, Mason was wearing a tailored business suit with a burgundy necktie. His suit was definitely thinner than my sweater, but *he* didn't look cold, not unless I counted the look in his eye when he said, "Oh, yeah? When?"

I felt my brow wrinkle in confusion. "What do you mean when?" I paused to think. "Do you mean, when did it happen?"

"That *was* the question."

"But you *know* when it happened. I just told you, it was right after school."

"And what time was that?"

As if he didn't know. "Around three o'clock."

"Right. Four hours ago."

"Oh." Finally, I got the message. "Uh, yeah. More or less."

"And you never thought to call?"

"You mean you?" I said. "Sure, I thought about it. But since it was handled, I didn't see the point of bothering you at work."

His mouth tightened. "Uh-huh."

"And just so you know, I *would've* told you if Willow hadn't mentioned it first."

"Right. And now you're gonna mention the rest."

"What do you mean?"

"The part you left out," he said. "I want to hear it."

"But you already did."

"I heard it from Willow," he said. "Now, I'm gonna hear it from you."

"But why? It's the same story."

His gaze bored into mine. "So it's true? She slapped you."

"Yes. But to be fair, that was only after I kicked her."

With a hint of sarcasm, he said, "In the ass?"

Jeez, what kind of maniac did he think I was? "No. In the shin."

"And why the shin?"

"Because she was standing on my foot, refusing to let me leave. And if *I* couldn't leave, Willow couldn't leave either."

"Is that so?"

"Yes. Unless you *wanted* Willow to drive off on her own."

"She's eight."

"Yeah, that's my point. And just look at it from my point-of-view. Veronica's standing on my foot, Willow's in the back seat, and I wanted to get the heck out of there."

"So you kicked her."

"Well, yeah, because at this at this point, I figure I've got two choices. I can either shove her away or kick her in the shin. And I figure if I try the whole 'shoving' thing, she might fall down and break something."

Only half joking, I added, "Plus, if she's lying on the pavement, I'd have to back over her to get out of the parking spot."

"Good."

I sighed. "No. It's not good. And besides, it's not like I'd actually do it. I'm just saying, she had me hemmed in, and I was a little short of options. And the *last* thing I wanted was to create a giant spectacle."

He gave me a skeptical look. "Uh-huh."

"And yes, I *do* realize there was a spectacle anyway. But trust me, it could've been so much worse. And it's not like I had any advance warning."

"Of what?"

"Of her showing up." I made a sound of frustration. "Like, if I'd known what Veronica looked like, she *never* would've gotten within ten feet of Willow."

He frowned. "Good to know."

I stared up at him. His words said one thing, but his expression said another. Unless I was horribly mistaken, he saw nothing good about any of this.

I could totally relate.

Still, I went on to make my point. "So maybe you should give me some photos – of the former nannies, I mean."

"Done," he said. "You'll have them tomorrow." He moved a fraction closer. "Now, you're gonna give *me* something."

As I craned my neck to stare up at him, I found myself getting lost in the intensity of his gaze – so lost that it took me a moment to realize the ramifications of what he'd just said.

He'd just agreed to give me the photos. This meant I *wasn't* about to be fired.

Well, that was good.

Probably.

Willow, I loved. And the job was shockingly easy for what I was paid. But as far as Mason, I didn't know what I felt. He distracted me to no end, even now, when we were supposed to be discussing his sister.

And now he wanted something? The truth was, I could think several things I'd like to give him. And none of them were decent.

Good grief. What was wrong with me, anyway.

Probably, it was some sort of apology, whether for making a scene or for not telling him right away what had happened.

Bracing myself, I said, "Okay, what?"

"The truth," he said. "Did you – or did you not – have coffee with my brother?"

CHAPTER 22

Mason

Shit.

It wasn't what I'd planned to say. I'd been planning to demand a written report detailing what had happened with Veronica, including a full account of their conversation – because I knew one thing for damn sure. *I hadn't heard the whole story.*

Not yet.

But sometime in the last few minutes, my thoughts had returned to my conversation with Chase, and I'd begun considering the possibility of Cami becoming just another notch in his bedpost.

I didn't like it.

She wasn't his type. She was too sweet, too responsible, and far too good for whatever he had in mind.

Don't get me wrong. *I loved my brother.* He had plenty of fine qualities, and I'd die for him if I needed to.

But if I had a daughter – or hell even a sister my own age – he'd be the kind of guy I'd warn her away from, *hard.*

Cami wasn't my sister. I realized this, just like I realized there was nothing brotherly about the way she made me feel, even now, as she stared up at me with apparent confusion.

After a long moment, she said, "Excuse me?"

"It's a simple question."

"Um, yeah. Well, I guess it is. But I'm not sure why you'd ask."

"So you're saying it's none of my business."

She hesitated. "Honestly I don't know. I mean, he's your brother, so I'm guessing *that's* why you're asking?"

Tonight, she was wearing jeans and a cream-colored sweater. Her cheeks were flushed, and her hair was long and loose. As she stared up at me, a cold breeze lifted the tendrils around her face, making her look like something out of an adolescent dream, the kind that ended happy in more ways than one.

As far as the question, I didn't know why I was asking. It would be easy to tell myself that I was asking for Willow's sake, making sure that Cami's attention didn't stray from her job.

But in my gut, I knew this wasn't the issue. Cami treated Willow like her own little sister. And if I were a betting person – which I wasn't – I'd bet just about anything that Cami would sacrifice herself long before she'd ever put Willow in danger.

The incident with Veronica had done nothing to change this belief.

I replied, "I'm asking, because I wanna know."

"But that's no kind of answer," she said. "And which brother do you mean, anyway?"

This should've been obvious. I had two brothers. My youngest brother, Brody, was engaged to her best friend.

So why the question?

Was she stalling?

I gave her a look. "If you're having coffee on the side with Brody, you've got bigger problems than Veronica."

She drew back. "Just what are you accusing me of, anyway?"

"Nothing."

"Are you sure?"

"If you heard an accusation, you heard wrong."

"Oh, really?" she said. "Because it *almost* sounded like you were accusing me of sneaking around with my best friend's fiancé."

She was wrong.

And she was *still* avoiding the question.

I said, "Hey, you asked which brother. Not me."

She was glaring now. "Just what kind of person do you think I am?"

The question hit harder than it should've. I thought she was a good person, a better person than I'd ever be. *So why was I hassling her?*

I didn't want to.

But she had this way of getting under my skin, making me feel things I hadn't felt in a long while. And whatever those feelings were, they were chafing like a broken blister, making me ornery as hell, even now when she'd technically done nothing wrong.

Deliberately, I softened my tone. "I was talking about Chase."

"Oh." Her eyebrows furrowed. "Really?"

"He said you met for coffee."

"Me? No." But then, she paused. "Oh, wait…"

I waited. And as I did, I silently considered how I might feel if she and Chase met for *more* than coffee.

I wouldn't like it.

She'd get hurt, and I'd get pissed. One thing would lead to another, and I'd be looking for a new nanny. *Again.*

See, it was an employment issue. Nothing else.

That had to be it.

Into her silence, I said, "And in case you haven't heard, he has a habit of banging the nannies."

She blinked. "What?"

"Yeah. Two so far," I said. "And if you wanna be number three…" My jaw clenched at the thought. "Do it on your own time."

She took an unsteady step backward, looking like she'd just been slapped. Too late, I realized I was acting like a total asshole. *Again.*

The truth was, I hadn't meant to say half of what I'd said during the last few minutes.

What the hell was wrong with me, anyway?

Cami was still glaring. "Oh, my God. You think I'm gonna sleep with your brother?"

"I don't know. Are you?"

"Hell no." Her hands flew to her mouth. "Shit."

I moved forward. "What?"

"I meant, 'crap.' No. I meant, 'crud.'" She groaned. "And I didn't mean to say, '*Hell* no.' I meant to say, '*Heck* no.'" She looked heavenward and groaned again. "Oh, for God's sake. You make me crazy, you know that?"

I knew the feeling. And yet, I *was* curious. "How so?"

"Isn't it obvious? Just listen to me. I'm cussing up a storm. Do you realize that until I met you, I went like three whole years without a single curse-word? Now, I'm turning into a total potty mouth."

"And that's my fault?"

"Well, it *must* be. I only do it around you."

Obviously, she was missing the flaw in her logic. "Right. *You* do it. Not me." I paused for emphasis. "Which means it's *your* problem, not mine."

"Hah! It can't be *my* problem, because if it were, I'd be cursing everywhere. Like, here's a good example. Do you know, today I wanted to curse Veronica up and down? But did I do that? Noooooo. I resisted."

She looked so cute, I almost smiled. "Was that *before* or *after* you kicked her?"

"It was before *and* after. So there!"

"Well, I guess you told *me*."

"Oh, please," she said. "I haven't *begun* to tell you."

"Is that so?"

"Definitely," she said. "Like for starters, that 'coffee' with your brother? I just realized what you're talking about, and you're reading way too much into it."

"Am I?"

"Yes. Totally. It was like two days ago, right?"

"You tell me."

"I'm *trying* to tell you," she said. "I had coffee with *Arden*, not Chase. But I did see him there."

"Where?"

"At that that little shop by your corporate headquarters. Arden and I are sitting there, minding our own business, when Chase walks in – with a half-naked blonde, by the way–"

If I were twelve, I might've snickered. "Oh yeah? Which half?"

"Oh, shut up," she said. "You know what I mean."

I did. When it came to women, Chase liked them on the trashy side, which made his apparent interest in Cami all the more maddening, unless…

I frowned. *Was he just yanking my chain?*

Shit. He probably was.

The dick.

And me? Like a total dumb-ass, I'd fallen for it.

This was a first, which posed a disturbing question. *Why this time?*

When I made no reply, Cami continued. "Look, I'm not trying to be judgmental or anything, but it *is* November, which *does* make it seem a tad odd when someone walks into a coffee shop wearing a bikini. And I don't mean a regular bikini either. I mean a thong bikini. Oh sure, she had little skirt over it, but the skirt was mesh and practically see-through." Suddenly, Cami threw up her hands. "And why am I telling you any of this?"

As she'd been speaking, I'd been trying not to wonder what *she'd* look like in a thong – not out in public, but in private, with just the two of us.

I didn't share. And that included glimpses of things that only a lover should see.

Absently, I replied, "Because I asked."

"Yeah, you did," she said. "But you were so off base, it wasn't even funny."

This was true. And yet, I almost felt like laughing.

Why?

Was it because she was so cute when she got flustered? Or was it because I was too damned relieved to hear that she and Chase wouldn't be hooking up any time soon?

Either way, this wasn't good.

"Anyway," Cami continued. "So *that's* the 'coffee' with your brother. And in case it wasn't clear, there was no 'banging' involved." Under her breath, she added, "Well, not with me, anyway. Who knows what he and the blonde did afterwards." She hesitated. "Or before."

With a final sigh, she asked, "And why am I even thinking about this?"

As I gazed down at her, it slowly dawned on me that my anger had morphed into something else, something a lot more dangerous – and not only to me personally.

Cami was a nice person. She deserved a nice guy. But me – I wasn't nice. Hell, I didn't even *want* to be nice.

Nice guys finished last – *and* wasted too much time doing it. *That wasn't me.* And it never would be, not if I could help it.

It was time to get back to business. "About Veronica," I said, "I'll need a written report."

Cami shook her head. "What?"

"Keep it under five pages. Typed. And don't omit anything." I gave her a hard look. "Because trust me, I have ways of finding out."

CHAPTER 23

Cami

I looked to Arden. "And then he tells me…" I did my best Mason impression. "I have ways of finding out."

Arden and I were sitting in the living room of the beach house that she and Brody had renovated earlier this year as part of the *Blast* reality show. The house had been in Arden's family for generations, but it wasn't until Brody had invested some serious time and money into its restoration that the house had morphed into something truly spectacular.

Today, the home looked brand new, but with all its original charm. Best of all, Arden and Brody were now living in the house together while they made plans for their upcoming wedding.

From the nearby sofa, Arden said, "You know what's funny? I bet he really does have ways of finding out."

"Oh, I'm sure he does," I said, recalling the background check that Mason had run on me, back in the beginning. "But if that's the case, why doesn't he get a report from *them* instead?"

"Maybe it's a test," she said. "You know, to see if you'll fib."

Knowing Mason, I could almost see it. "Or *maybe* he's just spreading the misery."

Arden gave a solemn nod. "Well, that's Mason for ya."

It was just past noon, and Arden had invited me over for lunch and coffee while Brody went into the office. Through the windows of the living room, I could see the endless waters of the Saginaw Bay shimmering in the afternoon sun.

The view of the water made me think of Mason's back patio, where we'd gotten into that heated discussion. I still wasn't quite sure how our conversation had gone so far off-track, but the whole thing had left me feeling confused and unsettled.

But hey, what else was new?

The truth was, I'd been feeling unsettled ever since Mason had walked into that club in Petoskey and turned my life upside-down.

"So," Arden said, "did you write it?"

"The report?" I rolled my eyes. "Yes. But only because I didn't have a choice. I mean, it's not like it was optional or anything."

"Are you sure?" she said. "Let's say you didn't do it. Do you think he'd fire you?"

I gave it some thought. "I don't know, but I *do* think he'd make me miserable."

"So are you?" she said. "Miserable, I mean?"

I sighed. "Well he's making me crazy. Does that count?"

It had been less than a day since Mason had demanded the report. And although he hadn't given me an official deadline, I'd gotten the distinct impression that if I didn't have it done by the time he got home tonight, he *wouldn't* be pleased.

Then again, it's not like he'd be pleased anyway. Now that I thought about it, he was looking less pleased with every passing day.

Last night, after our tense conversation on the patio, all three of us – meaning me and Willow, plus Mason – had eaten dinner together like we usually did whenever Mason was home.

In spite of the lingering tension, dinner had been surprisingly uneventful, with Willow doing most of the talking.

It was a good thing, too, because I'd been far too distracted to say anything intelligent. And forget making a decent dinner.

But at least *that* part was taken care of. All *I'd* had to do was pop the pre-made casserole into the oven and, after we'd finished eating, stack the dishes in the sink.

Sometime today – probably right now, in fact – Mason's daily housekeeper would do the rest of the cleanup while I visited with my friend.

The whole arrangement was entirely surreal, and I was still trying to get used to it.

During my first few weeks, I'd kept trying to clean up the dinner messes like I would at my own place, only to give up the habit entirely when the housekeeper worried out loud that she'd be out of work if I kept doing *her* job on top of my own.

I saw what she meant, but it still made me feel like a slug. After all, *my* only job was to watch out for Willow, and it hardly felt like a job at all.

All in all, I had nothing to complain about.

And I tried not to. But the truth was, Mason really *was* making me crazy.

As my thoughts churned, I looked to Arden and said, "Hey, can I ask you something? Do you think Mason's *ever* been happy?"

"With *his* childhood?" she said. "I doubt it."

"What do you mean?"

"Well, the way I hear it, Mason *really* got the short end of the stick."

"How so?"

She winced. "Are you sure you want to hear this?"

"Why wouldn't I?"

"Because the story's so grim. And I know you like happy endings."

Now, I really wanted to know, and not only for curiosity. For weeks now, I'd been wondering what made Mason tick. With this in mind, I practically begged Arden to tell me, anyway.

"Alright," she said. "But remember, you asked for it."

CHAPTER 24

Mason

Chase strolled into my office seven minutes late for the meeting.

I gave him a look. "The schedule said noon."

He glanced at his watch. "It's not even ten after."

"Yeah. And you're still late."

The three of us – me, Brody, and Chase – held this meeting once a month to discuss the company's direction and make sure we stayed on track.

The meeting was private, with no assistants, no transcripts, and nobody whose last name wasn't Blastoviak.

Chase ambled to my conference table and pulled out a chair. I was still sitting at my desk, preferring to get some work done while I waited.

Hey, *somebody* had to.

As Chase sat down at the table, he made a point to look around. "And why are you bitching at *me?* Brody's not even here yet."

"Yeah, well, I'll be 'bitching' at him when he shows up."

Chase grinned. "*If* he shows up."

"Meaning?"

"I'm just saying, he's got other things on his mind, you know."

My youngest brother – the guy who used our tools more than anyone – had gone soft maybe six months ago when a blast from his past had returned with a vengeance.

That blast had a name, Arden Weathers, who happened to be Cami's best friend. If I were in the mood to give Arden credit, I might admit that she was making my brother obnoxiously happy.

I meant that literally.

His happiness was obnoxious as hell. Just last week, I'd heard him whistling when he walked by.

Whistling.

Who the hell does that?

Not my little brother – or at least, not until Arden came along.

Arden and our family had a history. The history wasn't good.

But now, I was supposed to welcome her into the family like I'd welcome any *sane* person, maybe someone like Cami, who *wasn't* a truck-torching psycho.

For my brother's sake, I'd given Arden the official thumbs-up, but that didn't mean I was happy about it.

Good thing for Brody, he was happy enough for all of us, which might've made *me* happier, too, if only he weren't showing up late for meetings.

On the upside, his tardiness gave me and Chase a moment alone. I looked to him and said, "You're a real piece of work. You know that?"

He grinned. "Hell yeah."

It was the day after the patio conversation with Cami, and I was still pissed at Chase for yanking my chain with that story of meeting Cami for coffee.

I was even more pissed at myself for falling for it.

I said, "So you get what I'm talking about."

"No. What'd I do this time?"

My jaw clenched at the memory. "That coffee story."

With mock innocence, he asked, "What coffee story?"

He knew damn well what I meant. But hey, I'd spell it out if I had to. "You told me you had coffee with the nanny."

"Which one?"

"You *know* which one."

He lifted a single eyebrow, which annoyed the piss out of me, because it was one of the few things Chase could do that I couldn't.

Knowing Chase, he *knew* it annoyed me, which explained why he was doing it now.

In a voice filled with all kinds of innuendo, he said, "*Cami* the nanny?"

My fingers clenched. I didn't like the way he said it, almost like it was the title of a bad porno flick, starring her and him. In a tight voice, I replied, "She *is* the one you claimed to have had coffee with."

"I did not."

I gave him a good, long look. "You did. Right here in this office. Less than twenty-four hours ago."

"Oh, that?" he laughed. "No, what I *said* was I met her at the coffee shop, which I did."

He could laugh all he wanted, I didn't see the humor. "You know damn well how you made it sound."

"Do I?"

When my only reply was a murderous look, he said, "Hey, relax. I *did* meet her, just like I said."

"Right," I gritted out. "While you were on a date with someone else."

"It wasn't a date," Chase said. "It was a business meeting."

I recalled Cami's description of Chase's companion. "You mean the blonde in the bikini."

"Not just any bikini," Chase said. "A *thong* bikini."

Already, I was tired of his bullshit. "So I heard."

"Oh, relax," he said. "It really *was* a business thing."

Now this, I had to hear. "Oh yeah? What kind of business?"

"I was thinking of doing a tool calendar, the old-fashioned kind, with chicks in bikinis."

"Chicks?" My voice was flat. "In bikinis."

"Sure," he said. "You've seen them, right?"

"Chicks in bikinis?"

"No," he said, looking surprisingly sincere. "Chicks in bikinis *in* calendars. You know, something for guys to hang by their tool box. C'mon, you know what I mean."

I did know. I'd worked plenty of construction, and I'd seen my share of calendars, but very few of them were from recent years.

I said, "Isn't that a bit old-fashioned?"

At the conference table, Chase gave an easy shrug. "Call it retro."

Now here's the thing with Chase. Half of his ideas were batshit crazy. But the other half – well, they made us a shit-ton of money. The challenge was figuring out which idea fell into which category.

I said, "So you were auditioning her for a spot in the calendar?"

"Her?" he said. "You mean Cami the nanny?"

As he said it, an image of Cami in a bikini popped into my head. Her bikini was red, and her body was tight and sweet. She looked so good, I felt myself swallow.

Fuck.

Through gritted teeth, I said, "I meant the blonde."

"Oh, her?" Chase said in mock innocence. "She wasn't auditioning."

Yeah, right. "So, what *was* she doing?" I said. "It had to be *something*, unless she wears a bikini everywhere."

"She's a photographer," Chase said. "And a model on the side. She showed up like that to illustrate the look she'd be going for."

"In the calendar."

"Exactly." He leaned back in his seat. "But now that you mention it, maybe Cami *should* audition."

I recalled mentioning no such thing. "For the calendar? You're joking, right?"

With a smirk, he said, "I don't know. Am I?"

If I had *my* way, there'd be no calendar. But the truth was, Chase had the final say when it came to marketing and publicity. It was the deal we'd struck, back in the beginning, and I had to give Chase credit. He'd worked more than his share of miracles on the promo front.

His biggest miracle was that cable show, *Blast*. When he'd first suggested it, I'd thought he was out of his mind.

If I'd had the veto power, I would've vetoed the idea on the spot.

But I hadn't, and Chase had managed to sell his brainchild to the Home Network, pitching it as a sexy remodeling show starring three hot, single brothers who didn't always get along.

Hot – *his* word, not mine.

At the time, I'd figured the show would last one season at best. That was four years ago. Since then, its popularity had only grown, along with the sales of Blast tools.

The show was free advertising on steroids, which meant that I'd been willing to sacrifice some of my privacy to keep it going.

But Cami's privacy – I wouldn't sacrifice *that* for anything.

It was for Willow's sake – *and* her safety. Or at least, that was my working theory on why I'd never let it happen.

As far as any other theories, they were best ignored.

I told Chase, "Let's get one thing straight. Cami – she's off limits."

"Do you mean only for the calendar, or…?" He let the question hang there, unfinished. I knew why, too. He was still goading me, although I couldn't figure out why.

I mean, yeah, he'd been goading me for years, but the thing with Cami was holding his interest more than it should've.

I heard myself say, "You don't have a thing for her, do you?"

"Me?" he laughed. "No. But *you* do."

I frowned. "Says who?"

"You don't have to say it," he said. "It's written all over your face."

Shit.

This wasn't what I wanted to hear. Yeah, maybe I did find her interesting, but I'd never act on it. Female companionship – that was easy to find, *too* easy in some ways.

But a nanny for my sister? Now, *that* was difficult.

No way I'd be mixing the two.

I told Chase, "You're full of it."

"You can think that all you want," he said. "It doesn't make it true."

Wisdom from Chase. It was the last thing I needed.

And I was about tell him so when Brody ambled into the office, looking like he had all the time in the world.

I told him, "You're late."

He glanced at his watch. "It's only twelve after."

"Yeah. And you're still late."

At the table, Chase laughed.

I looked to him and said, "What's so funny?"

"That's the same thing you said to me."

"Yeah, because you were late, too."

Chase jerked a thumb toward Brody. "Not as late as him."

Brody looked to Chase and said, "What, you didn't tell him?"

I looked from brother to brother. "Tell me what?"

Brody replied, "I told Chase I'd be fifteen minutes late." He moved toward the conference table. "So in a way, I'm early."

Great. Now both of them were pissing me off. I looked back to Chase and said, "Why didn't you mention he was gonna be late?"

"Because we were busy." Chase looked to Brody and added, "Discussing Cami the nanny."

As Brody claimed a seat at the table, he looked to me and said, "Now *that's* funny."

If there was a joke, I didn't get it. "Why?"

"Because she's at the house with Arden right now."

I still didn't see the humor. "And why is that funny?"

"Because," he said, "she's probably talking about *you*, too."

I sure as hell hoped not.

CHAPTER 25

Cami

On the couch, Arden gave me a brief rundown of the Blastoviak family history, starting with the fact that their dad had a nasty habit of disappearing, sometimes for weeks, and sometimes for a whole lot longer. But he always came back eventually.

"But then," Arden continued, "the very last time he comes back, he stays only long enough to get the mom pregnant."

"With Willow, you mean?"

"Right. And according to Brody, as soon as their dad finds out that their mom's expecting another baby, he pulls a fade all over again, this time for good." Arden made a sound of disgust. "And then, the mom leaves too, the very next year."

I tried to imagine it. "So…she announces she's leaving? Just like that?"

"If only," Arden said. "No, what *she* does is announce that she's going on vacation."

"Seriously?"

"Oh, yeah. And she tells her sons they've got to hold down the fort while she's gone."

Silently, I worked through the details. At the time, Mason, Chase, and Brody would've been young men, more than capable of being on their own. Even Brody, the youngest son, would've been nearing his high school graduation. With two older brothers in the house, he might've done reasonably okay.

But Willow? She'd been just a baby. With a frown, I asked, "But what about Willow?"

Arden winced. "Apparently, she was part of 'the fort.'"

"So the guys were supposed to be watching her?"

"Oh, yeah. And the mom warns them that if anyone finds out she's gone, the government will swoop in and take Willow away, like into foster care or wherever, so they'd better keep their mouths shut."

"God, what a witch."

"No kidding," Arden said. "But anyway, so she leaves, supposedly for just a long weekend. But then, her vacation keeps getting extended. And she's telling them, 'Just a couple more days.' And then it's, 'Just a couple more weeks.' Finally, when she's been gone for like three whole months, she tells them – in a letter, no less – that she's not coming back at all."

My jaw dropped. "Really? But why?"

"Well, according to Brody, she said she was done with the whole 'parenting thing.'"

I shook my head. "But you're *never* done. Not really."

Arden gave me a look. "Sorry, but not everyone's parents are like yours."

Too late, I recalled who I was talking to. Arden's parents hadn't been all that terrific either. From what I'd gathered, they'd also spent plenty of time away, off doing their own thing.

I gave her a sympathetic look. "No. *I'm* the one who's sorry."

"Don't be," she said. "I'm just saying, some people are different, you know?"

I did know. I thought of my own mom, and I felt a surge of gratitude as I considered how lucky I'd been. I made a mental note to call her tonight and thank her for, well, everything, I guess.

"But what about Mason and Willow?" I said. "How'd *he* end up with sole custody?"

"He insisted on it."

At her words, something tugged at my heart. "Do you know why?"

"According to Brody, Mason wanted her to grow up in a stable home rather than being shuttled from place to place."

"You mean among the three brothers?"

"Or worse," Arden said. "She could've ended up with strangers. The way I hear it, Mason had to fight pretty hard to keep her out of the system."

As I listened, Arden went on to explain that Mason had been looking out for all of them for as long as Brody could remember. Even in grade school, Mason had been the one who'd made sure that his brothers went to school and did their homework, and that they had clean clothes and food in their lunch bags.

As I took all of this in, my heart nearly broke for all of them, Mason in particular.

When *I'd* been in grade school, I'd been a regular kid. It was true that we didn't always have a lot of money, but we did have a lot of love, and I never had to worry about the big things.

Looking back, my parents probably worried enough for all of us. And yet, they never shoved any of those burdens onto us kids.

I asked, "But what about their mom. *She* was there, right?"

"Well, the way it sounds, she wasn't home much, even before her so-called vacation."

Arden then went on to tell me that their mom had done her own share of disappearing – sometimes for hours, sometimes for days – while Mason kept the family from falling apart.

By the time I left Arden's place to pick up Willow from school, I was seeing Mason in a whole new light.

No wonder he was so serious.

Had he had a childhood at all?

To think, the guy wasn't yet thirty years old, but he'd been acting as a stand-in parent for nearly twenty years now. And, as far as I could tell, he never complained – well, not about that anyway.

And yet, he *did* have a way of surprising me, especially later that night when he read my dreaded report.

CHAPTER 26

Cami

In the dimly lit kitchen, Mason said, "I've got a question."

He wasn't the only one. Like right now, I was questioning why on Earth I'd chosen to get up for a bottle of water at two in the morning when I could've simply stuck my face under the tap in my private bathroom.

Sure, it would've been undignified, but not half as undignified as I felt now, standing in Mason's kitchen, wearing pajama pants, a thin tank top, and pink fuzzy slippers.

But in my own defense, the encounter with Mason hadn't been planned. Until now, I hadn't even realized that he was home. Earlier tonight, after picking up Willow from school, I'd received a text from him saying that he wouldn't be home for dinner, and that he'd see us in the morning.

At the time, I'd figured this meant that he had overnight plans. Whether those plans were for business or pleasure, I hadn't wanted to speculate, mostly because the thought of him pleasuring *anyone* was too unsettling to consider.

But now, here he was, standing in the kitchen, wearing the same business suit he'd been wearing this morning, before leaving for work.

And of course, he looked just as amazing as ever.

Oh sure, there was new stubble along his jawline, and his tailored suit had a few new creases here and there. *But man oh man, he was still something to look at.*

His shoulders were broad, and his hips were narrow. His hair wasn't quite as perfect as it had been this morning, but it was still thick and dark, framing his rugged face as we stood alone in the quiet kitchen.

In a low voice, he said, "And you wanna know what it is?"

I blinked. "What *what* is?"

"The question."

Oh, crud. Once again, I'd been caught with my head in the clouds. This didn't happen with anyone else, so why did it happen with him?

And why, oh why, was it happening now? But then it hit me. "Wait a minute. You *do* realize it's two in the morning."

"Yeah, so?"

"So my mind's hardly awake." *See, I wasn't distracted by the sight of him. My brain was just sleepy, that's all.*

He gave me a long, penetrating look before saying, "You look awake to *me.*"

Oh, please. I didn't look awake. I looked ridiculous. My pajama pants were too baggy, and my tank-top was too tight. *And don't get me started on the slippers.*

But hey, it could always be worse. Until I'd decided to get up for water, I'd been lying in bed, wearing only the tank top and panties.

I hadn't been able to sleep. And in a way, this was Mason's fault, whether he realized it or not.

When I'd first crawled into bed, I couldn't stop thinking about everything that Arden had revealed today at her house. And then, I'd spent way too long obsessing over the idea of Mason sleeping somewhere else – or rather *with* someone else.

I'd been wondering what he was doing, and exactly *who* he was doing it with. By now, I'd been living here for nearly two months, but I still hadn't met any of his dates, or female companions, or whatever you'd call them.

But I *did* wonder who they were and where Mason met with them, because by now, it was pretty obvious that he didn't bring any of his dates home. Or at least, he hadn't brought any home since *I'd* been around.

Still, I wondered more than I should've.

And if I were being totally honest, I'd been wondering such things for a while now.

But tonight, all of the wondering had made me thirsty and restless.

So, here I was. And, as far as the pajama pants, I'd only thrown on *those* just in case.

In case of what?

Well, in case of *this*, actually. Being caught in pajamas was bad enough, but to be caught in my panties? Now *that* would've been embarrassing.

Mason was standing near the kitchen's center island, holding a familiar document in his hand.

It was the report he'd requested after that incident with Veronica.

Before going to bed around midnight, I'd left the report on the island, thinking that Mason could simply swoop it up whenever he returned home.

I just hadn't expected the swooping to happen so quickly – or to find myself alone with him as he finished reading it.

And he'd definitely read it, alright. I knew *this* by the way he was holding it now.

The document was only three pages long, stapled together. But the first two pages were flopped over the side, leaving only the final page visible for his inspection.

But he wasn't looking at the report. He was looking at *me*.

Bracing myself, I said, "Alright, so what's the question?"

"I'm warning you, it's a tough one."

I feared as much. Although the report was relatively short, I'd left nothing out, not even the fact that Veronica had called me a whole bunch of four-letter words, and in return, I'd called her a few choice names of my own.

And that was *before* all the slapping.

And *after* the slapping? Well, I'd focused all of *my* energy on getting the heck out of there before things turned truly ugly.

Now in the kitchen, I prepared myself for round two – justifying myself to Mason. "Fine," I said. "Ask away."

"Alright," he said. "Tell me. What's a lunk-blaster?"

CHAPTER 27

Mason

Cami blinked. "Excuse me?"

Oh, man. She was so beautiful, standing there with her tousled hair and bedroom eyes. *And don't get me started on what she was wearing.*

As far as my question, it wasn't what I'd planned to ask. I'd been planning to ask why she hadn't called my security firm – or hell, even me – as soon as Veronica started making trouble.

But once again, I'd gone off-script. It wasn't just a problem. It was a *recurring* problem, which meant that I was in deeper trouble than I'd realized.

See, here's the thing about mistakes. If you make a mistake once, you can deal with it. But once you start making the same mistakes repeatedly, you've got to look deeper into the causes.

But me? I was looking deeper into Cami's eyes.

We were standing several paces away, and the only light in the kitchen came from the small motion-activated lighting that ran along the floorboards.

But that didn't change what I saw.

In front of me, I saw the person who'd been haunting my thoughts for too damn long. And that look in her eyes – it was distracting the hell out of me, making me want to drop the report and pose a whole series of *new* questions – questions I had no right to ask.

What was she thinking?

Did she have a boyfriend back home?

Was she wearing a bra under that tank top?

The answer to that last question was obvious, and I worked hard not to stare as her nipples visibly hardened in the quiet kitchen.

The kitchen wasn't cold.

And neither was she. Under my gaze, her cheeks grew rosy and her lips parted. For a long moment, neither one of us spoke.

In the end, it was Cami who broke the silence, asking in a breathless voice, "That's your question? Seriously?"

My gaze held hers. "Sure, why not?"

As I watched, her tongue darted out between her lips and grazed her upper front teeth. When my eyes followed the motion, she gave a little gasp and clamped her lips shut, as if to rein in whatever she'd been thinking.

Shit.

Did she have any idea what she was doing to me?

I sure as hell hoped not.

I put on my best poker face and made a forwarding motion with my hand. "So go ahead. Tell me."

"Sorry, what?"

"Lunk-blaster, what does it mean?"

"Oh." She blew out a long, trembling breath. As she did, my gaze strayed once again to her lips, and I felt myself swallow. She had nice lips – full, pink, and natural, too.

In my world, this wasn't as common as you'd think.

In the back of my mind, I wondered how long it had been since I'd kissed someone whose lips hadn't been pumped full of whatever to make them look more appealing.

But Cami, she was appealing just the way she was.

I wanted to kiss her.

Fuck.

From the other side of the kitchen, she gave a shaky laugh. "It's just an insult, that's all."

"But what does it mean?"

"I can't say."

"Oh yeah? Why not?"

"Because it's not kid-friendly."

I made a show of eyeing our surroundings. "You see any kids around?"

"No." She turned and glanced in the general direction of the staircase before saying in a much lower voice, "But Willow still might be able to hear."

She was wrong. The house was huge. Even the staircase was a decent walk away. I told her, "We both know that's not true."

"That's what *you* think," she said. "But when I was a kid, I heard my parents talking all the time, even when they thought I was asleep."

"Oh yeah?" I felt my lips curve into a reluctant smile. "So you were a little eavesdropper, huh?"

"No." She cleared her throat. "Not really."

I wasn't so sure. "Is that so?"

"I just have really good hearing, that's all."

"Uh-huh."

"And maybe *Willow* has good hearing, too." She glanced around. "So maybe we should talk somewhere else."

I recalled our last conversation. "Well, there's always the back patio."

With a rueful laugh, Cami said, "Oh, sure, because I didn't freeze enough yesterday."

I frowned. "You were cold?"

"Yeah, weren't you?"

"No." And now I felt like a dick. "You should've said something."

She bit her lip. "Why?"

"Because I could've done something."

"Like what?" she said. "It's not like you control the weather."

"No. But I could've brought you inside. Or loaned you my jacket."

"Oh stop it," she said. "You wouldn't do that."

She was wrong.

I would.

For Cami.

I stiffened. What the hell did *that* mean?

And now I was pissed – not at her, but at myself.

It wasn't just because I'd let her freeze. It was for the way I felt about it now, with a nearly primitive urge to protect her, not just from the cold, but from anything that threatened her comfort or safety.

Shit.

I was losing it – the calculated coolness that had served me well for most of my life. *I needed to regain it, and fast.*

When I spoke again, my voice came out several degrees colder. "Are you gonna answer the question or not?"

Her eyes narrowed, and the warmth in them cooled considerably. "Fine." She extended her arm and pointed to the nearby pantry. "In there."

I turned to look. "You're joking."

But already, Cami was stalking past me, heading toward the pantry door. She yanked it open and stomped into the glorified closet before turning once again to face me. "No. I'm *not* joking," she said. "So, are you coming or not?"

If this were anyone but Cami, I would've told her that we'd be talking where I damn well pleased. But her concern for my sister softened the edges, even as I said, "You want to talk in the closet?"

"It's a not a closet," she said. "It's a pantry."

"Which is a closet for food."

She gave me a stiff smile. "Excellent. If we get locked in, we won't starve."

Oh, man. The thought of being locked anywhere with Cami was a dangerous thing to consider. On the upside, the pantry had no lock, and Cami looked too annoyed to be interested in anything other than talking.

I might be a prick in every other way, but when it came to females, I was only interested in the willing. And from the *current* look in Cami's eyes, she'd rather kiss a cobra than get anywhere near *me*.

Good.

I shrugged. "Alright." As I strode through the open doorway, I said, "But I'm warning you…."

She backed up to make room. "Of what?"

Once again, the thing I'd been *planning* to say died on my lips. I'd been planning to tell her that she needed to make it quick. But instead, the thing that came out of my mouth was, "If we get locked in…"

"Yeah?"

I *almost* smiled. "The cereal's mine."

Damn it.

It wasn't just a joke. It was a corny joke. And I hadn't made one of *those* since grade school.

Oh, yeah. I was in trouble, alright.

And maybe, so was she.

CHAPTER 28

Cami

As I stared up at him, I *almost* wanted to snicker. "Was that a joke?"

With an expression that I couldn't quite decipher, he asked, "What do *you* think?"

I reached past him and shut the pantry door firmly behind us. "There *is* no lock so you must be joking."

His lips twitched, and he looked dangerously close to smiling. "Me? Nah."

I hadn't flicked on the pantry light, because I hadn't needed to. The pantry, like the kitchen, was equipped with low-level lighting of the motion sensor variety.

The light wasn't much brighter than candlelight, but it was still just enough to catch the amusement in Mason's eyes when I told him, "Either that, or you're crazy."

In a low voice, he said, "Am I?"

My pulse quickened. *He was definitely something.*

By now, I was pretty sure I was molesting him with my eyes. Trying to salvage some dignity, I broke eye-contact and glanced around the pantry.

As far as pantries went, it was shockingly clean and organized. It had nothing on the floor – no stacks of cans or stray water bottles. The entire space was clean and tidy, with food arranged on the shelves according to its type – soup in one section, pasta in another, cereal to my right.

On impulse, I grabbed a box of oat puffs and shoved it toward him. "Here."

He looked down at the box, but made no move to take it. "What's that for?"

With a smug smile, I said, "Cereal. So you don't starve."

"What, no cannibalism?"

"Well, you're not gonna eat *me,* that's for sure."

I froze. *Oh, God.* That came out so very wrong. And judging from Mason's expression, the double meaning hadn't escaped him.

Talk about embarrassing.

His voice was quiet in the near darkness. "You sure about that?"

I felt myself swallow. "Pretty sure."

Good grief. What was I saying?

His gaze grew speculative. "Uh-huh."

Dang it. He was standing so close, I swear, I could feel the energy pulsing between us, fueling my fantasies of catching him alone.

And now we *were* alone, which meant that I'd be smart to get out of here *fast*, before I did something truly asinine – like hurtle myself into his arms and beg for him to take me, right here in the pantry.

How humiliating would that be?

Almost too late, I recalled my reason for insisting on privacy. *Lunk-blaster.* He'd wanted to know what it meant. And if I didn't tell him soon and get the heck out of here, I was in serious danger of forgetting myself.

In a near panic, I whispered, "It's a mother-fucker, okay?" My hands flew to my mouth. "Shit! I mean, shoot!" I almost groaned out loud. "This is all your fault, you know."

With obvious amusement, he said, "Is it?"

"Yes, because I meant to *spell* it out, not blurt it out. And, as we've *already* established, you're the only person I curse around."

"So you say."

"What, you think I'm lying?"

His gaze held mine, and his voice softened. "I don't know what you're doing."

At something in his tone, I gave a hard swallow. "What does that mean?"

"Don't ask."

"Oh, I'm asking."

Once again, his gaze dipped to my lips. "Why?"

"Because I want to know."

"Trust me," he said. "You don't."

As he spoke, something in his gaze made my knees go just a little wobbly. My pulse jumped, and my body warmed. *Did he have any idea what he was doing to me?*

Or the things I *wanted* him to do to me?

Oh, boy.

He was so achingly close that I was finding it hard to breathe – not because we were in a confined space, but rather because lately, he was *always* having that effect on me.

By now, I was so disoriented, I could hardly think. Adding to my confusion, something about this seemed oddly familiar.

And then it hit me. "Oh, my God."

He frowned. "What?"

"This is almost exactly like the pantry where I had my first kiss."

His gaze grew speculative. "Oh, yeah?"

I almost cringed. "I don't know why I just told you that."

"So, who was the guy?"

As my thoughts swirled, heat flooded my face. "Nobody."

Mason gave me a long, inscrutable look. "It must've been *somebody* to make you blush like that."

Was I blushing? But of course, I was. Unfortunately, it had nothing to do with Anton McCormack, the guy who'd been my impromptu partner in that high school game of Spin the Bottle.

With an awkward laugh, I said, "Oh, please. I'm not blushing because of *him*."

"So why *are* you blushing?"

"Because of *you*."

His gaze warmed. "Oh, yeah?"

"Yes. You make it hard to think."

"But you're thinking *something*."

"Yeah, well, maybe *you're* thinking something, too."

"Am I?"

Was he ever. And unless I was mistaken, he was thinking the same thing *I* was thinking. If that was true, how crazy would *that* be?

When I replied with a slight nod, he said, "I'll tell *you* if you tell me."

"You mean what we're thinking?" I gave it some thought. "Alright. But you have to go first."

"Deal." His gaze held mine. "I was thinking I want to kiss you."

Oh, boy. "Well, um, that's a funny coincidence because… " I winced. *Was I really going to say it?*

Yes.

I was.

Finally, I just blurted it out. "*I* was thinking, I *wanted* you to kiss me."

His eyebrows lifted. "Wanted?"

"Want," I corrected.

His lips curved into a knowing smile. "Oh, yeah?" As he said it, he moved a fraction closer. Slowly, as if giving me the chance to back away, he lowered his head until our lips were barely an inch apart.

By now, my pulse was racing, and I was having a hard time catching my breath. Unable to stop myself, I closed the gap. When our lips met, his arms locked around me, yanking me tight against him as his mouth claimed mine like he owned it.

I heard a soft thud as the box of cereal hit the floor. *Funny, I hadn't even realized I was still holding it.*

But I didn't care. I didn't care about anything as I lifted my arms and laced my fingers around the back of his neck. As his mouth moved against mine, I kissed him back with all the pent-up passion I'd been holding in check for weeks now.

He was a great kisser. He was *so* great, in fact, that I moaned into his mouth and sagged against him as my core warmed and my insides grew slick with longing.

If I were feeling remotely sane, I might've wondered what the heck I was doing. But the truth was, any capacity for thought had vanished with that very first kiss – the best one I'd ever had.

By the time he pulled back, I was practically panting with need – raw and hungry, like I'd been starving for weeks.

Maybe I had been starving. *For him.*

He was still holding me. And I was still holding him. Against my pelvis, I could feel the proof of his arousal pressing against my hip.

And that's when I knew. If I had my way, I was going to be a *very* naughty nanny.

CHAPTER 29

Mason

I hadn't planned to kiss her. I hadn't planned any of this. But it felt so right, I knew that if we stopped now, I'd be kicking myself in the morning.

Hell, I'd be kicking myself no matter how this ended.

But how would Cami feel?

As we pulled back, I drank in the sight of her. Her face was flushed and her lips were parted as she stared up at me like she was reeling just as much as *I* was.

If that was true, we were in for one hell of a ride.

Still, I'd be smart to get a grip. She wasn't just my employee. She was Willow's nanny. *And I loved Willow a lot more than I loved myself.*

But Cami – she was something else. Breathlessly, she asked, "What are we doing?"

At the office, I had all the answers. Hell, even at home, I never wavered in my convictions.

Until now.

And Cami, she was a decent person, so I didn't want to lie to her. "The truth?" I said. "I don't know."

"Me neither." Her gaze met mine. "But I do know one thing."

"Oh, yeah? What's that?"

"Tonight, if we go our separate ways, I know I'll regret it."

Me, too.

I studied her face. "And tomorrow?"

"What about it?"

I didn't want to say it. But I had responsibilities beyond myself. *And so did Cami.* "You know this is a bad idea, right?"

She hesitated. "What do you mean?"

"I mean," I said, "it's not just about us." I looked deep into her eyes and willed her to understand. "I'm not gonna lie. *I want you.* I've wanted you for a while now."

"Really?"

"Is that such a surprise?"

"Sort of. I mean you never showed it."

I was finding this hard to believe. "Never?"

"Okay, maybe there were *sometimes* I sort of wondered."

"Well don't," I said, "because I'm telling you straight-up. If I had *my* way, I'd take you right here – and make damn sure you had nothing to complain about."

At this, she made a sound. It might've been a whimper, or maybe a soft moan. Either way, it went straight to my groin, making me want to pull her closer, to find all of her special places, to give her something to *really* moan about.

But not yet.

I had to say the rest – for *her* sake, if nothing else. "But," I continued, "if you wake up tomorrow and regret it, and it hurts Willow, we're gonna have problems."

She blinked. "What do you mean?"

"I mean, if you leave your job because you can't handle it…" I paused to let my words sink in. "I'll make damn sure you regret it."

"What?" She stiffened in my arms. "How?"

"It wouldn't be hard," I said. "A few phone calls, a few innuendos. And there's always bribes."

She swallowed. "Bribes to do what?"

"To make sure that if you leave before your term is up—"

"Wait, my term?"

"The nanny job. You agreed to stay 'til next fall."

"So?"

"So if you leave sooner because of *this*, I'm telling you up front, you'll have a hell of a time finding a new job."

Her fingers stiffened at the back of my neck. In a near-whisper, she said, "Oh, my God. You're actually threatening me."

"No. I'm letting you know in advance. Whatever you're offering, I'm not taking it at Willow's expense." I gave her a serious look. "And neither should you."

With a whispered scoff, she said, "As if I would. I adore Willow. You *know* that. But we *both* know I'm not gonna stay in this job forever."

"And no one expects you."

"But you just said—"

"No. What I *said* was, if you leave early because of whatever happens tonight, we're gonna have problems."

"You mean *I'm* gonna have problems."

"You *and* me." I paused. "And someone else." And that someone was my sister, who was happier than I'd ever seen her. And hell if *I'd* be the one to destroy her happiness in favor of my own.

Cami shook her head. "I don't believe you. Here we are, having some sort of moment, and you threaten my job."

"Not *this* job."

"Fine. My replacement job."

"Which you won't need if you stick with this one."

"That's a little heavy-handed, don't you think?"

"Maybe," I admitted. "And yet..." Deliberately, I softened my tone. "...you're not letting go."

It was no lie. Even now, her hands were still laced around the back of my neck. Our pelvises were still touching. And unless those pajama pants of hers were a lot thicker than they looked, she knew exactly how much I wanted her, even now.

She bit her lip. "Yeah, well... You're not letting go either."

She was right. I wasn't.

In spite of the tension, she felt perfect in my arms, like she'd belonged there from the beginning.

Forget letting go.

What I *wanted* to do was to yank her close and kiss her hot and heavy. I wanted to elicit that sound again, not just once, but over and over as I discovered what she liked and gave her more than she thought she could handle.

I was a good lover. I knew this, just like I knew that even though I had a talent for satisfying women in bed, I left them wanting in other ways.

The physical stuff, it was easy. But real intimacy, I didn't want it *or* need it. And once again, I didn't want to lie to her.

"And just to be clear," I said, "I'm not looking for a girlfriend."

"Good, because I'm not looking for a boyfriend either. And even if I were…" She shook her head. "Never mind."

The old "never-mind" thing. It was an age-old trick, one I never fell for. And yet, in what was becoming a bad habit, I said the opposite of what I'd planned. "No. Tell me."

She hesitated. "Well, I'm just saying, I don't think we'd make such a great couple."

"Agreed."

I meant it, too. Cami was light-hearted and sweet. But me? There was no lightness in my heart, and I had no sweetness to share beyond the scattered crumbs I gave my own family.

But hey, I was happy with who I was, and didn't plan on changing any time soon.

When Cami said nothing in reply, I added, "If you want, you can call it a one-time thing."

She chewed on her bottom lip. "You mean, like to get it out of our systems?"

"If that's the way you want to look at it."

She was a silent for a long, lingering moment. But already, I knew what she was going to say. I could see it in her eyes and feel it in the warmth of her body.

She wanted me just as much I wanted her.

Still, I waited in silence, letting her have all the time she needed. But in the end, it didn't take long. "Alright," she said. "And whatever happens, it stays between us. And *only* us."

CHAPTER 30

Cami

Only us?

As soon as those words left my lips, I almost groaned out loud – and not because Mason was so ungodly sexy.

Here I was, making it sound all romantic, when in reality it was more of a physical transaction, something that needed to be done so I could banish him from my thoughts, erase him from my fantasies, and get on with my life – a life that *didn't* include mooning after my elusive boss.

Quickly, I added, "I mean, it won't affect my job. That's all." And then, looking to recover some of my lost dignity, I said, "And it shouldn't affect *you* either. I mean, just so you know, if you fire me tomorrow, *you're* gonna be in trouble, too."

With a knowing smile, he leaned closer. At first, I thought he was going to give me another kiss. But he didn't. Instead, he bypassed my mouth entirely and brushed his lips against my ear. In a low voice, he said, "Don't you know? I'm *already* in trouble."

My breath hitched. *Oh, boy. So much for it not affecting me.*

Somehow, I managed to ask, "How so?"

"Because you're too fucking irresistible." His teeth grazed my earlobe, and he gave it a light nibble. "And, if you think you're going anywhere, forget it."

I gave a breathless laugh. "So we're gonna do it right here in the pantry?"

"Only round one."

"What's round one?" I asked.

"Well, it's not cereal."

At this, I actually giggled. "Oh, really?"

He pulled back and looked deep into my eyes. "But first, what I'm gonna do is get a good look at you naked."

I sucked in a breath. *Naked. With Mason Blastoviak.*

Now *that* was a thought. As my pulse jumped, I breathed, "Oh?"

"And before you ask, yeah, right here in the pantry."

It wasn't what I would've expected, but the thought of getting naked here, where the whole thing had started, well, it sounded slightly kinky. And for some messed-up reason, it only added to my excitement. I murmured, "Well, it *is* a nice pantry."

"Good to know." And with that, he pulled away, leaving me standing outside his embrace for the first time since that mind-blowing kiss.

I stifled a warm shiver as I considered what I was about to do – what *we* were about to do. The whole thing was entirely surreal. He was my boss. And my nemesis. And the secret fantasy that had been haunting my thoughts for weeks, maybe longer.

In a voice filled with sin, he said, "Now undress for me."

My breath caught. He wasn't just asking. *He was commanding. And heaven help me, I liked it.*

Still, I summoned up a saucy smile. "Are you gonna undress for me, too."

"Later."

"Why later?"

His eyes warmed. "Because ladies first."

Part of me was tempted to argue. After all, didn't "ladies first" mean that he'd do something for *me*, and not the other way around? But the more I thought about it, the more I liked the idea of watching *him* watching *me* as I peeled off my clothes in front of him.

He added, "But first, take three steps back."

"Why?"

"Because I want to see all of you. And if *I* back up, I'm gonna have to open the door." His tone grew teasing. "You don't want *that*, do you?"

No. I didn't.

But I wanted *something*, and that something was him. Without breaking eye-contact, I took a careful step backward, and then another, bypassing the tall wooden step-stool that I'd lugged into the pantry several weeks ago to help me reach items on the top shelves.

But none of that mattered now. I barely noticed my surroundings. All I noticed was *him*, the guy watching me with obvious interest as I took the final step.

Somewhere in the back of my mind, I realized that putting some distance between us was smart if he wanted a full-length view. But even better, it gave *me* a full look at *him*.

And boy, was he *ever* something to look at. His tailored suit fit like it was custom-made, which it probably was. He was still wearing his shoes – probably Italian – along with a classic red necktie.

From head to toe, he looked exactly like what he was – a wealthy, powerful man who was accustomed to getting what he wanted. And for whatever reason, what he wanted now was me.

And the feeling was more than mutual.

As he appraised me in the confined space, I appraised him too, marveling at his masculine perfection. He was tall and imposing, with broad shoulders, a narrow waist, and dark, smoldering eyes – eyes that made me feel nearly naked already in spite of the fact that I'd yet to remove a single item of clothing.

His gaze raked the length of me before he said, "Pants first."

I gave a shaky laugh. "Why?"

"Because I want to see you in your panties." Again, his tone grew teasing. "You *are* wearing them, aren't you?"

Yes. I was. And by some miracle, I was actually wearing one of my favorite pairs. They were black and lacy and definitely on the skimpy side.

Thank goodness for small favors.

Now if only the rest of my clothes were half as sexy. But they weren't.

If I'd known *any* of this was going to happen, I would've worn different pajama pants, maybe something silky or tight. And forget the pink fuzzy slippers. I would've left them in my closet and padded around barefoot if I had to.

With an embarrassed laugh, I said, "What about the slippers?"

His gaze dipped to my feet. "I like 'em."

I almost giggled. "You do not."

"Wanna bet?" he said. "Matter of fact, keep 'em on."

"But I can't." I glanced down. "I mean, logistically."

"Sure you can." His gaze drifted to my pelvis. "Matter of fact, just *lower* the pants."

"What do you mean?"

"Keep them on, but push them down."

This was also unexpected. Breathlessly I asked, "How far?"

"As far as your ankles," he said. "And do it nice and slow."

With a hard swallow, I moved both hands to my waist and gave the fabric a slow push downward, sliding the waistband first past my hips and then past the intersection of my thighs.

As I did this, I kept my gaze trained on the guy watching me, wondering if this was what he had in mind.

From the look in his eyes, it was exactly what he'd wanted. And he *wasn't* disappointed.

But when I started to bend my knees to push the fabric lower, he said, "Keep your legs straight." He gave me a long, lingering look. "I want to see you bend over."

I hesitated. "So, do you want me turn around, or—"

"No. I want you facing me." He smiled like he knew exactly what he was doing. "And as far as your ass, trust me. I'll be getting a good long look before the night's over."

"Oh, really?"

He gave a slow nod. "Now go ahead. I'm waiting."

Slowly, I did as he asked, feeling nearly obscene as I bent over and pushed my pajama pants down until the thick fabric was pooled over my slippers. I tried to watch him as I did this, but at the very end, the angle of my head made it pretty much impossible.

Still, when I straightened, I got a nice long look at Mason, watching me like I was the most beautiful thing he'd ever seen. With a slow smile, he said, "You're perfection. You know that?"

No. I didn't, not in the big scheme of things.

After all, I *knew* the kind of women Mason had been linked with in the past. *They* were perfection, at least in every photo *I'd* seen.

But me? I was just a normal girl.

And yet, I was feeling sexier than I ever had in my whole life as Mason's gaze raked the length of me, as if I *were* truly perfect.

In a quiet voice, he said, "Now the shirt. Nice and slow, remember?"

Oh, I remembered. And I was liking this far more than I might've anticipated.

I was wearing a thin tank top with no bra. With trembling hands, I reached for the lower hem and slowly started lifting it. So far, Mason and I had only shared a single kiss. And yet, I was already warm and slick with excitement.

It was totally crazy, but somehow this felt more intimate than the usual routine of groping under the covers in a traditional bed. And there was something in Mason's expression that made me feel like we were sharing a lot more than an impromptu peep show.

Taking my sweet time, I continued lifting the hem of my shirt, first up over my navel, and then up over my lower ribs. I paused for a long moment with only the underside of my breasts exposed and gave Mason a knowing smile of my own. "Should I keep going?"

"You'd better."

As our gazes held, I was very conscious of the cotton fabric clinging to my nipples. By now, they were so hard, they literally ached.

And that wasn't my only ache. Deep in my core, I was aching for Mason, wanting to be filled with his hardness until that achy feeling went away.

Or maybe, judging from the size of the erection I'd felt pressing against my hip, I'd be aching in a whole new way, a better way.

I wanted him.

Bad.

As I lifted my shirt and exposed my breasts, I felt no awkwardness, only lust.

It made no sense. I wasn't like this.

And yet, here I was standing there in Mason's pantry, with my pants down and my shirt up. *If it weren't for my panties, I might as well be naked.*

I *wanted* to be naked. With trembling hands, I yanked the shirt over my head and tossed it aside.

Mason smiled. "Now the panties."

By now, I knew what he meant. And I knew exactly how to do it. Slowly, I pushed down the silky fabric, first past my hips and then past my knees, and then lower still, until my panties were resting atop the pajama pants that were pooled at my ankles.

I should've felt ridiculous. But I didn't. I felt beyond sexy as I slowly straightened and gave Mason the view he'd been asking for.

From the look in his eyes, he was liking what he saw. With a sexy smile, he said, "I'm gonna make a liar out of you. You know that, right?"

I wasn't sure what he meant, but there was something in the way he said it that made my breath hitch with anticipation. "How so?"

Without breaking eye contact, he prowled slowly toward me, stopping only briefly to grab the nearby stool. The thing was heavy. I knew this from hard experience.

But Mason, he lifted it with one hand, like the thing weighed nearly nothing. He placed it by my side and then reached down to retrieve my discarded tank top. He placed on the seat and said, "Sit."

At that moment, I swear, he could've commanded me to do anything, and I would've done it without question. But when I went to sit on the stool, Mason reached for my hand and guided me gently down until my naked backside settled onto the discarded tank top.

I was sitting. And he was standing. My face was very near his pelvis, and at first, I thought he was going to drop his pants and give me a taste of his hardness – the massive erection I could see straining against the pricy fabric of his suit.

But instead, with his gaze locked on mine, he lowered himself to his knees directly in front of me and said, "Fuck the cereal. The only thing I want to taste is you."

CHAPTER 31

Mason

It wasn't what I'd planned on doing, but there was something about Cami that had me doing all kinds of things I never anticipated.

Or maybe it was because of that joke she'd made about me not eating her. It had gotten me thinking. And once I'd *started* thinking, I knew I wouldn't be happy until I'd had a taste.

And while I was at it, I was going to make her squirm until she begged for me to take her, like I'd been wanting to for far too long.

She looked almost ready to beg now. *No surprise there.*

The truth was, the begging happened more often than you'd think. But until now, there'd been no danger of me begging back.

But with Cami? *There was danger, alright.*

She looked so sexy with her tousled hair and naked body. Her eyes were warm and filled with lust. Her nipples were hard, and her smile was soft.

Man, I wanted this girl.

With a breathless laugh, she said, "I hope you don't mean cannibalism."

So she'd remembered the joke. *Smart.*

And sexy.

From between her thighs, I gave her a knowing smile. "Don't worry. I won't bite. Much."

With her pajama pants and panties bunched around her ankles, she was a sight for my jaded eyes.

I wasn't feeling jaded now.

Kneeling in front of her, I leaned forward and pressed my lips to the inside of her thigh. Her skin was warm and smooth, and she gave a light shiver when I trailed my lips higher.

She murmured, "This isn't what I expected."

Me neither. And I liked *that*, too. She had me surprising myself, which hadn't happened in a long while.

What was it about her, anyway?

When my lips drifted closer to the center, she made that same sound – that half whimper, half moan. My pulse jumped, and my erection throbbed. When I reached the intersection of her thighs and zoomed in on that special spot – *yeah, I knew the one* – she said on a ragged breath, "Oh, wow."

Wow was right. I tasted her with my tongue, and suckled her with my mouth.

I felt her hands in my hair, and heard the soft sounds she made as I learned exactly what she liked and filed it away for future reference – because I knew one thing already. One taste wouldn't be enough.

Already, her thighs were straining, and her pelvis was rising and falling – not a lot, but enough to let me know that I wasn't the only one loving this.

As I suckled her center, I lifted my hand and trailed my fingers along the inside of her thigh, loving the silky smoothness of her skin and the trail of goosebumps I left in my wake.

She was so responsive and so sweet, that I felt a warmth growing inside me – a warmth I hadn't felt in a very long time.

When I reached up and stroked her opening, she made a little moan that had me feeling like a teenager all over again – too eager and too ready for anyone's good.

But I hadn't been a teenager for a long time, and I knew the value of waiting. I decided right then and there that when I finally took her, it wouldn't be here in the pantry.

It would be up in my bedroom, where I could lay her across my bed, and do more than taste her.

As I suckled her center, I claimed her with my finger, and then another. She was sweet and tight, and so very wet that I almost moaned myself.

In a hoarse whisper, she said, "You're *really* good at that."

I smiled against her skin. "I know."

She started to laugh, probably at my arrogance. *Hell yeah, I was arrogant.* But I knew what I was good at, and I wasn't ashamed to admit it.

I turned her laughter into moans by nibbling at her clit just the way she liked while I caressed her insides with my fingers.

Oh, yeah, she was definitely on the edge.

I was tempted to let up, to take her almost there and back again maybe a few more times, before giving her the release she obviously craved.

But I couldn't stop, because I didn't want to. I wanted to hear her sounds and feel her convulse, and then take her up to my bedroom and claim her right and proper in my king-sized bed.

When she shuddered again and cried out her release, her slick walls closed around my fingers, filling me with the warm anticipation of what I'd be doing next.

But not here.

I smiled against her skin. Upstairs.

CHAPTER 32

Cami

Oh. My. God.

Mason was full of surprises. Gone was the cold and distant boss. And in his place was the best lover I'd ever had.

And we hadn't technically had sex.

Not yet.

But he *had* made me very happy. *No faking needed.*

After he'd given me the best oral sex of my life, he'd stood and taken off his suit-jacket. He'd wrapped it over my shoulders, telling me, "I'm taking you upstairs."

I loved that about him. He was the kind of guy who knew exactly what he wanted and wasn't shy about taking the lead.

It was so freaking sexy that I forgot to be self-conscious, even as I shrugged into his suit coat and let him pull me to my feet. I fell into his arms, where he kissed me hot and heavy, giving me a taste of not only his tongue, but of my own arousal, still fresh on his lips.

I should've been embarrassed, not only by the taste, but by the fact that my pajama pants – and my panties, too – were still down around my ankles, leaving my pelvis bare as I leaned into his kiss and gave as good as I got.

I couldn't help but whimper with excitement when he grabbed my backside and pulled me tighter against him.

By the time the kiss ended, I was so eager to go upstairs, I practically stumbled backward in my attempt to yank up my panties and then my pajama bottoms so we could make the mad dash for his bedroom – except it wasn't a dash at all.

Recalling the need to be quiet, we crept silently up the stairs and then into his moonlit bedroom, which was so spectacular, it would've put a five-star hotel to shame.

By the time his bedroom door closed behind us, both of us were so eager that we undressed as we walked, leaving our clothes to fall wherever.

Soon, we lay naked in his sheets. With an eagerness that should've embarrassed me, I yanked him closer and guided his massive erection to my slick opening. He was huge and hard, but I was warm and eager.

As our bodies joined, I wrapped my arms around his back and held on for dear life as we moved together in the moonlight.

Into my hair, he whispered, "God, I've wanted you."

"I wanted you, too," I admitted, not even trying to catch my breath. When his lips found mine, I kissed him back with a wild abandon that matched the movement of our bodies as we rode the waves of our excitement until we were utterly spent.

Afterward, we held each other close for a long time, until our breathing calmed and something like sanity returned.

Sane or not, I regretted nothing.

Maybe this was wrong, but it felt so achingly right, even now after our passion was spent. When Mason rolled onto his side, he didn't let go, and I savored the look and feel of him as we lay facing each other on his king-size bed.

With a sleepy smile, he said, "You're amazing. You know that?"

I smiled back. "You're amazing, too."

As our gazed held, I couldn't help but compare *this* Mason with the one who'd walked into that Petoskey nightclub all those weeks ago.

He was the same guy, but I was seeing a different side – a side I could definitely fall for if I wasn't careful.

And speaking of careful, I stifled a giggle. "I guess I should've mentioned this already, but I *am* on the pill."

His voice was quiet in the moonlight. "I know."

"Wait, how would you know?"

"I saw you pack, remember?"

"Oh." I smiled. "Yeah, I guess you did."

It was funny to think that barely two months had passed since he'd shown up out of the blue. But now, as I lay cradled in his arms, our tense beginning felt a lifetime away.

I said, "Can I ask you something?"

"Anything."

Funny, he looked like he actually meant it. I plunged onward before he could change his mind. "When you came to that club, you know, in Petoskey, how'd you know where I was?"

"Easy," he said. "I called your house."

"You mean my parent's house?"

He pressed his forehead to mine. "That *is* where you were living."

"And someone told you where I was? Seriously?"

"No. They said you were out clubbing. After that, it was easy."

"How?"

"I just looked for your car."

I didn't bother asking how he knew which car was mine. One thing about Mason, he knew all kinds of things.

Already, he knew all of my special spots and what to do when he got there. *And that was after only one time.*

Man, he was good.

I felt my tongue skim my upper lip and suddenly realized something totally hilarious. "Oh, my God," I laughed. "You know what's funny?"

He stroked my naked hip. "What?"

"I never got my water."

"What water?"

"Well, that's the reason I went down to the kitchen in the first place – to grab a bottle of water. But then, I got all distracted."

"Oh yeah?" he teased. "By what?"

"You *know* what," I said. "Trouble-maker."

With a smile in his voice, he said, "Is that a complaint?"

"Yes," I laughed. "It's a total complaint. In fact, where's your complaint department? I want to file a grievance or something."

"Do you now?"

"Definitely."

"Hang on." And with that, he pulled away and rolled to his other side, giving me a nice view of his muscular back.

I watched in perplexed silence as he reached down beside the bed and began rummaging on the floor for something.

I asked, "What are you doing?"

Without looking back, he said, "Resolving your complaint."

I didn't feel like complaining *now*. His whole backside was a sight to behold – from the muscles in his shoulders to the tight shape of his perfect butt.

Smiling at the view, I murmured, "Oh, really?"

He finished rummaging and turned back to face me. He was holding two bottles of water in one hand, holding them loose, near their caps. Looking way too smug, he replied, "Really."

I sat up in surprise. "You keep water in your bedroom?"

"I do *now*." He handed me a bottle and opened the other one for himself as he sat up beside me, resting his back against the massive headboard.

The water wasn't cold, but I hardly cared as I twisted the cap and leaned back beside him. I took a long, steady drink and kept on going. When I came up for air, my bottle was half empty.

Next to me, Mason, gave a low chuckle. "That bad, huh?"

I snuck a quick glance at *his* bottle. Unlike mine, it was still nearly full. Maybe I should've been embarrassed, but I wasn't. "Oh, it was bad, alright," I told him with a playful swat to his shoulder. "You almost killed me."

His eyebrows lifted. "Did I?"

"With dehydration," I clarified, lest he get the wrong idea. And besides, if amazing sex was *that* deadly, I would've been a goner in the pantry.

He smiled. "Well, we can't have *that.*"

My breath caught. His smile – it looked different, all warm and wonderful. Plus, it went all the way to his eyes, making him look younger and more carefree than I'd ever seen.

I was so mesmerized, I couldn't bring myself to look away.

Wow. So *that's* what sex did to him.

Still, I'd be foolish to think it was anything more than a physical release – not just for him, but for both of us.

A happy sigh escaped my lips. *Oh, but what a release it had been.* For me, there'd been multiple releases.

Imagine that.

There was only one downside. The plan had been for me to get Mason out of my system and return to a normal state-of-mind – one where I wasn't lusting after my enigmatic boss.

But the longer I thought about it, the more I realized that he wasn't *quite* out of my system. He still thrilled me beyond all reason. And the sex – it had been the best I'd ever had, with no close runner-up.

As our gazes held, I heard myself say, "I've got a question."

"Yeah?"

"What if I get thirsty again?" I hesitated. "Like tomorrow night for example."

Technically, my question was ridiculous. *Of course I'd get thirsty.* After all, no human could survive long without water – not even Mason Blastoviak, who hardly seemed human at all.

But surely, he knew what I was *really* asking.

Still, he remained silent as the question hung unanswered between us. As I watched, his smile faded, and his expression grew thoughtful.

What on Earth was he thinking?

I had no idea.

And by now I felt slightly foolish. Still, I couldn't seem to let it drop. "Like, let's say it's the middle of the night, and I want a bottle of water. Should I go to the kitchen, or…?"

Deliberately, I left the sentence unfinished, figuring it was up to Mason to fill in the blanks.

Finally he said with no trace of humor. "Or what? Keep water in your own room?"

I stiffened. *No. That's not what I'd meant at all.*

And surely, he knew this.

Mason *wasn't* stupid. So either he was deliberately misunderstanding, or this was his way of telling me that one night together was more than enough.

Well, this wasn't humiliating or anything.

But hey, that *had* been the deal, right?

With an awkward laugh, I said, "Never mind. I mean, I can always stash water under my own bed, right?" I hesitated. "Or I could stick my head under the tap, or, um…" I paused. "You know what? I think I'll stop talking now."

Deliberately, I clamped my lips shut and glanced around his bedroom. *Probably this was my cue to leave.*

I considered the logistics. *Should I just gather up my things and go?*

I had my pants, but my tank top was still in the pantry. *Should I ask to borrow Mason's suit jacket again? Or would that be too presumptuous now that we were done?*

I was still thinking when Mason said in a quiet voice, "Hey."

I turned to look. "Yeah?"

"You wanna know *why* I keep water under my bed?"

"Why?"

"Because of you."

I didn't get it. "Me?" And then it hit me. "Oh. So, you *knew* I'd end up here?"

But of course he had. I mean, that's what all the nannies did, right? One way or another, they all beat a path to Mason's door, with the possible exception of Veronica, who'd slept with his brother instead.

And now there was me.

Probably the script called for me to be grateful – not just for being allowed inside, but also for the in-room beverage service.

But I didn't *feel* grateful. Mostly I felt silly for being so easy to predict.

Before Mason could think to answer, I forced another laugh. "Never mind. Don't answer that." Again, I glanced around. This time, I spotted a plaid blanket draped over a nearby chair. "Hey, can I borrow that?"

"Borrow what?"

I pointed. "That blanket. You know, so I can return to my bedroom." I kept my gaze trained on the blanket. "I mean, now that it's over."

When Mason spoke next, his voice was softer than I'd ever heard it. "Cami."

Again, I turned to look. "Yeah?"

"You don't get it."

"I don't get what?"

"I wasn't keeping water under my bed for when you came to *me*. I was keeping it to stop *me* from going to you."

My breath caught. "What?"

He reached out and gently stroked the side of my face. "Do you know how crazy you've been making me?"

"Seriously?"

"Dead serious," he said. "There were times I'd leave my room in the middle of the night, and I'd happen to glance toward your bedroom door or hell, run into you in the kitchen. And then get I'd to thinking..."

When his words trailed off into silence, I couldn't stop myself from saying, "Thinking what?"

"About you. And this."

"Really?"

"Really," he said. "And I promise you this. If you're thirsty tomorrow night, my door – it'll be unlocked."

CHAPTER 33

Mason

She never came, not that night, nor the night after that.

I didn't get it. Whenever Willow was around, Cami acted like nothing had happened between us. There were no secret looks, no sly bids to get me alone, nothing except for the same warm professionalism she'd shown from the beginning.

And when Willow *wasn't* around? Neither was Cami.

If I were the kind of guy to question my own skills, I might've wondered if I'd left her wanting in the bedroom.

But I hadn't.

She'd been satisfied and then some. I knew this, just like I knew that when she'd left my bedroom near dawn, she'd left with a smile, along with every intention of returning.

Maybe she hadn't said so, but the look in her eyes had been crystal clear as I'd bundled her into the blanket and kissed her goodbye at my bedroom door.

Hell, I would've walked her back to her own room if only she hadn't insisted on going alone. *It wasn't a big deal.* Her bedroom was only a short walk from mine, and there were no wolves roaming my halls.

Well, none except me.

As far as the future logistics, I figured we had the next night to work out the details.

But we worked out nothing.

And why? It was because Cami never showed.

Another guy might've asked her what was going on, or maybe tried to get her alone for a repeat performance. *But that wasn't me.*

I wasn't looking for anything serious. *I wasn't looking for anything at all.* And yet, I couldn't stop thinking about her.

I started living for her smiles and watching her from the corner of my eye, wondering what would happen when she left my house for good. *Would Willow be the same?*

Would I?

I didn't think so. And slowly, I came to a startling conclusion. If I had a heart to give, I'd give it to Cami, assuming she'd accept.

But would she? Now I wasn't so certain. And this, too, was a new sensation. I wasn't sure how I felt about it.

I wasn't sure about anything.

And this, too, was a first.

After the first week, I stopped listening for a knock at my door. After the second week, I debated knocking on hers.

But I'd told Cami up-front that I wasn't looking for anything serious, so I refused to give her the wrong impression, to lead her on with promises of something I couldn't give.

She deserved better.

So I tried to let it go.

Tried. And failed.

At Thanksgiving, Cami went home for a long weekend to visit her family while Willow and I spent the holiday at Brody and Arden's place, where we had the first traditional Thanksgiving dinner we'd had in years.

It was nice. Or it would've been, if only I weren't missing a certain someone – Cami.

As far as her trip back to Petoskey, it was only fair to give her the time off, along with the use of the orange SUV to drive there and back. It was something we'd agreed on maybe a month earlier, before we'd given in to whatever urges had made us lose control.

When she returned from her vacation, it was more of the same. She was friendly during the day and avoided me at night.

It used to be, she'd spend her nighttime hours in the living areas, scrolling through her phone or reading on her tablet. Now, I didn't know what she was doing. I just knew she was doing it in her own private space, away from me.

And it was driving me batshit crazy.

Forget the sex. I missed seeing her around. I missed talking to her. I missed the way she challenged me when no one else would.

She wasn't anymore. Something had changed – and not for the better.

I let it go for maybe another week before deciding it was time to get some answers – for Willow's sake if not my own. If Cami was planning to make a move, I had to know.

That night, after Willow went to bed, I caught up with Cami in the upstairs hallway and said, "We need to talk."

From the look on her face, this wasn't what she wanted to hear. "About what?"

I gave her a look. "Guess."

"No."

This wasn't a word I was used to hearing. "What do you mean, no?"

"I mean *no*, I won't guess." She gave Willow's closed bedroom door a quick glance before adding in a hushed tone, "If you want to talk about something, just tell me what it is."

Cami was smart. She *had* to know what I wanted to discuss. But hey, if she wanted it spelled out, that was fine by me. "Alright," I said. "I want to talk about what happened."

"What do you mean?"

Now I, too, lowered my voice. "I mean, what happened between us."

"Oh." She frowned. "What about it?"

This should've been obvious. But I didn't want to be a dick about it, so for the first time in my adult life, I asked, "Are you mad about something?"

"You mean at you?"

I shrugged. "Sure, why not?"

With a shrug of her own, she said, "Alright. Then the answer's no."

I studied her face. "Bull."

In a low whisper, she said, "I'm not lying, so just let it go, alright?"

Let it go.

It was good advice. I knew this because I'd given this same advice to plenty of people over the years. Some had taken it. Some hadn't.

As far as those who hadn't, I never saw the point. *Until now.*

I replied, "I'll let it go when you tell me what's wrong."

"Why does something have to be wrong?" she asked.

"You tell me."

"Well maybe I'm just tired. Did you ever think of that?" She paused. "In fact…" She glanced toward her bedroom door. "Let's just say goodnight, alright?"

Now *I* was the one frowning. It wasn't even nine o'clock. I'd been living with Cami for months now, and had become familiar with her schedule. Her normal bedtime was still a few hours away.

I told her, "We can say goodnight after we talk."

Her mouth tightened. "Are you saying that as my employer? Or as something else?"

"I'm saying it as both," I said. "If something's up, I need to know."

"Oh, really?"

"Yeah. For Willow's sake."

She crossed her arms. "Now who's full of it?"

"Meaning?"

"Meaning you're not asking for Willow. You're asking for yourself."

She was only half right. Still, in the spirit of meeting her in the middle, I said, "Fair enough. But we *will* be talking."

She was silent for a long moment before saying, "You know what? That's probably an excellent idea. But not here."

On this, she'd get no argument from me. "Agreed."

If things were different, I might've suggested talking in my bedroom – for convenience if nothing else. The master bedroom was only a few paces away and insulated for sound.

But I was no fool. If Cami wanted to spend time in my bedroom, she wouldn't have spent the past few weeks hiding out in her own.

I flicked my head toward the stairway. "We can talk in my office."

Her chin lifted. "No."

I froze. *There was that word again.* "No?"

"We can talk out on the patio."

I didn't get it. My house was huge with plenty of places to talk in private. If she objected to my office, there was always the family room, the workout room, or hell even the basement if she wanted to put some serious distance between us and Willow.

So why the patio?

Maybe she wasn't thinking. But *I* was. She was wearing jeans and a little black T-shirt. With a pointed look at her bare arms, I said, "Outside? It's cold as hell."

With a tight smile, she said, "Isn't hell supposed to be hot?"

"I don't know," I said. "I'll let you know when I get there."

"Oh, please," she said. "You're the kind of guy who sends *others* to hell, not the other way around."

I gave her a tight smile of my own. "Thanks."

"It wasn't a compliment."

"Says you." *I wasn't joking.* When it came to judgment, it was always better to be giving than receiving.

And, if I hadn't known this already, the look on Cami's face was proof enough. If she were a judge, and I were the defendant, I'd be heading straight to the gallows.

It was a new sensation, and I didn't like it. When she made no reply, I said, "Good thing you're not mad, huh?"

"What do you mean by that?"

"You tell me."

"If you're implying that I lied when you asked, you're remembering it all wrong."

"Am I?"

"Yes. Because I never said I wasn't mad."

"Wanna bet?"

"What I *said* was, I'm not mad at *you.*"

"So you're mad at someone else?" I studied her face, wondering who had angered her, and what I could do to fix it. "You should've said something. You need help?"

She stared up at me with apparent confusion before saying, "Oh, I need help, alright."

With growing concern, I moved closer. "What kind?"

With a light scoff, she replied, "Probably psychiatric."

Something in my shoulders eased. *She was joking.* I knew this, because Cami was one of the sanest people I'd ever met.

And yet, she wasn't looking quite as sane as she'd been looking only a few moments ago.

Funny, I wasn't feeling so sane myself. I told her, "I know the feeling."

"Good."

No. It wasn't good. I replied, "Says you."

"Well there ya go," she said. "And I thought we were gonna talk on the patio."

"Not in *this* weather."

"Oh, please," she said. "It's not like it's snowing. And besides, the cold doesn't bother you. You said so yourself. Remember?"

"I was thinking of you, not me."

"Oh." She paused. "Well that's nice."

Her words said one thing, but her expression said another. I wasn't sure what was going on, but the more we talked, the less I liked it. She was acting like I'd taken her against her will.

And we both knew that wasn't the case.

I said, "Hey, there's always the pantry."

She stiffened, but made no reply.

And now I felt like a dick. "That was a joke."

"No it wasn't."

She was wrong. Maybe it hadn't been a good joke, but I *had* been joking. "And you know this, how?"

"Because you weren't smiling."

She didn't need to tell *me*. I felt like I hadn't smiled in weeks. "You don't need to smile to make a joke."

"Alright," she said. "Then your joke was in poor taste."

Shit. She had a point. And the truth was, I liked that about her, how she cut through the bullshit without kissing my ass.

She was one of the most genuine people I'd ever met, which made her recent behavior all the more baffling.

Whatever was wrong, I wanted to make things right.

Deliberately, I softened my tone. "Maybe."

"There's no 'maybe' about it," she said. "But you know what? It's not worth arguing about."

"Cami—"

"Forget it." And with that, she turned and walked away, heading not toward the stairway, but toward her own bedroom. Over her shoulder, she said, "See you on the patio."

I felt my eyebrows furrow. "I hope you're going for a coat."

I *knew* she heard me, but she didn't turn around. Instead, she disappeared into her bedroom and shut the door firmly behind her.

And me? I headed straight to the patio, because one way or another, I was going to get some answers.

CHAPTER 34

Cami

It was a conversation I'd been hoping to avoid – not because I didn't have the guts to face him, but rather because no good could come of it.

For me, anyway.

But now that he'd insisted, I was actually glad to stop pretending. Like a junkie in need of a fix, I'd been going slowly insane over the past few weeks – even more so because I'd been working so hard not to show it.

The truth was, everything about Mason was driving me crazy, and not in a good way. Even that reminder about grabbing a coat, it made me want to let him have it.

And I didn't mean the coat. I meant a piece of my mind, even if his reminder had been surprisingly thoughtful.

But even *that* was a problem. *And why?* It was because with a hatchet hanging over my head, I'd be a total idiot to *ever* let down my guard.

Still, I stalked to my closet and grabbed my warmest winter coat – not because he'd suggested it, but because it was nighttime in early December.

By the time I made it out to the back patio, Mason was already there, standing a few feet away from the back door. At the sight of him, I stopped in confusion. He was wearing the same thing he'd been wearing in the upstairs hallway – jeans and a long-sleeve shirt. *No coat.*

As I closed the patio door behind me, I gave him a pointed look. "Where's *your* coat?"

"I didn't need one. Is that a problem?"

"No. But it does seem odd that you'd tell *me* to grab one when you didn't grab one for yourself."

"Wanna know what's odd to *me*?"

"What?"

"Whatever is going on."

I stiffened. "What do you mean?"

"You're avoiding me."

I forced a laugh. "I am not."

"You are. And we both know it."

I knew no such thing. "Oh, please. I've been spending exactly the same amount of time with you that I used to." I hesitated. "I mean, before the incident."

He gave me a look. "The incident."

"Um, yeah. In the pantry. And later in your bedroom."

He frowned. "I've never heard it called *that* before."

I summoned up a stiff smile. "Your bedroom? What do you normally call it?"

He was still frowning. "Was that a joke?"

"Maybe," I admitted. "But you know what? You could probably use a little more teasing in your life."

"Is that so?"

"Yes." And then, fearful he'd take it the wrong way, I added, "And just so we're clear, I don't mean sexually."

"Good to know."

Was it? From the look in his eyes, I couldn't be sure.

I tried again. "I mean, I'm not playing hard-to-get, if that's what you think."

"I don't," he said. "So tell me what's on your mind."

There were so many things on my mind, I hardly knew where to begin. But in the end, it all boiled down to one thing. "Remember in the pantry, when you called it bad idea?"

From the look on his face, he wasn't happy with the reminder. "Yeah?"

"Well, you were probably right."

He studied my face. "*Probably* right?"

Dang it. "Definitely right. Which is why we were smart to keep it a one-time thing."

He looked at me for a long, silent moment before saying, "Is that right?"

"Definitely. I mean, everyone knows it's a terrible idea to donk your boss – *or* your employee, for that matter."

His eyebrows lifted. "Donk."

"Yeah. It's a non-swearword for…" *Gosh, how to put this?*

"Incident?"

I shook my head. "What?"

"You mean sex."

"Uh, yeah. Right."

His gaze locked on mine. "So you're regretting it."

Funny, he hadn't phrased it as a question. And now I felt slightly ridiculous. After all, I'd been more than willing. And he'd given me every chance to change my mind.

Did I have regrets?

Yes.

And no.

"If you mean the sex," I said, "I'm not saying I regret it. I'm just saying I'm not gonna do it again, that's all."

He gave me another look, this one longer than the last. "With me? Or with anyone?"

Now, it was my turn to frown. "So…Was *that* a joke?"

"Call it teasing," he said with a pale imitation of a smile. "Unless you can dish it out, but not take it."

"Oh, I can't take it, alright," I said. "And *obviously* I *am* going to have sex again."

"But not with me."

"Exactly."

Again, he studied my face. "So, are you gonna tell me why?"

"Oh come on," I said. "I shouldn't have to give you a reason."

"Is that so?"

"Sure," I said. "I mean, let's be honest here. You're probably *glad* I'm not beating down your door."

"Tell me, do I look glad?"

"Not really," I admitted. "But that's not the point."

"So, what is?"

"I'm just saying, I'm sure you've had plenty of one-night stands. Do you always explain to *them* why there's no second night? Or third? Or whatever?"

"No. I don't."

"See?"

"Right." His voice was cool in the darkness. "So you're calling it a one-night stand."

"Exactly."

"In case you're not familiar with the concept," he said, "a one-night stand is usually with a stranger, someone you don't expect to see again."

"Yeah, well, I've never had one, so…" I gave a loose shrug. "Anyway, so, it's settled?"

"No," he said. "Not 'til you tell me why you're angry."

"Who says I'm angry?"

"I can see it in your eyes."

Great. And to think, I'd been doing such a good job of pretending like everything was normal. And maybe I had. But now, under his intense scrutiny, my pretense was crumbling fast.

I made a sound of frustration. "Has it ever occurred to you that I might be mad at myself?"

"For what?"

"Alright, let's say you really like ice cream. And there's this pint in the freezer." I hesitated. "No. Not a pint. Something bigger and better."

At those words, *bigger and better*, my stupid eyes dipped toward his crotch – not because I was looking to make a point, but because, well, my eyes just lost track of the conversation, that's all.

And now I felt like a total idiot, even as I jerked my gaze upward to announce, "And just for the record, I'm still talking about ice cream."

From the look on his face, he was far from convinced. "Is that so?"

"Yes. And I'm trying to make a point if you'll listen."

"Go ahead," he said. "I'm all ears."

No. He wasn't all ears. He was a glorious hunk of masculine perfection – with a perfect face, a perfect body, and a perfect knowledge of how to use all those assets to turn girls like me into jelly.

As I stared up at him, visions from our night together drifted through my brain. But it wasn't his face, or even his incredible body, that made my pulse quicken in the shadows. It was the way he'd made me feel, all warm and tingly, right down to my toes.

And now I was all distracted. Desperately, I tried again. "Alright, let's say it's the middle of the night, and there's this ice cream. But you're not planning to lick it…" I cringed. "I mean eat it."

Dang it.

His lips twitched at the corners. "Uh-huh."

"And I don't mean cannibalism."

As I spoke, it wasn't lost on me that my metaphor was a minefield of dangerous innuendos, especially considering that any "eating" had been on Mason's part, not mine.

At the memory, I felt a frustrating warmth settle in my core, making my resolve falter, just as I'd feared.

After all, I'd been sticking to my own bedroom for a reason.

And now, Mason looked dangerously close to smiling.

I told him, "It's not funny."

"Am I laughing?"

"No. But you want to. I can tell."

His voice softened in the night. "Trust me. That's not what I want to do."

I felt myself swallow. "Then what *do* you want?"

When he replied, his voice was more tender than I'd ever heard it. "First, I want to hear what's wrong."

CHAPTER 35

Cami

He couldn't *truly* want to know. And yet, he looked so sincere that my stomach gave a traitorous flutter. *None of this was going how I'd planned.*

In my mind, I'd envisioned him reacting with cold indifference or worse, utter contempt, the kind he'd shown to Livia back in Petoskey when she'd been slobbering all over him.

But now, as he gazed down at me, he didn't look contemptuous at all. If anything, he looked concerned.

For me?

It almost looked that way.

Or more likely, I was simply getting swept away by my own emotions – the kind I'd been trying to ignore for weeks now.

But was it any wonder? The night was clear and cold, with a nearly full moon and a sky filled with stars. And yet, none of this could compare to Mason's incredible eyes as he gazed down at me with a look that made my pulse quicken in spite of all my good intentions.

I gave myself a mental slap. This was no time to let down my guard. Mason was notoriously ruthless. And, if I hadn't known this already, he'd made it perfectly clear in the pantry, when he'd explained the consequences I'd face if I failed to keep my emotions in check.

It was time to get to the point already.

I took a deep breath and plunged onward. "Alright, here's the thing. You remember that ice cream? In my story, I mean?"

"I remember."

"Well, sometimes, you know in advance you shouldn't eat it. And you *especially* shouldn't eat the whole thing. But it's the middle of the night, and it sounds *soooo* good. And you're thinking, 'I'll just have a little bit.' Or maybe you're thinking, 'Okay, I'll eat the whole thing, but it won't be *so* bad, because I'll hit the gym extra hard in the morning. Or maybe I'll make up for it by giving up ice cream entirely for the next week, or the next month. Or even forever–'"

"Why?"

"What?" I shook my head. "What do you mean why?"

"I mean, why give it up?"

"Because you can't have ice cream *all* the time."

"Why not?"

"Isn't it obvious?" I tried to laugh. "It's incredibly bad for you, especially in large doses." *And I did mean large.*

But Mason looked unconvinced. "Is that so?"

"Sure," I said. "And in case it wasn't clear, *you're* the ice cream."

"Am I?"

I nodded. "Yes. And that's not a good thing."

"Oh yeah? Why's that?"

"Well, for one thing, it goes straight to your thighs." As those word echoed out between us, I wanted to crawl into a hole and hide – or worse, scamper up to my bedroom and pleasure myself to memories of that blissful night.

See, I told you he was making me crazy.

Under my breath, I murmured, "Well, it does."

His voice was quiet in the shadows. "Does it?"

At something in his tone, my gaze dipped, not to *his* pelvis, but to my own, because the truth was, he'd done amazing things between my thighs. *And I'd loved every moment of it.*

By the time I looked up again, I felt totally ridiculous.

It was time to switch gears, and fast. I sighed. "Look, you threatened my career. In what world is that okay?"

"None," he said. "But that's not what I did."

I made a sound of protest. "It was, too."

"No. What I said was you'd regret it."

"Yeah, because you'd *make* me regret it – you know, by making it impossible for me to find a new job."

"Yeah. For nine months. Not forever."

"So?" I said. "That's still terrible."

"No. It's being up-front."

"Fine, I said. "And believe it or not, I actually appreciate it."

He gave me a dubious look. "Do you?"

"Yes. Because an advance warning is always better than a nasty surprise."

"Except it shouldn't have been a surprise."

I felt my brow wrinkle in confusion. "What do you mean?"

"You should've known there'd be trouble if you ditched Willow because you couldn't handle yourself."

"Oh, please," I scoffed. "*Me* I can handle just fine. It's *you* I can't handle."

"Is that so?"

"Of course it is," I said. "I mean, come on. You hold all the cards here."

"Meaning?"

"Isn't it obvious?" I said. "You're the employer. I'm the employee. You're rich. I'm not. You practically threatened me. But did I threaten *you*? No. I didn't."

"You don't *need* to threaten me," he said. "You hold some nice cards of your own."

I crossed my arms. "Oh yeah? And what cards are those? Go ahead, name one."

"My sister." His voice softened as he said, "She loves you."

"Oh." Those three little words went straight to my heart, and my eyes grew misty as I considered how much I'd enjoyed getting to know her. *Willow was a terrific kid.* And we really *did* get along. With a fond smile, I replied, "And I love her, too."

"No. You *like* her. Big difference."

And just like that, I wasn't smiling anymore. "Hey, you're not allowed to tell me how I feel."

"Fair enough," he said. "But if you leave, *you're* not gonna be devastated. She will."

"Oh come on," I said. "That's not fair. This job, we never said it was a permanent thing."

"I know," he said. "Which is why the deal was for the remainder of your term, and not forever."

"So I'm supposed to be thankful?"

"No. You're supposed to stick to your word. And you're forgetting something."

My chin lifted. "Oh yeah? What's that?"

"I gave you *mine*, too. In the pantry. You remember, right?"

I remembered a lot of things from that night. Unfortunately, most of them were X-rated and pretty darn distracting.

With an effort, I tried to focus on the reason I'd come to live here in the first place. It was for Willow, and *not* for her distracting older brother, who yes, *had* given me his word that he wouldn't fire me if things got complicated.

But he was still missing the point. "Just hear me out," I said. "I'm not saying I want to quit. I'm just saying that I don't like feeling threatened, that's all."

"Yeah? Me neither."

"Oh, get real," I said. "I'm no threat to you."

"That's what you think," he scoffed. "But forget *me*."

As if I could.

Mason continued. "About Willow, do you know, aside from family, you're the first adult she's connected with in years?"

Hearing this, something squeezed at my heart. "I am?"

"You know it's true."

I hadn't known for sure, but I *had* suspected. I murmured, "Yeah, I guess I can see that."

"And," he said, "if I wanted to be real prick, I'd ruin your job prospects for good."

I felt the blood drain from my face. "What, why?"

"So you'd stick around. And hey, I'd make it worth your while."

I was glaring now. "Are you freaking kidding me?"

"No."

I bristled, "Hey, if you ever—"

"Don't worry, I won't. Like I said, I gave you my word."

"Oh, that's nice."

His gaze softened. "Cami, listen. We both know I'm not being nice. But I *am* being fair."

"Fair to who?" I scoffed.

"All of us." And then, in a gentler tone, he said, "Look, Willow knows you're leaving next year. And she's okay with it."

"Not the way *you* make it sound."

"Hey, people come and go all the time," he said. "But hell if I'm gonna spend the next few months watching her wonder what she did to make you leave ahead of schedule."

I made a sound of frustration. "But I wouldn't be leaving because of *her*."

"Right," he said. "You'd be leaving because of me. And why?" He moved a fraction closer. "Because, like a selfish prick, I couldn't keep my fucking hands off you."

His words startled me. It wasn't just the profanity. It was the raw emotion I heard in his voice.

And then, there was the gist of what he was saying, along with all those memories his words conjured up. *It wasn't just his hands that were the problem.* It was his lips and his tongue. *And so much more.*

As the memories swirled, I stifled a warm shiver.

In a near whisper, Mason continued, "…although fuck knows I tried."

I knew the feeling. In a near whisper of my own, I replied, "Yeah, well I tried, too."

"I know."

Did he? I highly doubted it, considering that I'd been putty in his oh-so capable hands. "But you're missing the point," I said. "We *both* tried, but *I* was the only one who was threatened."

"And yet, it didn't stop you."

"Exactly!" I said. "See, that's where the ice cream comes in. I knew I should've stopped. But I didn't. And hey, I'll be honest. The 'ice cream' was probably the best I'd ever had, okay?"

His lips curved into a knowing smile. "Only probably?"

God, he was so cocky, and with good reason, too. But that didn't change anything.

"Alright, fine," I said. "It was the best. But so what? I mean, you don't blame the ice cream if you can't resist. You blame yourself."

"So you're angry at yourself? That's what you're saying."

"More or less."

"Sorry but I'm not buying it."

He didn't look sorry. He looked way too sure of himself, *as usual,* which prompted me to say, "Listen, there's something you need to hear, for your sake, not mine."

"Oh, yeah?"

"Definitely," I said. "When it comes to women, you've been playing on easy mode for way too long. You think just because you're rich and famous, and yes, obnoxiously hot, that anyone would just *love* to sleep with you, no matter how you act *outside* the bedroom."

Or the pantry.

But that was beside the point.

Mason gave me an inscrutable look. "Good thing you're immune, huh?"

"No. I'm not immune," I said. "But I *have* come to my senses. I mean, seriously, there's such a thing as dignity, you know."

The words had barely left my lips when I heard a sultry female voice call out from somewhere in the distance, "Mason?"

I stiffened. That voice – it sounded eerily familiar.

But no, it couldn't be.

"Oh, my God!" the voice squealed. "It *is* you!"

With growing dread, I looked toward the sound. Unless I was mistaken, it was coming from the other side of the river.

Sure enough, someone I knew all too well was standing on the back patio of the mansion directly opposite us.

At the sight of her, I stifled a curse – and not a *kid-friendly* curse either, but a *real* curse, the kind that sailors make when their ships collide with sea monsters.

I heard myself say, "Livia?"

CHAPTER 36

Cami

Oh yeah. It was Livia alright. She was standing on the back patio of the same mansion where that unfortunate nanny had been forced to crawl through the window, however many weeks ago.

But it was definitely Livia.

She was wearing a short black skirt, black ankle boots, and a tight white blouse with a very high neckline.

I watched in growing confusion as she gave us a big smile and a friendly wave.

When I gave her a tentative wave back, she called out, "Cami? Is that you?"

Before I could even think to answer, she strode toward us, stopping only when she reached the edge of the river.

With a laugh, she called out over the darkened water. "Funny seeing *you* here!"

Yes.

It was.

And I couldn't help but notice that she'd called out to Mason first. When I turned and gave him a perplexed look, he appeared to be just as delighted as I was.

Under his breath, he said, "Fuck."

No kidding.

But I didn't say it, because I'd been cursing far too much already. And yet, I *did* feel like it.

The last time I'd seen Livia had been in Petoskey.

After that night at the club, we hadn't parted on the best of terms. Afterward, we'd played telephone tag for maybe a week until she'd left me one scorcher of a voicemail informing me that I was – in her words – a "total ingrate" for not accepting the job at her dad's jewelry store.

Considering that I was never offered the job – not officially, anyway – her message seemed more spiteful than anything.

I hadn't returned the call.

This wasn't as unusual as you'd think. My friendship with Livia had always been an on-again, off-again sort of thing. And judging from her demeanor now, we were on again with a vengeance.

With another smile, she called out, "Small world, huh?"

I knew Livia. It wasn't that small.

Still, I *was* curious.

When I made a move toward the river, a hand on my elbow made me turn to look.

Mason frowned. "What are you doing?"

Wasn't it obvious? "I'm gonna get closer."

"Why?"

"Oh, I dunno," I said. "Maybe to cut down on the yelling?"

"Forget it. That chick's crazy."

"Oh, please. I've known her since kindergarten."

"So?"

"So yeah, she's a little enthusiastic, I guess. But she's not crazy-crazy." *Or at least, I sure hoped not.*

Mason replied, "Says you."

"Well, you're not gonna stop me," I said.

He looked at me for a long silent moment before saying with a marked lack of enthusiasm, "Hang on. I'll get the lights."

"Sorry, what?"

"The landscape lights," he said. "I don't want you tripping on the way."

I saw what he meant. Although the mansion across the river was fully lit, our patio, as well as the rest of Mason's yard, was still cast in shadows.

This posed an interesting question. *Just how did Livia know who we were?*

But of course, the answer should've been obvious. She knew, because her arrival in Bayside was no accident. And her arrival *here*, directly across from Mason's place, was so devious, I hardly knew what to think.

I bit my lip. Maybe she *was* crazy-crazy.

As for Mason, he looked so disgruntled, I couldn't resist teasing, "You know, instead of turning on the lights, you could always escort me to the river's edge."

His eyebrows furrowed. "What?"

"I'm just saying, I'm sure you're more familiar with the terrain."

My statement was deliberately ridiculous. The so-called terrain was maybe a hundred feet of manicured perfection.

He said, "You think I won't."

I almost laughed in his face. "I *know* you won't."

"Oh yeah? Why not?"

"Because," I said, "I saw how much you enjoyed her company the first time around."

"Yeah, well maybe it's not *her* I'm worried about." And with that, he took my hand in his. With a tender squeeze, he said, "I'm ready when you are."

I glanced down at our hands, now joined. As my fingers closed reflexively around his, I tried not to notice how right it felt to be standing here holding hands by the light of the moon.

In spite of the cold, his hand was warm and steady as it held my own. And there was something about that squeeze – as light as it was – that made me want to turn *not* toward the river, but back toward the house, where we could do a lot more than hold hands.

Now that was crazy-crazy.

I mean, hadn't I *just* told him that we were done with the physical stuff?

Yes. I had. And I was determined to stick with that plan, even if it killed me – which it just might.

So I gave a quick nod and let Mason guide me toward the river's edge, where Livia was waiting.

By the time we arrived, she wasn't smiling anymore.

As I watched, her gaze zoomed in on Mason, and then on me. With a little frown, she called out, "So, are you guys a thing, now?"

Mason replied, "Hell yeah."

I whirled to look. "What?" And then it hit me. *What a total snork-weasel.* He was only saying that so Livia would set her sights elsewhere. Under my breath, I hissed, "I am *so* gonna get you for this."

Without bothering to lower his voice, he replied, "You promise?"

Oh, I'd give him a promise, alright.

From the other side of the river, Livia called out, "That's a little unprofessional, don't you think?"

I turned and called back, "Excuse me?"

"I mean, he *is* your boss, right?"

On this, she had a point. Still, her comment grated. Livia had practically begged for this job, and not because she'd been dying to look after Willow. If Mason was *her* boss, a little "unprofessionalism" wouldn't have bothered her in the least.

Thank goodness Mason hadn't hired her.

For Willow's sake.

Not mine.

Much.

Still, I had to face facts. I *had* been unprofessional, especially in the pantry. In fact, if I looked up "unprofessional" in the dictionary, I just might find a picture of myself, being pleasured by Mason where the family's food was stored.

Sure, the thought was ridiculous, but the point was still valid.

And what about now?

I mean, here I was, at the river's edge, safe and sound. And yet, I'd made no move to retrieve my hand from Mason's.

But in my own defense, his hand felt very nice – not just big and warm, but strong and tender. The unlikely combination went a long way in explaining why he'd been such an amazing lover.

I felt myself swallow. He'd been good with his hands…and other parts, too.

Great. And now I was all distracted again.

Livia had asked me something. *But what?*

In the end, it was Mason who replied on my behalf. "Forget Cami," he told her. "What the hell are *you* doing?"

I almost smiled. It was vintage Mason – rude, abrasive, and obnoxiously direct. But sometimes, I decided, those traits weren't *all* bad. In fact, at this particular moment, I could totally see their appeal.

And besides, his question was entirely valid.

What *was* she doing across the river?

Sure, I had a theory, but it was too horrifying to consider – until Livia confirmed it herself by calling out, "Oh, you don't know? I'm their new nanny."

CHAPTER 37

Cami

As soon as the patio door closed safely behind us, I whirled to Mason and said, "She doesn't even like kids."

"Good thing," he said.

I stared up at him. "Why?"

With a low scoff, he replied, "Have you *seen* the kids across the street?"

Yes. I had. This was assuming, of course, that he meant what I *thought* he meant. Just to be sure, I said, "You do mean across the river, right?"

He nodded. "River, street…you get the idea."

It reminded me of a similar conversation I'd had with Willow. "I'm just curious," I said. "Who started that?"

"Started what?"

"Calling it a street instead of a river."

With a rueful smile, Mason said, "You can't guess?"

"So it *was* Willow?"

"Well it wasn't me," he said. "When we moved in, she was still in pre-school. She started calling it a street the day she saw her first boat 'driving' past our back yard. I guess the name stuck."

It made total sense, and yet I was a little surprised to hear Mason going along with it. It was sweet and just a little silly.

I liked it. As I gazed up at him, I said, "So *you* say it that way because *she* says it that way?"

"Yeah. Why?"

In spite of my lingering annoyance with Livia, I couldn't help but smile. "I guess I figured you for a more literal type of person."

The truth was, I'd figured lots of things when it came to Mason. Some of them had turned out to be true. And yet, the longer I lived here, the more I realized that he also had a softer side. It was the side he showed to his sister.

And to me.

Well, sometimes, anyway.

With a casual shrug, Mason said, "Eh, it helps if we use the same lingo."

"Oh, really?" I teased. "Does this mean you're going to be using *my* lingo, too?"

He looked intrigued. "Like what?"

"Well…" I gave it some thought. "Like lunk-blaster."

Although it was an obvious joke, he appeared to give it serious consideration. "Well, I'd use *that* before 'donk.'"

I saw his point. As far as words to describe sex, donk was totally lacking. But the strangest thing was, the term had seemed perfectly fine until now.

Meaning until Mason.

After my encounter with *him*, the word seemed utterly ridiculous. *Why was that?* Was it because sex with Mason had been too incredible for such a silly word? Or was it because he made me feel things that I'd never felt before?

What those feelings were, I didn't want to speculate. And yet, I *was* speculating, not just now, but during the past few weeks. Now, as my thoughts churned, I heard myself say, "What would *you* call it?"

"Call what?"

Embarrassment made me hesitate until curiosity won out. "Like, you know how I say 'donk' to describe a certain act. What's your slang word?" The question had barely left my lips when a sudden recollection made me freeze. "Wait. Never mind."

Mason studied my face. "Why?"

"Because I already know."

"You know what?"

"What your word is," I said. "It's 'bang', right?" With an awkward laugh, I added, "As in, you don't 'bang' the Help."

Meaning me.

And yet, he had.

Mason frowned. "I shouldn't have said that."

I tried to laugh. "No kidding, especially because you did." I lifted my hands and made little air-quotes between us. "Bang the Help, I mean."

"Cami…" His voice softened. "Whatever you are, you're not the Help."

It was such a nice thought. But it wasn't accurate, and it seemed silly to pretend otherwise. "I am, too."

"Listen—"

"No. It's okay, honest. I mean, I took this job knowing full well what I was getting into."

His gaze locked on mine. "Did you?"

"Well…" I bit my lip. "Maybe I didn't anticipate *everything* that would happen, but I *did* know that I'd be your live-in employee, and thus—"

"Don't say it."

"Why not?" I said. "I am what I am, for now anyway. And honestly, this is a really good job. I probably shouldn't tell you this, but sometimes it doesn't feel like a job at all."

"Is that so?"

I nodded. "Willow – she's amazing." I smiled through my awkwardness. "And she's *really* fun, too."

With surprising tenderness, he said, "And so are you."

I wasn't sure which word he meant – fun or amazing. Regardless, it was such a lovely thing to say, especially coming from Mason, who no one would describe as warm and fuzzy.

And maybe if he'd been somebody else – *anybody* else – I might've gotten lost in the tenderness of his words. *Or his eyes.* Or the memories of what we'd shared during that one incredible night.

It hadn't been donking.

Or banging.

It had been something else entirely – for me, anyway.

And this was definitely a problem, because now that I'd seen Mason's other side – meaning his tender side, not his naked backside, even though that *had* been pretty spectacular – I was having a hard time remembering that the nanny gig was only a job.

And Mason? He was my boss.

Whatever we'd shared that night, it couldn't happen again – not because of Mason's threat, but because it was slowly dawning on me that I just might be falling for him, although heaven knows why.

I mean, it's not like he'd ever fall for *me*.

Probably, he'd never fall for anyone.

I still hadn't replied to his compliment, mostly because I didn't know what to say. In the end, I settled on, "Well, you're pretty amazing yourself. I mean, look at everything you've accomplished. It really *is* something to be proud of."

The compliment landed with a thud.

Instead of smiling, Mason frowned as he said, "Thanks."

"I mean it," I assured him.

"I know." And yet, he didn't look any happier.

I cleared my throat. "Anyway…I should probably get to sleep. See you tomorrow?"

Mason shook his head. "I'm leaving for Kentucky, remember?"

At the sudden recollection, I almost winced. "Oh, that's right."

Even though Mason's youngest brother, Brody, handled most of the construction stuff for their remodeling show, every once in a while Mason and Chase needed to show up on-site and make an appearance.

This was one of those times. "And you'll be gone five days, right?"

When he answered in the affirmative, I should've been relieved, but mostly, I was stupidly sorry to see him go.

Still, I'd be a fool to let him see it. So with a friendly smile, I wished him goodnight and headed up to my bedroom alone, where I slept fitfully and woke at the crack of dawn – just in time to see Mason's car ease out of the driveway while I watched from my upstairs window.

As I watched, I whispered, "See you next week."

CHAPTER 38

Cami

I was sitting at the kitchen table, doing homework with Willow, when a light knocking sound made me pause.

I glanced toward the sound. Unless I was mistaken, it had come *not* from the front of the house, but from the rear. I asked Willow, "Did you hear that?"

She looked up from her homework. "Oh yeah. Twice."

"Sorry, what?"

"They knocked a minute ago, too…only a lot quieter."

Funny, I hadn't heard. It was nearly dinner time, and I wasn't expecting anyone. With a perplexed smile, I said, "Oh. Why didn't you say something?"

She made a face. "Because I know who it is."

"Really? Who?"

"It's the kids across the street."

"You mean those older kids? Across the river, right?"

She gave a decisive nod. "Right."

Well, that was strange. Going for a joke, I said, "So, do they swim across or what?"

"Nah. They have a dinghy. It's their dad's, but they use it when he's not home. They're not supposed to, but they still do."

From what I'd seen so far, those kids did a lot of things they weren't supposed to do. Happily, this was Livia's problem, not mine.

Still, I got to my feet, intending to answer the door and be done with it.

Willow spoke up. "Oh, you don't have to answer."

I paused. "Really?"

She nodded. "If you do, they'll just run away. They do it all the time."

I'd been living here for months now, but this was the first time anyone had knocked on the rear door. "Seriously?"

"Oh yeah. But mostly in the summer."

If nothing else, this explained the lack of knocking until now. I asked, "And they always run off?"

"*Almost* always," she said. "But this one time, they hit the nanny with a water balloon." Her eyes brightened. "Except it wasn't filled with water."

"Oh?" I was almost afraid to ask. "So, what *was* it filled with?"

"Milk, I think." She leaned forward to announce, "And it wasn't *their* nanny either. It was *my* nanny."

I frowned. *Well, that was ominous.*

"Oh?" I repeated.

Willow nodded. "But it was okay, because she wasn't very nice."

I hesitated. As the only adult in the room, it was probably my responsibility to tell Willow that whether someone was nice or not, they still didn't deserve to be hit with a milk balloon.

And yet, I couldn't help but recall my encounter with Veronica, back in that school parking lot. She'd bothered Willow. And *then*, she'd stomped on my foot.

I felt my eyes narrow. *Boy, what I wouldn't have given for a nice milk balloon then.*

As I envisioned it, my thoughts strayed to the other nannies. At least two of them had tried to get all naughty with Mason. The recollection bothered me more than it should've, even in spite of the fact that I was in no position to judge.

Still, I decided that if one of *them* had been hit with the milk balloon, maybe this wasn't *so* terrible.

In fact, I sort of liked the idea.

What did that say about me?

Nothing good, that's for sure.

Just then, I heard the knocking sound again, except this time it was a whole lot louder.

Willow said, "Yup, it's them, alright."

I asked, "How can you be sure?"

"Because they always do that," she said. "They start out quiet and get louder if you don't answer." She smiled. "But then they go away."

It was one of the craziest things I'd ever heard. It wasn't just because of the knocking either.

It was early December, and even though the river hadn't yet begun to freeze over, it was long past boating season.

I just had to ask, "And what does Mason think of all this?"

"I dunno," she said. "He's never home when they do it."

Considering that Mason worked long hours and traveled regularly, this wasn't terribly surprising. I made a mental note to mention it when he returned home.

But now, I was beyond curious. "Wait here," I said. "I'm gonna check the monitor." And with that, I turned away and strode toward the first-floor media closet.

Once inside, I consulted the oversized video monitor, which channeled nine live feeds from strategic cameras placed outside the house. I zoomed in on the panel that showed the back-patio door.

Yup, we definitely had company.

But it wasn't the teenagers.

It was Livia.

CHAPTER 39

Cami

I stared at the monitor. On the screen, Livia was wearing an outfit similar to what she'd been wearing the other night, along with the same black ankle boots.

As I watched, she lifted both of her fists and pounded again on the patio door.

Just yesterday, I'd called Livia to demand answers on what exactly she was doing here in Bayside. She hadn't answered *or* called me back.

She'd *also* ignored all of my texts, including one I'd sent just this morning, asking what she hoped to accomplish by taking a job that was so opposite of everything she liked.

As if I didn't know.

And now, here she was, literally at the back door.

To see me? Doubtful.

Probably she was here to see Mason.

I gave a low scoff. *Good luck with that, sister.*

Mason had been gone for two days now, and wouldn't be returning for three more. This gave me the perfect opportunity to get some answers *without* an audience.

By the time I reached the back door, Livia was knocking yet again. When I yanked the door open, she gave me an accusing look. "It took you long enough."

Yes. It had. Normally, I'd feel guilty for making a visitor wait, but considering Livia's recent behavior, I was short on guilt, and long on irritation.

I leaned sideways to peer around her. Sure enough, I spotted a bright red dinghy pulled up onto the river bank directly behind Mason's house.

I had to give Livia credit. She was showing a surprising amount of initiative.

I looked back to her and said with a sarcastic smile, "Can I help you?"

With a sarcastic smile of her own, she said, "Yeah. You can switch."

"Switch what?"

"Kids," she said. "Mine are monsters."

I rolled my eyes. "Oh, please. You think all kids are monsters."

"Yeah, but *you* only have one monster. I have two. And they're bigger."

"Which means," I reminded her, "they don't require as much care."

"That's what *you* think," she said. "Their mom lives in Italy, and the dad is *always* gone. I know why, too."

"Why?"

"Hello? Because his kids are monsters."

I sighed. "So you said."

"That's why they need a nanny, you know."

I gave her a look. "Because they're monsters?"

"No. Because the dad has sole custody. And he's gone *all* the time, which is a real bummer."

"You mean for the kids?"

"Well, yeah. That too." She leaned forward. "But I *meant* because he's super-hot."

I'd never seen the guy. "Oh?"

"Yeah, totally." She smiled. "And I think he likes me."

This wasn't a surprise. After all, *every* guy liked Livia, with the possible exception of Mason. And for some reason, this made me want to smile.

As far as the dad across the river, I couldn't help but ask, "But how can he like you if he's never home?"

"Well, sure he's gone all week. But he's almost always home on the weekends." She giggled. "Plus, we talk *all* the time on the phone. He's got this *great* accent, too. It's super sexy."

I shook my head. "Wait, I thought you liked Mason."

"I did," she said. "But now that I know he's yours, I figure I'll focus on the bird in the hand, you know?"

Mason wasn't mine. And yet, for some strange reason, I didn't correct her. *What did that mean?*

It was something I'd need to think about later.

But for now, I couldn't help but appreciate Livia's loyalty. It made me feel just a little bad for assuming the worst of her. And to be totally fair, I'd never once seen her go after another girl's guy.

With looks like hers, she definitely could've.

Even at the club in Petoskey, it's not like Mason had been my boyfriend. He'd been a prospective employer, and I'd already turned down the job – which meant that he was technically fair game.

I guess.

As I tried to sort it out, I looked to Livia and said, "Just how long have you been working there, anyway?"

She gave it some thought. "Oh, a couple of months now."

I did a double-take. "And I'm just *now* seeing you?"

"It's the kids," she said. "They keep me super-busy." She smiled. "And then, there's the dad on weekends."

By now, I hardly knew what to think. I decided to switch gears. "Hey, did you get my messages?"

"What messages?"

"I left a voicemail on your cell phone, and few texts, too." I hesitated. "But I didn't hear back."

Livia frowned. "Yeah, because the monsters stole my phone."

"Seriously?"

"Oh yeah. And I *just* found it this morning." She grimaced. "Wanna know where?"

From the look on her face, I wasn't so sure. And yet, I *was* morbidly curious. "Where?"

"In the cat box."

Hoping for the best, I said, "Like, where he sleeps?"

"No. Where he pees."

Now, *I* was the one grimacing. "You mean the *litter* box?" I wasn't even sure what surprised me more – that the kids had done something so disgusting, or that Livia had cleaned out a litter box.

When she replied with a disgruntled nod, I said in a gentler tone, "So, you're on litter-duty, too, huh?"

"Me?" she scoffed. "No way. He's got a service who does *that*."

"But you just said—"

"Okay, so it wasn't *me* who actually found the phone, but the phone was still mine."

"So, what are you gonna do?" I asked. "Like… can you clean it?"

"Me? Hell no," she said. "I called Lorenzo on the land line. He's sending me a new one."

"Wait, who's Lorenzo?"

She grinned. "The dad."

"Oh. Well, that's nice."

She gave a happy nod. "I know, right?" She glanced past me, toward the interior of Mason's house. "So, aren't you gonna invite me in?"

"Gosh, I'm really sorry." Oddly enough, I meant it, too. Still, I continued. "But I can't. We're in the middle of homework. And besides, I'm not supposed to have company without prior authorization."

"What do you mean?"

"I mean, it's not my house. This is a job, remember?"

With a perplexed look, she said, "But I thought Mason was your boyfriend."

Dang it. Regardless of my mixed feelings, it was definitely time to come clean. Reluctantly, I admitted, "Actually, he's not. He was just kidding."

"But I saw the two of you holding hands."

"Right. Because he didn't want me to trip."

"Oh, please," she said. "I saw the way he looked at you."

I sucked in a quiet breath. "What?"

"I don't know what you're doing in the bedroom," she said. "But it's obviously working."

Technically, we'd started out in the pantry, but there was no way I'd be sharing *that* little nugget with Livia – or anyone else while I was at it.

Even Arden, she was my best friend in the whole world, but I hadn't told her a single thing about what had happened between me and Mason.

It was incredibly frustrating, too, because I would've loved to tell her everything. But she was engaged to Mason's brother, and the last thing I wanted was to get the family talking – or even worse, put Arden in the awkward position of having to lie to Brody.

And besides, I told myself, it hardly mattered. My encounter with Mason had been a one-time thing. It was over and done. *Now, if I could only stop thinking about him.*

To Livia, I said, "I'm not doing anything anywhere. Seriously, there's nothing between us."

She laughed. "You are such a liar."

"Oh come on. You don't know that."

"Sure, I do," she said. "I've known you since kindergarten." She leaned closer to say, "So tell me, does he fuck as good as he looks?"

I winced. "Will you *please* be quiet?"

"Why? Because of your no-cursing policy?"

"No," I whispered. "Because his little sister is in the kitchen."

"Oh, alright," she said, not looking too happy about it. "But seriously, let me in, okay?"

"I'm really sorry," I said yet again. "But I can't."

She sighed. "Fine. You want the truth? I'm locked out."

I glanced past her. "You mean out of the house?"

"Yes, if you *must* know."

"How'd *that* happen?"

"I'll tell you how," she said. "Those little monsters tricked me."

"But how?" I persisted.

"They *told* me – which was a total lie by the way – that Mason Blastoviak was in his backyard naked."

I couldn't help but laugh. "Why would they say that?"

"Because they're monsters, that's why. And just so you know, I wouldn't have *done* anything. I just figured I'd take a peek, you know?"

As someone who'd had *more* than a peek, I couldn't exactly blame her.

She gave another sigh. "And now I can't get back in."

I asked, "So…did you try the windows?"

"What?"

"The windows," I repeated. "If the doors are locked, you could always climb through a window."

She gave me a look. "Are you freaking kidding me?"

"No. I've seen it done before." I leaned around her and pointed to same window that I'd seen the other nanny use. "Try *that* one."

She rolled her eyes. "Gee, thanks for the help." And with that, she turned and began stalking back toward the dinghy.

From the open doorway, I watched in morbid fascination as she climbed in and used the attached paddles to navigate across the river. When she reached the opposite bank, she disembarked and yanked the dinghy back onto dry land.

When she strode to the house and tried the appropriate window, it opened just like I'd predicted. She turned around and gave me a perplexed look.

When I waved, she hesitated for only a moment before smiling and waving back. And then, she turned and crawled in through the open window.

When she slammed it shut behind her, I shut the patio door and returned to the kitchen, hoping like crazy that Willow hadn't caught any of our conversation.

But as it turned out, my hopes were in vain.

CHAPTER 40

Cami

Willow asked, "Is Mason *really* your boyfriend?"

Oh, crud. To think I'd returned from the patio over twenty minutes ago, and Willow hadn't said a single word about it. *Until now.*

Mostly, she'd been talking about how surprising it was to discover that a friend of mine was working as a nanny right across the river.

On this, I could totally relate.

In spite of everything, I liked Livia. And yet, she'd opened up a real can of worms by sharing personal details where Willow might overhear.

As I mentally ran through our recent conversation, I felt the blood drain from my face. *Oh, my God.*

What if Willow had overheard that one comment? The one about Mason fucking as good as he looked.

With growing dread, I asked, "Just how much did you overhear, anyway?"

"A lot," she said. "Your friend talks really loud."

No kidding.

Still, I summoned up a smile. "So, did you hear what she said about him being a faker?"

Willow's eyebrows furrowed. "I dunno. Maybe."

"Yeah, she said that he faked as good as he looked. I think she meant something about the TV show."

Willow eyed me across the table. "Really?"

I nodded. "Oh, yeah. Like on TV, he doesn't seem as nice as he does in person. But then, once you get to know him, he seems really different."

As I said it, it suddenly struck me how true this was. Oh sure, Mason still had his hard edges. But there was a softer side, too. And the funny thing was, I liked *both* sides of him in a crazy sort of way.

Across from me, Willow was nodding now. "Oh, I know," she said. "People say he's mean, but he's not."

I stiffened. *So someone had been bad-mouthing Mason to Willow? If so, I didn't like it.*

I asked, "Who says he's mean?"

"Everyone at school," she said. "They all watch the show."

Of course they did. Sure, it wasn't a kids' show, but not only was *Blast* insanely popular, it starred three brothers who lived right here in the area.

Of those brothers, Mason was probably the most interesting – not because he was flashy, but because he was blunt to the point of rudeness and so private that he was hard to figure out.

To Willow, I replied, "Well, they just need to get to know him, that's all."

"Oh, I know," she said. "But is he your boyfriend?"

Oh, boy.

Again, I hesitated. I didn't want to lie to her. And happily I didn't need to. But still, I felt slightly dishonest when I said, "No. We're just friends, that's all."

"But are you sure?" she said. "Because I heard your friend say he was."

"Yeah, but she was just teasing me."

Willow eyed me with obvious suspicion. "Are you really, *really* sure?"

"Sure, I'm sure."

And I was.

I mean, hadn't I just told him a few days ago that we were back to business as usual?

And let's say we *were* planning to do the horizontal hokey-pokey again, that still wouldn't make him my boyfriend.

But what *would* it make him?

My donk-buddy?

I really hated the sound of *that*.

To Willow, I added, "But he's not *just* my friend. He's also my boss. And if your friends ask, you can tell them that he's a pretty good one, too."

And I meant it. In reality, working for Mason hadn't been half as bad as I'd feared. In fact, I'd actually come to admire him, especially for the way he cared for his sister.

Willow said, "It's okay if you are."

I'd been so lost in my thoughts of Mason, I'd lost track of the conversation. "Sorry, Sweet Pea, I'm not following. It's okay if I'm what?"

"I mean, it's okay if he's your boyfriend." She gave me a hopeful smile. "I don't mind, honest."

At the eagerness in her eyes, something tugged at my heart. More than anything, Willow wanted a regular family. She hadn't said so directly, but from little things she'd said over the past few months, I knew exactly where her thoughts were leading her.

I tried to look at it from her point-of-view. If Mason and I ever became a couple, and maybe even got married, nothing would need to change. I'd never leave, and Willow would finally have a mom – or at the very least, an older sister who adored her.

The three of us would be a family.

It was such a pretty picture, and her eager eyes held such hope that I felt my own eyes grow just a little misty.

She really *was* a terrific kid – which is why I refused to get her hopes up, only to see them dashed later on. With an encouraging smile,

I said, "Well, lots of girls like Mason, so I'm sure that when the time is right, he'll meet someone really nice."

She frowned. "I don't want someone nice. I want you."

As she said it, I couldn't help but recall Mason's concerns regarding how Willow might react if I left my nanny job ahead of schedule.

The way it looked, those concerns were completely valid.

Still, I knew a minefield when I saw it. Hoping to distract her, I teased, "Oh, so I'm not nice, huh?" With a friendly laugh, I said, "I see how this is."

"But you *are* nice," she said. "You're just not *too* nice. To him, I mean."

I was intrigued in spite of myself. "How so?"

"Like with the other nannies – they were way nicer to *him* than they ever were to *me*."

Hearing this, I wanted to slap Veronica all over again – and maybe hit her with a nice milk balloon while I was at it.

I told willow, "That's because *some* people don't know a good thing when they've got it."

But me? I knew. This was a terrific job. And I was incredibly fond of Willow, which meant I had one heck of a conversation ahead of me – not with Willow, but with Mason himself.

If I were smart, I decided, I'd have this conversation sooner rather than later.

And boy, was he gonna love this.

CHAPTER 41

Mason

On the phone, Cami said, "There's something I need to tell you."

I'd figured as much. She'd sent me a text maybe ten minutes ago, asking me to call her when I had the chance.

No emergency.

That's what she'd texted.

But now, judging from the tone of her voice, her news wouldn't be good.

It was just past eleven o'clock at night, and I was alone in my hotel suite after a full day of swinging a hammer in front of the cameras.

The construction work, I liked. *The cameras, I could do without.* All I wanted now was to get the hell out of here and return to business as usual – except my thoughts hadn't been on business, and there was nothing usual about my state-of-mind.

In fact, it was so *unusual*, I'd been on edge all day. *Yesterday, too.*

The truth was, I'd been off-kilter for a while now. And it wasn't getting better. *It was getting worse.*

Into the phone, I said, "Just tell me."

"Well, first, let me assure you, everything's fine."

I frowned. As soon as anyone says, *"Everything's fine,"* that's when you know, everything's gone to shit. *Was it about Willow?*

My grip tightened on the phone. "What happened? And first, cut to the chase."

Cami paused. "What do you mean?"

"Tell me how it ended."

"Alright," she said with a shaky laugh. "It ended with everything being fine. How's that?"

My fingers relaxed, and I almost smiled.

Nobody ever teased me.

Nobody but Cami.

Whatever she was calling about, it was no disaster. I knew this, because I knew the caller. Cami wouldn't be joking if Willow were in trouble.

"Point taken," I said. "Now tell me the rest."

I listened as Cami explained that her psychotic friend – the new nanny across the river – had knocked on the back door of my house earlier today and had started asking questions about what she'd seen the other night.

Cami went on to say, "We were holding hands, remember?"

Hell yeah, I remembered. I wasn't the hand-holding type. And yet, holding hands with Cami had felt different. *Better. Nice.*

I wanted to do it again – that and other things. But Cami – she had other ideas. *No more physical stuff between us.*

Logically, I agreed. We'd be smart to call it a one-time thing and move on.

Hell, it shouldn't have happened the first time.

And yet, I wasn't feeling very logical, not when it came to Cami. In a careful voice, replied, "I remember."

"And when Livia asked if the two of us were an item, you said, 'yes.' You remember *that*, too, right?"

Oh yeah. I remembered all too well. It had been messing with my head ever since. The truth was, I hadn't meant to say it. But once I'd thrown it out there, I hadn't wanted to take it back.

This, too, was messing with my head.

I'd been on travel for two days now, and I'd been corresponding with Cami by text – not about us, but about household stuff, checking in on Willow and her schedule.

At least a dozen times, I'd pulled out my phone, intending to call Cami and hash things out between us. There was just one problem.

For the first time in years, I didn't know what to say.

And the thing I *should* be saying – that she was right to make it a one-time thing – well, it wasn't sounding so good. But neither was anything else.

My fault. Not hers.

I'd grown up in a messed-up household, with parents coming and going even when they promised to stay.

And me? *I was majorly fucked up.*

I knew this, just like I knew I wasn't capable of love – or at least, not the romantic kind.

And why? It was because I didn't believe in it.

Love was just a word. It was the term people threw around when they wanted to make someone feel better about their own shitty choices, or when they wanted to bang some boxer in Miami instead of staying in town to care for their own family.

In my mind, I could still hear my mom telling me, "But I love him" as Willow slept in the second-hand crib a few feet away.

At the time, I'd been twenty-one. I'd been too old to be living at home, except I was the one paying the bills and making sure my brothers kept out of trouble, especially Chase, who kept raising hell, even while taking marketing classes at the local college.

But me? I'd skipped college entirely and gone straight to work – learning the tool-and-die trade while forming the raw foundation of what would later become Blast Tools.

Finally, I'd been in the home stretch, ready to claim my freedom to go out on my own.

But then came Willow.

She'd been sweet and helpless – and cute as hell. But my mom had left for Miami anyway, telling me that she'd be back in a few days.

I'd known it was a lie.

It didn't take long before I was proven right.

Again.

If that was love, I wanted no part of it.

On the phone, Cami asked, "Are you still there?"

Shit. I was doing it again. Lately, it had been hard to focus, and even harder to pull my head out of the clouds. I replied, "Yeah. I'm here."

"So, naturally," Cami continued, "Livia assumed that you were my boyfriend, and she happened to call you that when Willow was listening."

I stiffened. "So Willow thinks I'm your boyfriend."

"Right. Sort of."

"And you didn't set her straight?"

"Of course I set her straight."

I'd heard such stories before – not from Cami, but from plenty of others – former nannies, women I'd dated, or hell, even women I *hadn't* dated. Too many had decided that Willow was their ticket to my heart – as if I had one.

Just the thought of them pissed me off. *Willow wasn't a pawn. She was my sister. And my responsibility.*

In a tight voice, I said, "How?"

Cami hesitated. "Sorry, what?"

"*How* did you set her straight?"

"You mean Willow? I told her that you and I are just friends."

I frowned. *Just friends.* It was a phrase I'd used plenty of times myself. But for some messed up reason, I didn't like Cami saying it – not about me.

I told her, "I'm not your friend."

"Excuse me?"

"I'm your employer," I said. "And I'm sure as hell not your boyfriend."

I felt like a dick for saying it, but that didn't mean it wasn't true. Cami and I weren't a couple.

And we needed to keep it that way – because if we didn't, I knew exactly how things between us would end, with Cami bolting for the exit and Willow wondering what she'd done wrong.

Girls like Cami – they were never happy with a casual thing, at least not for long. And yet, a voice in my head whispered, *"But you banged her anyway."*

Yeah. I had.

Except, it hadn't felt like banging.

It had felt like something else, something with real meaning, assuming there *was* such a thing.

And now, I was pissed off – not at Cami, but at myself. *What the hell was I doing?*

On the phone, Cami still hadn't replied, which meant it was my turn to ask, "Are you still there?"

She was quiet for another long moment before saying in a strained voice, "Oh, I'm something."

Yeah. She was.

And that "something" was pissed off. I could hear it in her voice just the same as if she'd called me every name in the book.

When I said nothing in reply, she said, "So let me get this straight. You're saying we're not even friends?"

"Not if I'm signing your check."

Regardless of my other flaws – plenty as they were – I knew one thing for damned sure. Business and pleasure – they were dangerous to mix.

And yet, I had.

On the phone, Cami's tone grew sarcastic. "It's direct deposit, remember?"

"What?"

"Those 'checks'?" she said. "They're direct deposits. And just so you know, if you bring up that bonus check again, I swear, I'm gonna…" With a sigh, her words trailed off, leaving dead silence in their wake.

The silence hung there like a dark, empty void. And me? I made no move to fill it with empty platitudes. I felt like shit for hurting her feelings, but I'd feel even shittier if I gave her the wrong idea.

I wasn't a relationship kind of guy.

In the end, it was Cami who broke the silence. "You know what? I don't even know why I'm arguing."

"Yeah, you and me both."

"I *meant* about the check-signing. Because yes, I *do* realize that you're the one supplying me with money for a service. But just so we're clear, that service *doesn't* include taking your crap."

At the word "crap," I almost smiled. Silently, I waited for her to correct herself, to claim that she'd said the c-word, or make up some funny non-curse word to take its place.

But she didn't.

Instead, she said, "You know what? You really can be a jerk sometimes. You *do* realize that, don't you?"

I did. But it wasn't something I dwelt on. With a tight shrug, I replied, "Hey, I've been called worse."

"How's this for worse?" she said. "You're being a total lunk-blaster. And you know exactly what I mean by that."

"So you're calling me a mother-fucker."

"Well you're certainly acting like one." She made a scoffing sound. "And thanks *so* much for rubbing it in my face."

"Rubbing what?"

"You *know* what," she said. "Look, so we 'banged', okay? And yeah, I didn't think we had some big romantic connection or anything. But I *did* think we were at least friends. And just because you sign my check, that doesn't give you the right be a, well, whatever you are."

I was an asshole.

But I didn't say it, because from the tone of her voice, she already knew.

With another sigh, she said, "Now, do you want to hear the rest of it or not?"

"The rest of what?"

"The reason I called."

Shit. "There's more?"

"Of course there's more," she said. "That's why I'm still on the phone, because I'll tell you one thing, if I *weren't* calling about Willow, I would've hung up on you a long time ago."

"Thanks for the warning."

"Yeah, well you're not welcome," she said. *"Anyway*...I called because I thought you should know that Willow *wants* us to be boyfriend-and-girlfriend."

Son-of-bitch. "What?"

"Yeah. She didn't come right out and say it, but trust me, that *is* what she's hoping for."

"Shit."

"No kidding," Cami said. "And yes, I *do* realize that's not what you want, which is fine, because it's not what I want either." Her voice rose. "Especially now."

That made me pause. *Especially now.*

What did that mean?

But I didn't ask – because I was better off not knowing.

And Cami – she'd be better off, too, because I'd rather accept her hatred than risk breaking her heart – and Willow's, too, while I was at it.

So instead I kept my mouth shut and listened as Cami went on to tell me, "So, all I'm saying is that you might want to be extra-careful in front of Willow from now on."

I was still thinking about Cami. *What was so different about her, anyway?* Absently I murmured, "Careful how?"

"Just don't act too act friendly," she said. "And don't say or do anything to give her the wrong impression."

"Done."

"Excellent," she said. "And just in case it's not clear, you can act the same way when it's just the two of us alone – because one thing's for damn sure, we will *not* be getting 'friendly' again." Under her breath, she added, "Asshole."

And with that, she hung up without saying goodbye.

I stared at my cellphone for a long moment before tossing it onto the bed. This wasn't the first time I'd been hung up. And it wouldn't be the last.

But it *was* the first time I cared.

CHAPTER 42

Cami

Mason didn't even try to call me back.

That was fine by me. I wasn't the kind of person to hang up on someone just to make a point.

In fact, I wasn't the kind of person to hang up at all.

Now that I thought about it, he was probably the first person I'd ever hung up on in my whole life.

Good. Because he totally deserved it.

Even now, after a full day of replaying our phone conversation, I was so angry, I could hardly see straight.

But, like a total sap, I was hurt, too.

We weren't even friends?

What did that mean? He didn't even *like* me?

Fine. Because I didn't like him either. *Not anymore.*

It was nine-thirty at night, and I'd just put Willow to bed when my cellphone buzzed with an incoming text. With my heart in my throat, I yanked the phone from my pocket and glanced at the display.

It was Arden.

She wanted to know if I could talk.

My shoulders slumped in disappointment. It's not that I wasn't happy to hear from her, but I'd be lying if I didn't admit it that might've been at least a *little* nice if Mason had texted to apologize.

Or hey, a phone call might've been even nicer.

But Mason – he hadn't contacted me all day, not even to check on Willow.

Maybe it was a compliment of sorts, like he realized that I'd surely let him know if something was wrong. Still, it bothered me more than it should've – and *not* because of Willow herself.

At the realization, I literally groaned. *Great.* Now *I* was the nanny who spent too much time obsessing over Mason and not enough time on the kid I'd been hired to care for.

All day, I hadn't been myself. And even though I'd tried not to show it, I realized all too well that I'd been only half-listening as Willow told me about her day at school.

Now, as I stared at my cellphone, I couldn't decide what to do. There was only one topic I felt capable of discussing. Unfortunately, it was the same topic I'd be smart to avoid, especially while Arden was in Kentucky with all three brothers – Brody, Chase, *and* Mason.

But then, my pulse quickened. Maybe, if I were really crafty about it, I could get Arden to tell me something about Mason's current mood *without* arousing her suspicion.

With that in mind, I tapped the call button and waited for her to answer.

I didn't need to wait long. She answered almost instantly. And then, with barely a hello, she said, "I've got a question."

"Oh, yeah?"

"Yeah. By any chance, is there a nice family emergency you could rustle up? Like maybe some sort of house-fire? Or maybe a flood?"

"Sorry, what?"

"Cripes, I'd even take pestilence."

With a weak laugh, I asked, "Why pestilence?"

"Because I'm not picky," she said. "I'm thinking that if you could find a reason for Mason to come back home, the rest of us could breathe a little easier."

I sat up straighter on the sofa. "What do you mean?"

"He was *such* a crab-ass today."

For some stupid reason, I almost wanted to smile. "Really?"

"Oh, yeah," she said. "And I mean above and beyond, even for him."

"So…you're saying he was in a bad mood?"

"No. He's *normally* in a bad mood. Today, he was in the worst mood I've ever seen."

"Really? How so?"

"Well for starters, he flipped out on Brody."

"Oh." This wasn't what I wanted to hear. "He did? Why?"

"For *whistling*."

I felt my brow wrinkle in confusion. "You mean…like, wolf-whistling or something?"

"No. Like when you whistle a happy tune."

"Really?"

"Oh, yeah. There Brody is, looking at plans for the new kitchen, and he's kind of whistling, you know, to himself. And Mason happens to walk by. And he stops and gives Brody this look. You should've seen it. It was like he wanted to clobber Brody with a two-by-four."

"Wait, why a two-by-four?"

"Don't ask me," she said. "I'm just glad he wasn't holding a hammer."

I hesitated. "You *are* joking, right? I mean, you don't seriously think that Mason would ever take a hammer to Brody?"

"Okay, maybe not a hammer," she said. "But I'm telling you, the look he gave Brody, it really *was* scary."

I could totally envision it. Still I couldn't resist saying, "But that's hardly flipping out. I mean, the way you talked, I half expected to hear that Mason was yelling or something."

"Hah! You know Mason. He doesn't *need* to yell to be scary. And besides, it wasn't *just* the look."

"It wasn't?"

"No. Because after he gives Brody the look, Brody says to him, 'What's *that* look for?' And Mason says, 'You're whistling.' And Brody says, 'Yeah, so?' And Mason says, 'You need to stop.' And then–"

"Wait," I said. "Did Mason say *why?*"

"Why what?"

"Why Brody should stop whistling. I mean, did Brody ask?"

"Oh yeah. And you wanna know what Mason says?"

"What?"

"He *says* that it's pissing him off."

I Iuh. "Well that's weird."

"Yeah. And it gets even weirder – because Chase comes along and catches the tail end of the argument. And you *know* how he is."

I did know, but it wasn't from being Willow's nanny.

Even before I'd started working for Mason, I'd spent countless hours watching the *Blast* remodeling show. Chase was a notorious trouble-maker. It's not that he came across as malicious, but he *did* have this way of pushing people's buttons.

And now on the phone, Arden was saying, "So you can probably guess what Chase does next."

I winced. "You don't mean—"

"Oh yeah," he said. "He starts whistling."

I couldn't help it. I laughed.

But Arden wasn't laughing. "And Mason," she continued, "he looks like he's gonna pop. And for some stupid reason, this only makes Chase do it more."

I was still laughing. I wasn't even sure why. I mean, yeah, it was funny, but even to my own ears, my laughter had a sinister edge, like I was glad to see Mason tormented by his own brother.

This wasn't like me.

I was definitely losing it.

Through my laughter, I said, "But that's so childish."

"Yeah, tell me about it. Anyway, the *next* time Mason tells him to stop, Chase says, 'Oh yeah? Make me.' So…one thing leads to another, and before anyone knows what's happening, Mason takes a flying leap at Chase."

And just like that, I wasn't laughing anymore. "You're kidding."

"I wish," she said. "And of course, the whole thing is caught on camera."

Oh, God. I could totally envision it. "But what was Brody doing?"

"What else? He was *trying* to separate them."

"Did he have any luck?"

"Not really," she said. "I mean, there's two of them and only one of Brody. And the camera guys – they're no help at all, because all *they* want is the footage."

"So, what happened?"

"So eventually, a couple of carpenters step in and help Brody yank Mason and Chase away from each other. And by now, they're both covered in blood–"

"Oh, my God," I said. "So they *seriously* hurt each other?"

"No. But Chase ended up with a bloody nose when his face hit something."

I bit my lip. "You don't mean Mason's fist?"

"No," she said. "And that's the other crazy thing. It was like neither one of them wanted to go full-boar on the other one. But Mason was still royally ticked, even *after* the scuffle."

"And what about Chase?"

"Oh, he was loving it. After they were pulled apart, he laughed his ass off."

I frowned. "And what did Mason do?"

"Well, he wasn't laughing. I can tell you that. And I think he's gonna have a black eye."

I cringed. "You *think?* Or you *know?*"

"Well, the last time I saw him, his eye looked a little swollen. But that was hours ago."

"So, where is he now?" I asked.

"Probably at the hotel."

"So he left after the fight?"

"Not *right* after," she said. "He stuck around for maybe an hour, but then he *had* to leave."

"Why?"

Sounding beyond annoyed, she replied, "Because Chase is *still* whistling."

I couldn't help but snicker. "Seriously?"

"Oh, yeah. And you can tell he's totally loving it. But Mason isn't. And the whole time, the camera guys keep following both of them around, like they're waiting for Mason to totally lose it."

"So…did he?"

"No. But I could tell he wanted to."

"Gosh, I'm so sorry," I said. "That sounds *really* stressful."

"Yeah, tell me about it." She sighed. "And what's Mason's problem, anyway?"

It was a good question.

At the moment, I wasn't thrilled with Mason myself. Still, I had to say, "Well, as far as the fight, it sounds like Chase was the one who started it."

"No. *Mason* started it by complaining about the whistling."

"Yeah, but afterward, Chase was totally goading him."

"Maybe," she said, "but that's no excuse to get violent."

"I never said it was. I'm just saying, it sounds like Chase got exactly what he wanted. I mean, you said he was happy, right?"

"Sure, but what about Brody?" Arden said. "*He* didn't want that. Do you know, he's got *three* houses going? And his brothers, they're *supposed* to show up and look pretty for the cameras.

"Yeah, well…"

"Do you know what they're *not* supposed to do?"

"What?"

"Cause a giant ruckus on a work site. Do you know, we lost a whole day of progress thanks to *your* boss?"

Hoping to lighten her mood, I teased, "Don't you mean *your* future brother-in-law?"

"Oh, please," she said. "He hardly considers me family."

I couldn't disagree, but I *could* sympathize. "Yeah, well, maybe he will after the wedding."

"Oh, please," she said. "You don't believe that any more than I do."

"Well…Maybe I'm trying to look on the bright side."

"With Mason?" she scoffed. "There *is* no bright side."

"Oh, come on," I said. "That's not *quite* true. I mean, he's really good to Willow."

"Yeah. And terrible to everyone else."

"But that's not true either," I said. "He's really good to his brothers, right?"

"Not today, he wasn't."

"Yeah, but we all have bad days. Why should Mason be any different?"

"I'll tell you why," she said. "Because *all* of his days are bad. I swear, he never smiles."

This wasn't true either. In fact, now that I thought about it, Mason had been smiling a lot more than he used to. And not just at Willow. *At me, too.*

Of course, there'd be no smiles *now*. After all, we weren't even friends.

On the phone, Arden was saying, "I'm not even sure he's human."

As she said it, I couldn't help but recall how cold he'd been during our last phone conversation.

No. Not just cold.

Cold *and* cruel.

Who knows, maybe Arden had a point. Maybe he *wasn't* human.

And honestly, why was I bothering?

With the way Mason was acting now, he didn't deserve a champion. No, what *he* deserved was a good kick in the pants – if not physically, then definitely verbally.

And just three hours later, I had my chance to give it to him.

CHAPTER 43

Cami

I was half asleep when my cell phone buzzed on the night stand. With a start, I sat up and glanced at the nearby clock. It was past midnight.

I picked up the phone and studied the display. I had a text. *It was from Mason.*

Oddly enough, it was identical to the one Arden had sent me earlier in the night. It said, *"Can you talk?"*

I blew out a long, trembling breath. *I could. I just didn't know if I wanted to.*

I was still trying to decide when my cellphone buzzed again. It was another text, *also* from Mason. This one said, *"You were right."*

I bit my lip. *Right about what?*

During that tense phone conversation, I'd said a lot of things. *And so had he.* Some of those things stung, even now.

And if I were being totally honest, I wasn't just hurting over the thing he'd said about us not being friends. I was hurt by the way he'd coldly informed me that he wasn't my boyfriend.

As if I expected him to be.

The idea was completely ludicrous. He and I were total opposites. He was hard. I was soft. He was tough. I was a peace-maker by nature. He was rich. I wasn't exactly poor. But compared to him?

Oh yeah, I was a total pauper.

In my darkened bedroom, I was still staring at his latest message. I was dying to know what he meant, but dreaded the thought of going another ten rounds with my impossible boss.

In the end, I decided to split the difference by texting him back. *"Right about what?"*

His reply came almost immediately. *"You're awake."*

"Maybe."

"Can I call you?"

Huh. That was weird. Mason was the kind of guy who didn't ask permission – well, other than the time we'd gotten frisky in the pantry. But that was a total anomaly in more ways than one.

I was still trying to come up with a decent response when my phone buzzed yet again. *"Say yes."*

And right on the heels of *that* text, came another. *"You know you want to."*

I felt my lips twitch like they wanted to smile. But I shouldn't be smiling. Mason had been totally awful. And yet, judging from his texts, he was willing to meet me more than halfway.

After all, I wasn't telling *him* that *he* was right – because he wasn't.

In the end, curiosity won out. I didn't give him a "yes," but I did send him a text with two little letters. *"Ok."*

I'd barely hit "send" when my phone buzzed with his incoming call. Bracing myself, I answered with a quiet, "Hey."

His voice was quiet, too. "Hey."

It felt so embarrassingly good to hear his voice, although for the life of me, I couldn't figure out why. "So…What's up?"

"There's something I need to tell you."

"Oh yeah? What's that?"

"You were right."

"So I hear. But about what?"

He paused for a long moment before saying, "I was an asshole, just like you said."

I frowned. "But I never said that."

In a tone that was almost teasing, he said, "Didn't you?"

And then, it hit me. "Oh, my God. You heard that?"

"Heard it. *And* digested it." With a faint laugh, he added, "Deserved it, too."

I could hardly believe my ears. Still, I had to tell him, "Just so you know, I didn't mean for you to hear that. I was talking to myself."

"Why? *You're* not the asshole." When he spoke next, his voice was nearly a caress. "Cami?"

"Yeah?"

"I'm so fucking sorry. I know you don't like swear words, but it's the only way I can tell you. The things I said – I did a sorry job of it. You deserve better."

I felt myself swallow. "Really?"

"You know it's true," he said. "And you wanna know what I just figured out?"

By now, I was nearly breathless. "What?"

"If I could love anyone, it would be you."

My heart lifted, and then sank as I digested the full implication of his words. On the surface, it was such a sweet sentiment. But deep inside, where it counted, I wasn't so sure. "What do you mean?"

"I mean, I don't believe in it."

"In what?"

"Love."

My breath hitched. "Oh."

"And I like you too much to lie."

By now, I was chewing on my bottom lip. *He liked me.*
So we were friends after all?

I should've been happy. But when I searched my heart, I found no happiness, just disappointment, which made no sense whatsoever. *We weren't even a couple.* I heard myself say, "I never expected you to love me."

"No. But you would eventually."

"You don't know that."

"I do," he said. "And I like you too much to hurt you."

There it was again. *He liked me.*

From Mason, it was a huge compliment. *So why did I feel so empty?*

Now I didn't know what to say. He was hurting me *now*, even if that wasn't his intention. I wasn't even sure why I was hurting. I mean, it's not like we made any promises.

Stiffly, I said, "I see."

Except I didn't. *Not really.*

"And I *would* hurt you," he said. "I wouldn't mean to. But I would."

"But why?"

"Because it's not my thing. I don't believe in it. And *you* do."

I shook my head. "It?"

He said it again. "Love."

That word – it sounded so good from his lips. But the sentiment, it was all wrong. "But you love your family," I said. "And they love *you*."

With a rueful laugh, he said, "Not today."

I winced. "Yeah, I heard about the whole whistling thing. How's your eye, by the way?"

"Eh, it looks like shit. But I'm fine." His voice softened. "It's *you*, I want to talk about."

"What about me?"

"Listen," he said, "I think you should find a new job."

CHAPTER 44

Cami

My mouth opened, but no sound came out.

On the phone, Mason said, "Are you still there?"

I bolted upright in the bed. "Oh, I'm here, alright. Are you seriously firing me?"

When he spoke again, his voice was very quiet. "No."

"Are you sure?" I said. "Because it sure sounds like it."

"Don't worry, I'm gonna pay you."

"For what?"

"The rest of your term – I'll pay you through the end. And if you want to find another job, you can get paid for that, too."

I gave a snort of derision. "So what is this? Some family tradition?"

"What do you mean?"

"I mean, you're not the first Blastoviak to try to such a stunt. Trust me. I know."

"It's no stunt," he said. "It's a real offer."

"An offer?" I said. "Or a command?"

"No one's commanding you to do anything."

"Oh yeah?" I said. "So you're *not* commanding me to leave?"

"It's not like that."

"Isn't it?"

His voice was quiet in the night. "No."

"Why not? Because you're paying me for the privilege?"

"I'm paying you because it's fair."

"To who?"

"You," he said. "Look, it was my mistake, not yours. So *I'm* paying for it, not you."

"And what about Willow?"

"What about her?"

"You were the one who was *so* determined that I should stay through the end. And now you're paying me to leave? Do you realize how insane you sound?"

"Fuck yeah, I realize. And you wanna know why?"

"Why?"

"Because I *am* insane." He made a scoffing sound. "Shit. I don't mean clinically. I just mean, I haven't been thinking straight. But I do know one thing."

"Oh yeah? What's that?"

"It's nobody's fault but my own. So I'm gonna make it right."

"No you're not," I said. "What you're *trying* to do is write a check to make a problem go away. And I'm here to tell you, I'm not having it."

"Meaning?"

"I'm not leaving. If you're paying me, I'm staying."

"Is that a joke?"

"No." My jaw clenched. "Because unlike you, *I* can be an adult about it."

"And I can't?"

"Obviously not," I said. "Have you listened to yourself? Here, you go on and on about how much you care about Willow, and then, when things get a little dicey, you think you can just whip out a wad of cash–"

"I thought it was a check."

"Yeah. And *I* thought you cared about your sister."

His voice grew ragged. "You think I don't?"

"No. What *I* think is you're not thinking straight, just like you said. I mean, come on. Earlier today, you jumped your own brother. That's not exactly normal, you know."

"Trust me," he said. "It was a long time coming."

"I don't care. I'm just telling you, you're full of it." Now that I was going, I couldn't seem to make myself stop. "And as long as we're having it out, here's a question. Why on Earth do you keep hiring nannies in your own age group?"

"As opposed to what?"

"Like some nice grandmotherly type." I made a sound of irritation. "Or are you worried they'll get all 'naughty' with you, too?"

"That's not it."

"Are you sure?" I said. "What, you think no one can resist you?"

"No. What I *thought* was Willow would like someone around the same age as me, so we'd be more like…"

I waited, but he never did finish the sentence. "Like what?" I said. "A regular family?"

"Shit. I dunno."

"Yes, you do," I said. "So you go out and hire hot single chicks – me excluded of course and—"

"Why not you?"

"What do you mean?" I asked.

"Why are you excluded?"

I sighed. "Because I'm not the hot single type. I'm just a regular girl."

"Trust me, Cami. Whatever you are, it's not regular."

I rolled my eyes. "Yeah, sure. But the point remains, you keep having the same problem over and over. But what do you do? You keep hiring the same type of people. And then, you act all surprised when the inevitable happens."

"And what's that?"

"When like total idiots, they fall for you."

Shit.

I hadn't meant to say it. But as soon as I did, I realized all too well that I *had* fallen for him. And it wasn't because he 'banged' like a Trojan or made my knees turn to jelly.

It was because for some messed up reason, I actually liked him. No. I *more* than liked him.

I loved him.

I loved his mind and his devotion to his family. I loved his strength and the way he'd sacrificed his own freedom to give Willow a home. I loved his smiles, as rare as they were. I loved his protective streak, even as maddening as it was sometimes.

But there was something I *didn't* love.

It was the fact he didn't love me.

Maybe he was right. Maybe he didn't have it in him. Or maybe, he simply hadn't met the right person.

Either way, I'd meant what I said. *I wasn't walking away.*

Meaning from Willow, not Mason.

Him, I could totally do without – now, anyway.

On the other end of the phone, Mason had grown utterly silent. I knew why, too.

It was time to set him straight.

"And just so you know," I said, "I'm fine with keeping things professional. Like I already told you, I won't be knocking on your bedroom door. So unless you *are* planning to fire me, I'll see when you get home."

And with that, I hung up on him for the second time in two days. And I didn't feel the least bit guilty.

CHAPTER 45

Cami

When Mason returned two days later, I figured we'd at least talk about it. Or maybe he'd simply fire me and call it good.

But *neither* of those things happened. Instead, Mason walked in from the garage the same as usual and dropped his suitcase by the door. Wordlessly, he walked into the kitchen, looking like he wanted to be anywhere but here.

Willow and I were sitting at the kitchen table – not doing homework, but finishing up a giant jigsaw puzzle of frolicking puppies.

At the sight of Mason, Willow jumped up from her chair and hurtled herself into his arms. Watching, I felt my eyes grow misty, wishing I could do the same.

And wishing I could slap him silly.

But the way it looked, somebody already had.

Just as Arden had predicted on the phone, Mason had one heck of a shiner around his left eye. Unfortunately, it did little to diminish his appeal.

Our gazes met for the briefest instant before I looked back to the puzzle. Still, from the corner of my eye, I drank in the sight of him as he crouched down to return Willow's hug.

His hair was tousled, and his face was grim, even as Willow clutched him tight.

When Willow pulled back, she asked, "What happened to your eye?"

With a ghost of a smile, he replied, "Eh, I was wrestling with Chase and must've banged it."

Banged.

God, how I'd come to loathe that word.

And not too long afterward, I came to loathe *him.*

The real loathing started later that night, after I put Willow to bed. With my heart in my throat, I wandered back downstairs in search of Mason, figuring we'd need to talk sooner or later, unless we were planning to pretend that nothing had happened.

And me? I wasn't good at pretending.

I found Mason in his home office, going over some paperwork behind his massive desk.

When I knocked on the edge of his open door, Mason looked up and frowned. "Yeah?"

I hesitated. "Don't you think we should talk?"

With a look of utter indifference, he replied, "About what?"

I stared from the open doorway. "You know. About everything." I hesitated. "And my job."

He returned his attention to his paperwork. "It's still yours if you want it."

"Sorry, what?"

He was still looking at the papers. "The job. Stay or go. Your choice."

I stiffened. "Gee, how flexible of you."

Finally, he looked up. "It was your idea, not mine. So, like I said, you choose, and I'll handle it."

Oh, I'd give him something to handle, alright. I slipped into his office and shut the door quietly behind me. "That is *such* a crock," I said. "You practically fired me."

With a stiff smile, he said, "I did more than that."

I drew back. "What's *that* supposed to mean?"

"You *know* what it means," he said. "So, are you staying or quitting?"

"Oh, that's nice." I did my best Mason impression. "So, are you firing me or not?"

"Not," he said.

I searched his face. "But where do we go from here?"

"That's up to you," he said. "You're smart. You'll figure it out."

Me. Not us. In my whole life, I'd never been so irritated by a compliment. "I can't be too smart," I said. "Or I would've seen it the same as you."

Looking almost bored now, he said, "Seen what?"

"That it was a bad idea. *You* know." I lowered my voice. "For us to sleep together." A bitter scoff escaped my lips. "You told me. And I guess I should've listened, huh?"

His jaw clenched. "Yeah. You should've."

His words felt like a slap. "So you're saying this is *my* fault?"

"No. It's mine," he said. "I take full responsibility."

It was a decent sentiment. And yet, his cold businesslike approach was making me just a little bit crazy.

And besides, we all knew it took two to tango.

I muttered, "Well, I'm sure the shareholders will be delighted."

"I don't have shareholders."

"I know," I said. "I was being sarcastic."

"*I* wasn't," he said. "I answer to no one." He gave me a hard look. "And maybe you should remember that."

I crossed my arms. "Maybe I will."

Once again, he looked down to his paperwork. He picked up a random document and frowned. "Now, if we're done, I've got stuff to do."

I stood there in front of his desk, staring as he set aside the first document and picked up another.

Part of me wanted to lunge for his paperwork and scatter it to the floor. And then, assuming I had his full attention, I could tell him exactly what I thought of his icy demeanor.

His words from the other night haunted my thoughts. *"If I could love anyone, it would be you."*

What *was* that, anyway?

Just a line? Maybe an easy way to give me the brush-off?

He'd also claimed to *like* me. But that couldn't be true. Because if you truly like someone, you don't sit there shuffling through paperwork while they stand in front of you like…well, an employee, actually.

I froze. *Oh.* That's exactly what I was – his employee.

The Help.

But of course, I *did* have a choice in the matter. I mean, I could walk off right now and let him replace me with nanny number-eighty-seven, or whatever it was. By now, he probably had several agencies on speed dial.

But Willow – *she'd* be the one who'd suffer.

Over the last few months, I'd seen her really blossom under the love and stability I'd been trying to provide.

And what if I left now?

It was only two weeks until Christmas, and we'd made all sorts of plans – to bake Christmas cookies with Arden, to put up a giant Christmas tree, and to decorate the house for the first time ever – at least according to Willow.

Did I have the stomach to walk away now, just because I'd been unable to resist my boss?

I shook my head. *No.*

I didn't.

And I *couldn't.*

Right then and there, I decided that regardless of whatever was going on between me and Mason, I'd still keep my promise. Even if it killed me, I'd stick around until next fall.

For Willow's sake.

Not mine.

And certainly not Mason's.

The lunk-blaster.

He was still sorting through his paperwork, but he surely realized that I hadn't left. So either he truly didn't care, or he was making a point to ignore me.

Either way, I was more than ready to move on.

I said, "I've got a question."

Without looking up, he said, "Yeah?"

"Christmas is two weeks away. And as you know, I'm planning to spend the week at my parents' place."

This was something we'd discussed a couple of months ago, before everything had gotten so crazy between us.

It had been a good plan, especially because, thanks to Arden, Willow wouldn't be left in the lurch. On Christmas Day, she and Brody were planning to host a traditional Christmas dinner at their beach house. They'd invited Willow and Mason. Chase, too. *Plus me.*

But as much as I'd appreciated the offer, I'd decided to take the opportunity to spend the holidays with my own family.

And now, more than ever, I was beyond eager to see them.

Or maybe, I just felt like running away, at least for a little while.

To Mason, I continued, "And about the vehicle, the one I drive for my job. You know how I took it home for Thanksgiving? I just wanted to make sure that it's still okay if I drive it home for Christmas."

Without bothering to look up, he said, "You don't need to ask."

"Sure I do."

"No. Because you already know the answer." Finally, he looked up. "I said it was fine weeks ago. Nothing has changed."

I felt my gaze narrow. "A lot has changed, and you know it."

"Not the way *I* see it," he said. "So take it. Or don't. Your choice."

I stared at him for a long silent moment. Even though he was technically talking about the vehicle, his words were filled with hidden meaning.

Take it or don't.

Stay or leave.

Scream or strangle him.

So many choices, so little time.

With a sound of disgust, I said, "Fine. I'll take it. Thanks *ever* so much."

"You're welcome."

He didn't mean it any more than I did. But hey, that was fine by me. I'd had more than enough of Mason Blastoviak.

Not just for tonight. But for a lifetime.

CHAPTER 46

Cami

The next couple of weeks passed in a long, depressing blur. Oh sure, I tried to be festive for Willow's sake, but it was tough going.

Even as we decorated the house and picked out Christmas presents for Mason – from Willow, *not* from me – my heart was heavier than it had been in a long time.

Mason and I weren't exactly ignoring each other, but we *were* acting like polite strangers – or more accurately, like boss and employee.

Him being the boss of course.

On the upside, things across the river offered just enough distraction to stop me from wallowing in my own misery.

To my surprise, Livia was still toughing it out with the two unruly teens, which was pretty incredible, considering that she'd lasted only three days at her *last* job, which was a hundred times easier than her current gig.

For the previous job, she'd been working as a hand model in her dad's jewelry store, where her primary responsibility had involved trying on the merchandise.

Not even kidding.

But her nanny job? It looked like something else entirely. From the back window, Willow and I had a front-row seat to all the theatrics between her and her teenage charges.

They locked *her* out.

She locked *them* out.

One time, they *all* got locked out and had to break a back window when the *usual* window got stuck.

And forget taking a dinghy across the river. Winter weather had arrived with a vengeance, dropping the temperatures so low that the river finally began to freeze. And although the water wasn't completely frozen over, the icy surface would be a detriment to almost any watercraft – dinghies included.

As far as the antics between Livia and the teenagers, to me, the whole thing seemed seriously unhinged. But apparently, they thought otherwise. I mean, why else would they keep on doing it?

Livia had come from money. Technically, she didn't need to work at all, so there was no reason for her stay if she was truly that miserable – unless she really *did* have a thing for the dad.

And then, there were the teenagers themselves. They were too old for a nanny in the traditional sense. But the way it looked, they were liking their *non-traditional* one a lot better – if only because she gave as good as she got.

I had to give Livia credit. She was proving to be a tough nut to crack.

But me? I wasn't tough.

Every time I saw Mason, my heart squeezed just a little, even as I debated going for his throat, speaking figuratively, that this.

But it wasn't until the day before my holiday departure that I made a fool of myself all over again, but in a totally different way.

CHAPTER 47

Mason

The way it looked, she hated me.

Good.

It was better than the alternative.

For her sake, not mine.

Was it killing me? Fuck yeah. But I'd rather die a thousand deaths than hurt someone I cared about. And I *did* care for Cami, in my own messed-up sort of way.

But she was still my employee, which meant that certain responsibilities had to be taken care of. With this in mind, I texted her from my home office asking her to stop by my desk when she had the chance.

She never showed.

I'd sent the text at seven o'clock, two hours before Willow's usual bedtime, thinking we could get the formalities out of the way and move on with the rest of our evening.

For me, this meant handling some year-end paperwork that I'd been putting off.

For Cami, this meant packing for her trip. I knew this, because three hours after sending my text, I could still hear her going up and down the stairs, and then out into the garage, loading up the SUV with whatever she was taking to Petoskey.

I felt like a dick for not offering to help, at least with loading the suitcases. But that was something a boyfriend – or hell, even a friend – would do. And, as we'd already established, *that wasn't me.*

Cami was leaving tomorrow afternoon and wouldn't be home until after the new year.

Home. At the thought of it, I frowned at my desk. This wasn't Cami's home. It was *my* home and Willow's.

But somewhere along the way, I'd come to think of it as Cami's home, too. This wasn't the case. *Her* home was nearly three hours away, with a family she'd known all her life.

Eventually she'd find a teaching job and move out on her own, but one thing was fairly obvious. She'd be leaving *this* home at the end of her term.

That was months away, so I tried not to dwell on it, just like I tried not to dwell on what might've been, if only I were capable of giving her the one thing I couldn't.

Love.

She deserved it.

And maybe I did, too. But I wasn't willing to take more than I could give, and I knew she'd only end up hating me if I tried to fake it.

Hell, she hated me now, and I hadn't done half the damage I was capable of.

When eleven o'clock came and went, and Cami still hadn't showed, I left my home office in search of her.

I found her upstairs in her bedroom, rummaging in her closet. I stopped just outside her bedroom's doorway and said, "Did you get my text?"

She was standing on her tiptoes, trying to reach a box on the upper shelf. Without looking in my direction, she said, "Yeah, I got it."

From the open doorway, I asked, "So why didn't you show?"

"Because it was ridiculous."

I felt my eyebrows furrow. "What, the text?"

"No. The summons."

"It wasn't a summons," I said. "It was a request."

"Whatever it was, it was silly." She stopped and gave me a no-nonsense look. "If you want to talk, come out of your office once in a while. Willow might like that, you know."

I gave her a hard look. "Yeah? And how about *you?*"

"What do you mean?"

"Would *you* like it?"

"Not particularly."

"Good. Then consider it a favor."

She was glaring now. "So, let me get this straight. You're blaming me for the fact you've been avoiding your sister?"

"There's no blame," I said. "I've been busy."

"You've *always* been busy," she said. "But you've never been distant. And just in case it's not clear, I meant from Willow, not from me."

She was wearing dark jeans and a black turtleneck sweater. Her hair was loose and her eyes were flashing with anger. She looked so sexy, I wanted to leave the doorway, yank her into my arms, and kiss her like I had in the pantry.

Shit. What was it with me and closets lately?

But I knew what it was, and it had nothing to do with the location. It had to do with the girl *in* the closet.

Cami.

She was the sweetest thing I'd ever known, even now, bristling with hatred.

When I said nothing in reply, she said, "And remember, I'm leaving tomorrow for a whole week."

"Nine days," I corrected.

"Fine. A week and two days then. The point remains. I hope you're not planning to hole up in your office the whole time."

"I'm not."

"Good. Because starting tomorrow, she's off school."

"Yeah, so?"

"So I hope you're planning to spend some time with her."

I felt my jaw clench. "You think I won't?"

"I don't know what to think. Do you realize, you haven't had dinner with her in like two whole weeks?"

I said it again. "Yeah, so?"

"So, what are you gonna do when I'm gone? Make her eat alone?"

No. I wasn't. And the truth was, I'd been keeping to myself for Cami's sake. As far as Willow, I'd been planning to make it up to her over the Christmas break, when it would be just the two of us – along with some part-time help from the housekeeper and Arden, who'd made noises about having Willow over to bake Christmas cookies.

I told Cami, "Don't worry. It's handled."

"Good." And with that, she returned her attention to the box. She stood on her tiptoes and reached up to grip the bottom.

"Hang on," I said. "I'll get it."

"I'm fine," she said.

"Yeah, until the box hits you in the head."

She stopped and gave me a look. "Would you care?"

"Hell yeah, I'd care. What? You think I wouldn't?"

"I have no idea," she said. "You're the most confusing person I've ever known."

Another guy might've asked her what she meant. But me – I didn't need to ask. *I already knew.*

The next time she reached up for the box, I didn't bother asking permission. I strode into her room and joined her in the closet.

With a sigh, she stepped aside, letting me grab it from the top shelf. The thing was heavy – not for me, but surely for her.

As I set the box on the floor beside us, I said, "What's in there, anyway?"

"Rocks."

I gave the box another glance. "You're joking."

"Yeah. I am. It's Christmas presents for my family."

I almost smiled. "So you got them rocks?"

"No, but as long as we're talking, there's something you should know."

"Oh yeah? What's that?"

"Everyone – and I mean *everyone* – has problems. But there's no need to spread the misery. And yeah, maybe you got a raw deal with your family. And yeah, maybe you've spent too many years picking up the slack. But don't you think it's time for you to move on?"

This wasn't what I'd come for. My jaw clenched as I replied, "From what?"

"From whatever baggage you've got stored in that heart of yours."

Her words found their mark. *If she only knew.* Still, I gave her a stiff smile. "Haven't you heard? I don't have one."

"Yeah, well goodie for you." She sighed in obvious irritation. "So what did you want, anyway?"

I wanted her.

I wanted to pull her into my arms and feel her softness against my hardness, to clutch her tight and pretend to be somebody else, somebody who didn't have a lump of coal where their heart should be.

But I wasn't that guy. Hell, I didn't even *want* to be that guy. Guys like that were too vulnerable, too weak, too unable to protect those they cared about.

And God help me, I cared about *her.*

So instead, I reached into my back pocket and pulled out a plain white envelope – no card, no sentiment, nothing but her name – first *and* last, just to make sure there was no misunderstanding.

I held out the envelope between us. "Your bonus."

She frowned. "What?"

"Your Christmas bonus," I said. "I figured you'd want it before you left."

She was still frowning. "I didn't know I'd be getting a bonus."

"Yeah, and I didn't know I'd be getting a lecture." And with that, I pushed the envelope closer. "Now take it. I've got things to do."

Finally, she reached out took it from my hand. "So…should I open it now, or…?"

"It's a bonus, not a gift." And with that, I stooped down and picked up the box, the one containing gifts for her family.

She gave me a worried glance. "Wait, what are you doing?"

"I'm loading it up."

"You don't need to. I can get it."

"Maybe. But if you can't, and break your neck on the way down, it'll be a shitty Christmas for Willow."

And me.

But I didn't say it. Because the thought of anything bad happening to Cami was impossible to bear – and not only because Willow would be devastated.

I'd be devastated, too.

With the box in-hand, I turned and left her bedroom. Over my shoulder, I said, "I'll load it in the back. If you want to move it later, be my guest."

CHAPTER 48

Cami

A thousand dollars. That was the amount of my Christmas bonus. The envelope had contained ten crisp hundred-dollar bills, *brand new* bills from the look and feel of them.

And of course, I felt awful. After Mason had left my bedroom and loaded up the box, I never saw him again – not that night nor the next morning.

And now I felt guilty for not getting him a Christmas present at all. Yes, I realized that he'd made a point to inform me that the bonus wasn't a gift. *But wasn't it standard procedure to get your boss at least something in return?*

It was mid-morning, and I was still trying to decide when Arden called to say, "Hey, I'm going to the mall for some last-minute things. Do you and Willow want to come?"

I hadn't planned on it. Tomorrow was Christmas Eve, and snow had been falling all morning – not enough to be dangerous, but enough to make me glad that I'd be leaving for Petoskey in just a few hours.

Tonight, the weather was supposed to take a serious turn for the worse, and I had a three-hour drive ahead of me. My vehicle was already loaded, which meant that I could leave town the moment Mason returned home to watch Willow.

As I glanced out the window, I tried not to worry. Given our recent hostilities, Mason might even decide to work late, which would leave me stuck driving through a nighttime blizzard.

Or more likely, he'd tell me that I had to wait until the snow cleared – not for my own safety, but for the safety of his vehicle and to prevent Willow from being sad if I wrapped myself around a telephone pole.

But would Mason be sad?

Not hardly.

Other than his concern for his family, he was the coldest person I'd ever met. And yet, I swear, I'd seen glimpses of true warmth under his icy exterior, like there was another version of himself just dying to come out.

Regardless, he was driving me insane, even now.

Unable to resist, I took Arden up on her offer and met her at the mall, where I explained how crazy Mason was making me.

As Willow played in the kiddie area, I even confessed that I'd slept with him over a month ago.

But as it turned out, Arden already knew.

I asked, "But how?" And then I paused. "Oh, my God. Did Mason tell Brody?"

"Are you kidding?" she laughed. "That guy's more tight-lipped than anyone I know – meaning Mason of course." She gave me a sympathetic smile. "No. I figured it out on my own."

"How?" I asked yet again.

"It wasn't that hard," she said. "I'm just embarrassed I didn't see it sooner."

I tried to smile. "Actually, there wasn't much to see. I mean, it was just the one time."

But already, Arden was shaking her head. "No. I don't think so."

"But it was," I insisted.

"I'm not talking about the sex," she said. "You really like him. And if you don't mind me saying…" She cringed. "…I think you might be in love with him, at least a little."

At one time, it had been *more* than a little. But now? I was pretty sure I hated him. Or at least, I tried to hate him.

"Oh, please," I said. "What do I look like? A masochist?"

"Not a masochist," she said. "But you always see the good in people. Even me."

"Yeah, but you really *are* good."

"Not all the time," she said. "I'm stubborn and temperamental and *way* too likely to fly off the handle. *But you?* You're the most serene person I've ever met."

I almost laughed in her face. "Not lately."

"Oh, come on."

"I'm serious," I said. "You should've seen me last night. Here Mason comes in to give me a Christmas bonus, and what do I do? I read him the riot act."

Her surprise was obvious. "Really? What'd you say?"

"Nothing that will a make a difference."

"Oh, I don't know," she said. "Ever since you showed up, he *has* seemed at least a little different."

"But how would *you* know?" I asked. "You hardly see him."

"But Brody does," she said. "And just the other day, he mentioned something about Mason seeming more human." She gave me a significant look. "Good *and* bad."

I was intrigued in spite of myself. "How so?"

"Well, for a while there, it sounded like Mason was actually lightening up."

"In what way?"

"According to Brody, Mason was smiling a lot more, and even joking once in a while." She frowned. "But then, when all of us were in Kentucky, he was as miserable as I'd ever seen him."

"Yeah, well…at least Chase was happy."

Arden rolled her eyes. "Chase is *always* happy – well, as long as he's up to no good."

From watching their cable show, I couldn't disagree. But *Chase* wasn't my problem. It was his older brother who was making me nuts. "Back to Mason," I said. "I've got to get him a Christmas present. Any ideas?"

She winced. "A whistle?"

"I'm serious," I said. "I need to find *something*, and I don't have much time." I snuck a quick glance at Willow, who was still playing with the other kids. "And we're supposed to be getting that blizzard tonight."

"Not *tonight*," she said. "Later today."

"What?" I shook my head. "I thought it wasn't hitting 'til midnight."

"It *was*. But the forecast changed." With a look of concern, she said, "Wait a minute, you're not leaving *today*, are you?"

"Well, that *is* the plan."

"Oh, crap. Then you'd better leave now. If you hurry, you can probably miss the worst of it. I hear it's supposed to be *really* bad."

"Yeah, but they always say that." *It was true.* I'd lived in Michigan my whole life, and one thing I knew from experience – the weather was almost never as bad as the forecast.

Plus, I was from Petoskey, which was three hours north and more prone to winter weather. I was no stranger to snow – *or* driving in it.

But Arden looked far from comforted. "Seriously, you really *should* leave right away, just to be safe."

I was touched by her concern, but I had to face facts. "I *can't* leave now. Mason won't be home for a few more hours yet."

"So?"

"So I can't leave Willow alone." I went on to explain that the housekeeper had the day off, which meant that I had no backup for emergencies.

"Hey, *I* know," Arden said. "Why don't you let *me* take her? We were planning to make Christmas cookies anyway. We could do it today instead of tomorrow."

I bit my lip. *It was so very tempting.* "Are you sure you don't mind?"

She smiled. "Oh come on. It'll be a blast. I love Willow. And Brody's working late, so the timing's perfect."

I gave Willow another worried glance. "I wonder if Mason would agree."

"How about this?" Arden said. "I'll have *Brody* let him know. They're both in the office today. Brody can swing by and tell Mason so you don't have to."

Recalling last night's encounter, I decided this was probably a good idea. And besides, a Christmas bake-a-thon would do Willow a lot of good. Even though I'd been trying like crazy to be in a festive mood, I swear, there were times when she looked almost worried about me.

This was the *last* thing I wanted.

So after a quick lunch, I sent Arden and Willow on their merry way, thinking I'd just snag a quick gift for Mason, drop it off at the house, and be on *my* way, too.

But nothing happened the way I'd planned. *Not even close.*

CHAPTER 49

Cami

Three hours later, I was still at the mall. It wasn't that I *planned* to be there, but I was having the hardest time finding a decent gift for Mason.

Probably, I should've gotten him a necktie and been done with it – except I knew that Mason's neckties probably cost more than my entire outfit, which granted was nothing special – just jeans and a fuzzy sweater, plus my thick winter coat, which felt way too warm for the crowded shopping mall

But then, as I wandered from shop to shop, the crowd began dwindling at an alarming rate.

I knew why, too. Judging from conversations I heard in passing, the blizzard had come earlier than expected, catching all of us by surprise.

I was even more surprised when the mall announced they'd be closing early due to bad weather. Today was the day before Christmas Eve. It was one of the busiest shopping days of the year.

That's when I knew it was serious.

And along with *this* knowledge came a sickening realization. There was no way on Earth I could leave for Petoskey *now.* Cripes, at this rate, I'd be lucky to get out tomorrow – unless by some miracle, the snow cleared just as quickly as it had arrived.

After all, this was Michigan, not Florida. Once it stopped snowing, the plows and salt trucks would get to work, clearing at least the main roads faster than you could say, *"Get me the heck out of here."*

But if the weather didn't let up? In that case, I'd be spending another day – or maybe more – with my impossible boss and *not* my own family.

By now, I wanted to kick myself. And I *especially* wanted to kick myself when I received an incoming text from Mason, saying "*Where are you?*"

Two could play at this game. I texted back. "*Where are YOU?*"

He replied. "*Home.*"

Oh, crud. This meant that if I was still determined to get him a gift, he'd be home when I dropped it off. *Talk about bad timing.*

He texted me again, mimicking my own text from a few moments ago. "Where are YOU."

With a sigh, I texted back, "*At the mall.*"

In reply, he texted back three little letters. "*WTF.*" Almost immediately, this was followed by another text containing only a question mark.

I frowned. *Talk about rude.* I texted back, "*Meaning?*"

"*You need to get your ass home.*" And *this* text was followed by *another* text. "*Now.*"

Oh, for crying out loud. By now, I felt like hurling my cellphone against the nearest wall. I was only shopping because of him. Yes, it had been my own decision, but the point remained.

If it weren't for Mason Blastoviak, I'd already *be* home – and I didn't mean the place I'd been living for the past few months. I meant my *real* home, with my real family, people who actually *liked* me.

But Mason? *He* didn't like me. Oh sure, he *said* he liked me, but his words and actions were so opposite, I was having a hard time believing any of the nicer things he'd said.

But boy-oh-boy, did I remember the bad stuff. *That* was burned into my brain like a flaming Christmas tree.

I shoved the phone back into my purse and marched toward the nearest department store. I was halfway there when my cell phone rang. With a sigh, I pulled it out and glanced at the display.

It was Mason. *Of course.*

When I answered with a curt hello, he said, "What the hell are you doing?"

"Shopping. That *is* what people do at the mall, isn't it?"

"Not if they know what's good for them."

My fingers clenched around the phone. *Speaking of things not good for me.* In a stiff voice, I informed him, "If you're talking about the snow, I know it came ahead of schedule. And I *know* it must be bad, because the mall's closing early."

"Not early enough," he grumbled.

I made a sound of frustration. "Just why do you care, anyway?"

"Is that a serious question?"

"Yes. It is, in fact." Speaking slowly, pronouncing every single word, I said, "Why. Do. You. Care?"

"I care because of Willow," he said. "Now are you leaving or not?"

His words stung, although for the life of me, I couldn't imagine why. I mean, I already knew I was expendable. And besides, hadn't I already decided that I hated him?

I replied, "Of course, I'm leaving. Didn't you hear the part where I said the mall's closing?"

In a tight voice, he said, "When?"

"Five minutes. There, you happy?"

"I'll be happy when I see you pulling in the driveway."

With a bark of laughter, I replied, "Hah! You? Happy? I'd drive through a *dozen* blizzards to see *that*."

"Meaning?"

"Oh, stop," I said. "You know what I mean. You're so damned determined to be miserable."

"So you're cussing now?"

"Hell yeah, I'm cussing. And there's a lot more where *that* came from."

"Oh yeah? Hit me."

With a stiff smile, I said, "Do you mean that *literally*? Because I'm pretty sure they sell boxing gloves."

"If you mean the mall on Wheeler, they don't."

"What?"

"The sporting goods store moved last month."

"Oh, for God's sake," I said. *"Now* you're joking with me?"

"It's no joke," he said. "They moved to Woodside."

By now, I felt like screaming. "Alright, you really want me to let you have it?"

"Sure, why not?"

"Alright." I lowered my voice to a raw hiss. "You're being a total snork-weasel. Me? I like roses and balloons – yellow, by the way. And cookies. But what do *you* like? *You* like being miserable. But has anyone ever told you that misery is contagious? Well, *I'm* here to tell you, Mason Blastoviak, that you're not making *me* miserable. Not anymore. Now if you'll excuse me, *I've* got a stupid present to buy."

And with that, I ended the call and marched straight into the nearest department store. I stalked directly to the menswear department, where I found a sales associate – some guy in his twenties – standing behind the main counter.

When he saw me coming, he gave me an apologetic smile. "I'm sorry, but we're closing."

As If I didn't know. "When?"

He glanced at his watch. "Two minutes."

"Terrific," I said. "I know *exactly* what I want." I yanked Mason's envelope from my purse and retrieved one of those hundred-dollar bills. I slapped it onto the counter and said, "Give me the ugliest tie you've got."

The guy frowned. "You serious?"

"Dead serious," I said. "If there's an ugly tie contest, I want *this* tie to win – first *and* second place."

The guy gave a slow nod. "You know what?"

"What?"

He grinned. "I know just the thing."

CHAPTER 50

Cami

Soon, I was striding toward the mall's main entrance with Mason's new necktie stuffed deep into the pocket of my winter coat.

The clerk had offered free gift-wrapping, but I hadn't had the heart to take him up on it, not with the mall closing early and everyone so anxious to leave.

So instead, I'd asked him to simply stuff my purchase into a small plastic shopping bag and call it good.

If the tie got wrinkled, all the better.

By now, the mall was practically empty, which was pretty surreal, considering how crowded it had been when I'd first arrived with Arden and Willow.

My steps faltered. *Willow.*

Oh, my God. I stopped in the middle of the main thoroughfare and squeezed my eyes shut in dawning mortification.

That's why Mason had contacted me. *It had to be.*

He was notoriously protective when it came to his little sister, which totally explained why he'd been so insistent that I leave the mall immediately. If *I* had a child, or cripes, even if Willow were still with me, I would've left long ago.

I tried to think. Arden had promised to tell Brody to tell Mason that Willow would be baking cookies at Arden's place. But with multiple people in the line of communication, it would be incredibly easy for the message to get delayed.

Plus, Mason had obviously left work early. Apparently, he hadn't been pleased to find his sister gone when he returned home. Given the horrible weather, I couldn't exactly blame him.

Crud.

Now, I'd need to apologize for flipping out on him. *Again.*

My shoulders slumped. *This day just got better and better.*

With growing dread, I trudged onward until I reached the main entrance. What I saw through the big glass doors made my eyes widen in surprise.

Outside those doors, I didn't see a regular snowstorm. I saw a raging blizzard, even by Petoskey standards.

One time for a school project, I'd had to look up how many inches of snow Petoskey averaged in any given year. The total was over a hundred inches, nearly four times the national average.

And yet, what I saw in the mall parking lot left me speechless. The wind was raging, and the snow was falling so hard, I could hardly see beyond the sidewalk outside the glass doors.

Great. Now I owed Mason a double apology.

As far as the blizzard, I wasn't *that* worried for my own safety. Mason's house was only twenty minutes away, and the SUV had four-wheel drive, along with tons of safety features.

Plus, I was more than willing to take my time. *If the drive took me an hour, so what?*

In fact, *two* hours would be even better, considering what awaited me at Mason's place.

With a sigh, I reached into my purse and pulled out my gloves. Before braving the snow-covered roads, I'd need to call Mason and explain that Willow wasn't with me, if only to keep him from venturing out himself.

On second thought, I decided, I'd just send him a text.

The less contact the better, right?

Stalling, I decided I'd first make it to my vehicle and take it from there.

With my head down, I trudged through the swirling snow, trying my best to keep from falling on my backside in the slippery parking lot.

I wasn't even sure what was more frustrating – that the weather had caught me by surprise or that Mason had been annoyingly correct about the need to leave quickly.

He hadn't been caught by surprise. And he'd warned me, too. *But had I listened?*

No.

But then again, he'd only called me like fifteen minutes ago, which would have made nearly no difference – except for the fact that he'd now have the pleasure of saying, *"I told you so."*

Terrific. Something else to look forward to.

On the upside, the blazing orange SUV was impossible to miss, even now, with the visibility so awful.

In my purse, my cellphone was buzzing every minute or two, just like it had been doing ever since I'd ended the call with Mason. Into the swirling snow, I muttered, "Jeez, hang on, will ya?"

By the time I reached the SUV, I was a freezing, snowy mess. As I yanked open the driver's side door, my phone buzzed yet again.

With a muttered curse – a *real* one, by the way – I practically dove into the driver's seat and slammed the driver's side door shut behind me. Without wasting any time, I started the SUV's engine, figuring I'd let it warm up while I caught up on my messages.

From Mason, there were half a dozen texts along with a couple of phone calls, too. *No voicemails.*

As far as the texts, they were more of the same, urging me to head home ASAP. He meant *his* home, of course, because by now, it was pretty darn obvious, my plans for driving to Petoskey today were utterly ruined.

And on top of *that*, the SUV's windshield was completely covered in snow – not the fluffy kind that could be easily brushed off, but the icy kind that required defrosting.

This meant I still had at least five more minutes before I could even think of leaving the parking lot.

To Mason, I tapped out a quick text. *"Willow's safe at Arden's. Making cookies. Not shopping. Ok?"*

I waited for the return text, because in spite of Mason's *many* other annoying qualities, I had to admit, he was really diligent when it came to correspondence about his sister.

But no return text came.

Was he making me wait because I'd made *him* wait?

Or – *oh, God* – what if he was on the way to pick her up? He was so protective sometimes that I could totally see him doing it, hopping into his car and coming out after her.

With a frown, I picked up my phone and texted again. *"Ok???"*

No response.

Dang it. I should've texted him sooner.

While the SUV thawed, I figured I'd hop into the back seat and rearrange some of the things I'd tossed into it last night – clothes mostly, along with some extra blankets and Christmas presents – some of them already wrapped, and others in need of boxes or bows.

Normally, I'd be a lot more organized, but last night, I'd been so angry, I swear, I did more throwing than arranging.

And even though I obviously couldn't leave for my trip any time soon, there was at least a decent chance I'd be able to leave tomorrow morning – assuming it *ever* stopped snowing.

A quick glance out the side window wasn't encouraging. If anything, it was snowing harder.

Unwilling to brave the weather so soon – or risk getting locked out of the vehicle – I crawled over the center console and tumbled into the back seat.

Dignified? No.

But hey, dignity had been scarce on the ground, especially lately.

I was in the back seat for less than a minute when suddenly, the two front doors opened at exactly the same time. A split second later, two strangers in ski masks hopped into the vehicle. One claimed the driver's seat while the other claimed the passenger's side.

I swear, my heart leapt out of my chest. What the hell?

CHAPTER 51

Cami

From the back seat, I yelled, "What are you doing?"

In unison, they both turned to look. Their ski-masks were pitch black, just like their bulky black winter coats. The masks covered most of their faces, leaving only their eyes and mouths exposed.

The one in the driver's seat demanded in a voice that was all masculine, "Who the hell are you?"

"I'm the owner of the vehicle," I said. "Who the hell are *you*?"

Before he could even think to answer, the person in the passenger's seat – a female, judging from her voice – yelled, "You are *such* a liar!"

I shook my head. "What?"

Her tone grew snippy. "It's not 'your' car."

Legally speaking, she was correct. I mean, it's not like my name was on the title. But it was still my vehicle as far as *these* two jokers were concerned. I shot back, "It is, too."

"Hah! It belongs to Mason Blastoviak, not *you.*"

I blinked. "Wait, how would you know?"

"It's a custom color," she said. "Any idiot knows *that*. What, you don't watch TV?"

Obviously, she was referring to the brothers' cable show. I told her, "I've watched it plenty."

"Then you should know, the color is Blast Orange, the same as their logo."

Through gritted teeth, I said, "And *you* should know that I'm *not* in a good mood. So get out."

"No, *you* get out."

"Forget it," I told her. "I'm not going anywhere."

Maybe I was being foolhardy, but the way I saw it, I'd be even *more* foolhardy to give up the vehicle, along with all of my belongings, just because two idiots in masks decided they wanted to take the Blast-Mobile for a spin.

Or maybe I'd simply had enough.

I told them, "So get out before I call the police."

But they *didn't* get out. Instead, the guy turned forward and shifted the vehicle into drive.

Again, I yelled, "What are you doing?"

"I'm getting the hell out of here."

"Why?"

"So the police don't catch us."

Oh, for God's sake. "I haven't called them *yet,"* I said. "Just let me out." I paused. "Wait, no. I mean, *you* get out!"

But already, the guy was pulling forward. *Shit.* Way too late, I recalled that I'd shoved my cellphone back into my purse, which I'd stupidly left in the passenger's seat.

Was she sitting on it right now?

Probably.

The female looked to the male and said, "Hey, I wanna drive!"

"Forget it," he said. "You drive like shit in the snow."

"I do not!"

"Oh yeah?" he said. "Tell that to my truck."

"Hey, that wasn't my fault!"

"Well, it sure as hell wasn't *my* fault."

I spoke up. "I don't care whose fault it is. Stop the car!"

In the passenger's seat, the female made a scoffing sound. "It's called an SUV, you know."

I blinked. "What?"

Her tone grew snotty. "*You* called it a car. But it's not."

Well, this was just terrific. "Yeah, but *I* only called it that because that's what *you* called it."

"When?" she demanded.

"When you first showed up. *Uninvited*, by the way."

"Yeah. Well, maybe it was *you* who was uninvited. You ever think of *that*?"

I wasn't even sure what she meant. And already, we were leaving the mall parking lot. The driver took a right, fishtailing on the slick road, as we headed not toward the city, but toward the rural area surrounding it.

It was the same road I'd taken to reach the mall – *and* the same road I would've taken to return to Mason's, if only I'd been the one driving.

Already, the SUV was sliding all over the place, making me wonder how long we'd even stay on the road.

Not long at this rate.

And now I didn't know what to do. I wasn't even buckled up. *Should I buckle up?*

It would be a whole lot safer. And yet, that felt way too permanent for my liking, as if I were settling in for a long haul.

Just then, something buzzed in the front seat. *My cellphone.* It *had* to be.

Sure enough, the masked female shifted in her seat and then pulled out my purse from underneath her backside.

I watched in growing indignation as she started rummaging through it.

"Hey!" I yelled. "That's mine."

"Not anymore, it's not."

With a sound of defiance, I lunged forward and grabbed for it, only to have her yank it further out of my reach.

The driver yelled, "Ditch it!"

I turned to look. "What?"

Just then, the passenger's side window slid down. *His* doing, not *hers*. He looked to his companion and yelled again. "What are you waiting for?"

"Fine," she muttered and tossed my purse straight out the window.

I whirled in my seat, hoping to see where it landed. But all I saw was swirling snow.

I turned back to the front and yelled, "What'd you do *that* for?"

The guy replied, "Because I'm not a dumb-ass, that's why."

"Well, you can't be too smart," I said, "because you're gonna be in big trouble." My words sounded hollow, even to my own ears. Probably, I should've jumped out when I had the chance.

Who was the dumb-ass now?

Me, apparently.

In the front seat, the guy said, "Get real. Who's gonna catch us?" And with that, he hit the button to shift the car into four-wheel drive. Immediately, the vehicle gained a smidgen of stability.

I asked, "When you're done driving, are you gonna give me the car back?"

The guy replied, "It depends."

"On what?"

He lifted his hand and jerked a thumb vaguely toward the passenger. "It's up to her."

I sputtered, "Wait, why is it up to her?"

The female turned to me and said, "Well, it sure as hell isn't up to you."

The words had barely left her lips when I spotted an oncoming car, the first one we'd seen for at least a mile or two. I groaned, "Oh, my God." And then, I hollered out, "Seriously, stop!"

The female made a sound of annoyance. "You already said that!"

"Yeah, but…" My words trailed off as the vehicle sped past us, going way too fast for the slick conditions.

Damn it. Just as I'd suspected, I knew that vehicle. It was Mason's. I whirled in my seat and stared out through the rear window.

My stomach clenched. It was his, alright.

And if there had been any doubt before, the fact that it was actually turning around confirmed all of my worst suspicions.

The way it looked, he was coming after us – or more accurately after his sister, who wasn't even in the car.

I sucked in a breath. *Oh, shit.*

It was time to buckle up, and fast.

CHAPTER 52

Cami

In the passenger's seat, the masked female yelled, "Oh, my God. It's *him!*" She was looking forward in the rear-view mirror. But then, she whirled around to stare out the back window.

I turned to stare, too.

In the driver's seat, the guy said, "Him who?"

"Who do you think?" the female said. "It's Mason Blastoviak."

I whirled to face her. "Wait, how do *you* know?"

"None of your business," she said, turning to look at her companion. "I think he's coming after us."

The driver said, "Oh, fuck."

For once, we were in total agreement. I asked, "So, are you gonna stop?"

"Not *now,*" the guy said. "That fucker's crazy."

Mason was *not* crazy. Oh, sure, he was a little abrasive and very protective when it came to people he cared about. But crazy? I didn't think so.

But soon, I was reevaluating that opinion. The further we went, the more slippery the roads became. And yet, Mason wasn't slowing down.

And neither were we. When the driver took a hard right on the next country road, we nearly spun out, coming dangerously close to slamming into a telephone pole. *Good thing I'd buckled up.*

And so had they.

But enough was enough. Pushing against my seatbelt, I leaned forward to say, "Seriously, just stop, alright?"

The driver's bare knuckles were white on the steering wheel. "Forget it."

"Fine," I snapped. "Then let me out."

"If you want out, go ahead. But I'm not slowing down."

And he wasn't.

The funny thing was, we weren't driving much faster than the posted speed limit. But that was a small comfort, considering the dangerous conditions. The roads were slick, and the visibility was horrendous.

And yet, when I turned to look behind us, I could still make out the hazy outline of Mason's vehicle.

I bit my lip. His car was fast, but that would be little help if he couldn't keep it on the road. After all, *he* didn't have four-wheel drive.

No, what *he* had was a reckless disregard for his own safety. When I saw him come dangerously close to spinning out, I screamed, "For God's sake, will you *please* stop the car!"

The guy didn't stop. But then again, he hadn't stopped the other times I'd asked either. Going for a new approach, I took a deep, calming breath and tried again. "Seriously, just stop the car, alright?"

With a sarcastic snort, the female said, "It's not a car. It's an SUV, remember?"

This again? I made a sound of annoyance. "You called it a car first."

"Yeah, well you called it one *last*."

"It doesn't matter what we call it," I said. "You still need to stop."

From the driver's seat, the guy said, "Shut up! You've got no say in this!"

The female turned to face him. "You'd better be talking to *her!*"

"I'm talking to both of you," he said. "Now, zip it! I'm trying to drive."

Did I really need to say it? "You wouldn't *need* to drive if you'd just pull over."

He glanced in his rear-view mirror and cursed under his breath. "I can't. He's gaining on us."

Knowing Mason, he'd keep gaining on us. Or he'd die in a ditch. Or, maybe he'd end up twisted around a telephone pole. Just the thought of it made my heart clench and my mouth go dry.

I told the driver, "You can't outrun him, you know."

He hollered back, "Didn't I tell you to shut up?"

"Don't you get it?" I said. "He thinks *Willow's* in the car."

"Who the fuck's Willow?"

"His little sister."

For the tenth time, I said a silent prayer of thanks that she *wasn't* in the vehicle – *and* a silent curse that Mason apparently believed otherwise.

The female looked to me and said, "Can't you just call him? Tell him Willow's not here?"

Seriously?

How soon they forget.

"Suuuuure," I said. "Just turn back and retrieve my purse. You know, the one you tossed out the window?"

From the driver's seat, the guy said, "We're not goin' back for nothin'."

I told him, "Well, you can't drive forever. Eventually, you'll run out of gas." *Assuming we didn't slide into a ditch long before that.*

He gave the rear-view mirror another glance. "Yeah, well maybe *he'll* run out first."

"Or *maybe*," I said, "he'll catch up with us and beat you senseless for kidnapping his little sister."

The driver shot back, "But his sister's not even here."

"I know," I said through clenched teeth. "But Mason doesn't know that, does he?"

The guy glanced toward his female companion and said, "Why'd you throw out her purse for?"

"Don't blame *me*!" she yelled. "It was *your* idea!"

The guy made a sound of disgust. "Since when do you listen to me?"

As they bickered back and forth, I whirled in my seat to study the road behind us. Snow was falling so hard, I could hardly see anything. Even Mason's black sedan – it was a gray, hazy blur amidst the swirling snow.

As far as the road itself, we were now on a long country stretch, with very few houses and no other vehicles in sight.

Through the rear window, I was still eyeing the fuzzy outline of Mason's car. The way it looked, he was having a heck of a time keeping it on the road. And was it any wonder, given the conditions?

But he wouldn't give up. I knew this, just as sure as I knew my own name.

One thing about Mason, he always got what he wanted. *Including me.*

God, I'd been such an idiot.

And I wasn't getting any smarter, considering that I was more concerned for *his* safety than for my own. And now, I could only imagine his disbelief when he caught up with us and learned that his chase had been all for nothing.

Willow wasn't here.

And me? *I wasn't family.*

I was "The Help."

The driver said, "Fuck! He's not giving up!"

I couldn't resist. "Told ya."

As I watched through the rear-view mirror, the sedan lurched forward, as if Mason had abandoned all reason. My stomach clenched. *Oh, God.*

I whirled forward and yelled to the driver, "Seriously, just stop, alright?"

"No way," he said. "I told you, that guy's fucking nuts."

I whirled again to look behind us. *Oh, yeah.* Mason had definitely lost his mind. Already, the sedan was closing in on us fast, like he was putting the pedal to the metal in spite of a million fluffy reasons to do just the opposite.

Suddenly, his sedan shifted lanes and roared forward. Within mere moments, it passed us in a blur of speed and disrupted snow.

The guy in the driver's seat said, "What the fuck?"

But then, a split-second later, Mason's car swerved directly in front of us. The female screamed, and I might've too.

It was like Mason *wanted* us to hit him.

The thought had barely crossed my mind when that's exactly what happened. With a sickening crash, our SUV slammed into the back of Mason's sedan and sent both of our vehicles spinning.

I heard a series of bangs as airbags deployed all around us – in the front and even on the sides. The guy in the driver's seat gave a girlish scream as we spun like five times before coming to a slow stop in the shallow ditch.

Frantically, I glanced around. *I was okay.* And so, apparently, were the two idiots in front, because already, they were arguing about whose fault it was.

The female yelled, "You should've swerved!"

He yelled back, "I *did* swerve!"

"Yeah, but you swerved too much!"

"What? You wanna drive?"

"I can't now," she said. "The car's toast."

Was it? I wasn't so sure. Yeah, maybe the front end was severely crumpled, but it's not like we were in a twisted heap of burning metal.

My heart clenched. *But what about Mason?*

Here in the back seat, I was surrounded by tangled clothes and tumbled boxes. Still, I yanked off my seatbelt and lunged toward the side window. The side airbag had deployed at hip level, leaving my view unobstructed. *Thank God.*

And yet, thanks to the swirling snow, I still couldn't see beyond a few feet.

But then, the snow cleared barely enough for me to spot Mason's car on the opposite side of the road, where it had apparently found a ditch of its own. The rear of his sedan was a banged, crunched-up mess.

As far as the front, I couldn't be sure either way.

As I took in the damage, something squeezed at my heart. *Was Mason alright?*

I reached for the door handle and gave it a frantic tug. *Nothing happened.* In the front seat, they were still arguing.

Ignoring them, I gave the door handle another tug. *Still nothing. Stupid safety features.*

I hollered out, "Unlock the door!"

Both of them ignored me and kept on bickering.

Great. Already, the snow was kicking up again, hiding Mason's car from my desperate view. With growing anxiety, I stared through the snowy mist.

And then I saw him, striding forward like a gladiator heading into battle. He wore a dark business suit, a red necktie, and a look so ominous, I felt myself swallow.

In his right hand was a hammer – silver on the business end with a blazing orange handle. It was their trademark Blast Demolition Hammer, which he was wielding like a weapon.

I murmured, "Oh, my God," before hollering out to the idiots in front. "At least roll down the window!"

I wasn't even thinking of escape. I knew I'd make it out eventually. But now more than anything, I needed to let Mason know that his sister wasn't here, before he killed someone in a brotherly rage.

But did they listen?

No.

They kept on bickering.

As I watched in growing horror, Mason strode to driver's side window and lifted the hammer high. A split second later, the window shattered in a hail of broken glass that instantly silenced the bickering.

Mason used the sharp end of the hammer to puncture the airbag. And then, he tossed the hammer aside and reached into the car with both hands. He grabbed the guy in the driver's seat and yanked him out through the now-open window.

The guy hollered out, "What the fuck?"

As for his companion, she practically dove for the passenger's side door and shoved it open with no trouble.

But me? I was still trapped by the child safety locks.

I watched in stunned disbelief as she slammed the passenger's side door shut behind her, and then headed *not* for her companion, but in the opposite direction, toward the nearby woods.

Well, so much for loyalty.

As for Mason, he slammed the driver up against the side of the car, just inches from my face. He hauled back and hit the guy in the dead center of his ski mask.

With my face pressed against the back window, I hollered out, "Willow's not here!"

Mason called back, "I know," just before hitting the guy again, this time in the stomach.

Huh?

By now, the masked car-jacker was babbling and cussing up a storm. *And so was I.*

Obviously, Mason still wasn't getting it. I scrambled over the center console and dove into the driver's seat. As I did, Mason called out, "What the hell are you doing?"

"I'm trying to get out!"

"Don't," he said. "There's broken glass."

As if I didn't know.

I glanced down at my hands and thanked my lucky stars that I was still wearing my gloves and coat. If the shards of glass were cutting me, I sure as heck didn't feel it.

Or maybe I was just too numb to feel anything but desperation.

I needed to stop Mason before he murdered the guy.

I grabbed the front door handle and gave it a hard yank. The door wasn't locked, but when I tried to push it open, I was met with hard resistance in the form of the guy's backside, which was blocking just enough of the door to keep it from swinging open.

I stuck my head out the front window and yelled, "Didn't you hear me? I *said* Willow's not here. She's with Arden."

Now Mason was gripping the guy by his shoulders, holding him firm against the car. Without letting go, he looked to me and said, "And I told *you*, I know."

"Yeah, but—"

"Hang on." And then, almost as an afterthought, he tossed the guy aside, sending him stumbling toward the road. The guy regained his balance for only a moment before he slipped and fell hard on his backside.

With a string of curses, he scrambled up and then bolted through the swirling snow, heading in the same direction as his female companion.

I watched for only a moment before I looked back to Mason. The snow was still falling in big fluffy blobs, lending a Christmas card quality to our surroundings.

The picture would've looked oh-so serene, if only there weren't two banged-up vehicles and a very ticked-off guy standing just outside the SUV.

He didn't look serene. *Far from it.*

His gaze locked on mine as he said, "I didn't come for Willow. I came for *you*."

My breath hitched, and my mouth fell open. I hardly knew what to say. I wasn't even sure what he meant, not for certain. After a long moment, I said, "Really?"

His gaze softened. "Is that such a surprise?"

It was, actually. And yet, I was so stupidly touched that I shoved open the driver's side door and hurtled myself into his arms.

When his arms closed around me and gathered me close, I gave a happy sigh against his chest. He felt so warm and strong, and so very real that I didn't even wonder if this was all a dream.

It wasn't. It was the happy end to what had been a nightmarish day. *Until now.*

When I pulled back to search Mason's face, his lips claimed mine, and I sagged against him, relishing the intensity of his kiss and the strength of his embrace.

At that moment, I didn't even care that my trip was delayed, or that I'd been scared out of my wits. All I cared about was the guy holding me close and kissing me like he meant it.

By the time I pulled back to gaze up into his eyes, I felt warm and wonderful all over, even in spite of the bitter cold. With a smile, I said, "You're totally crazy. You know that, right?"

He grinned. "Hell yeah."

Now, I couldn't help but laugh. "I feel like I should yell at you or something."

"Oh yeah? Why's that?"

"Because," I said, "you could've been killed."

"Me? Nah. I'm indestructible."

This wasn't true. Mason might *look* indestructible, but he was made of flesh and bone like anyone else. Still, he was the most breathtaking thing I'd ever seen as he stared down at me with something that looked a lot like love.

With another laugh, I fell back into his arms and said, "But seriously, why on Earth would you do that?"

His reply was a long time in coming. But when it *did* come, quieter than I might've expected, it hit with all the force of a hammer. "For Willow."

I blinked. "What?"

"Willow," he repeated. "If anything happened to you…"

He didn't bother finishing the sentence, because after all, he didn't need to.

And me? I'd made a total fool of myself.

Again.

CHAPTER 53

Mason

Cami stiffened in my arms. "Oh."

Shit. It would be easy to say that I'd misspoke. *But I hadn't.* And yet, those words hadn't been my first choice.

I'd almost said something else, something a lot more dangerous, because it was something I didn't believe in.

I'd almost told her that I loved her.

And more.

But now, I said nothing.

Instead, I held her tight, soaking up the feel of her as the blizzard raged around us. Even now, I felt a primal urge to protect her body with my own, to keep her warm and safe, and to shelter her from anything that might hurt her.

Including me.

But abruptly she pulled back. She stared up at me for a long moment as I drank in the sight of her. Her hair was wild and flecked with snow. Her face was flushed, and her lips were parted, like she had something she wanted to say, but didn't know how to put it.

In the end, all she said was, "Well, this is awkward."

"Cami—"

"Forget it." She moved back until we were no longer touching. "It's fine." With a shaky laugh, she said, "I mean, thanks for the rescue. It was, um, really something."

And now, she looked ready to cry.

I moved toward her. "You're upset."

She backed away. "Of course I'm upset. I was just car-jacked. I mean, that's enough to upset anyone, right?"

It was a lie.

I could see it all over her face.

It wasn't the car-jacking that had upset her. *It was me.*

At a low rumbling sound, both of us turned to look. Coming up the road was an oversized red pickup with a big silver snowplow on the front.

When I looked back to Cami, she was waving her arms to get the truck's attention.

I asked, "What are you doing?"

She kept her eyes on the truck. "Hitching a ride."

"You're joking."

"Nope. No joke here."

"But we don't need a ride," I said. "We've got two vehicles. We'll get one running."

"Wrong," she said. *"You've* got two vehicles. But me? I've gotta go."

"Wait—"

"Just stop it!" She whirled to face me head-on. "You know what? You knew damn well what I thought. And you kissed me, anyway. You let me think you gave a rat's ass about me as more than a fucking nanny." Her voice broke. "What kind of monster are you, anyway?"

It was a good question.

I had no answer. And even if I had, it would've been silenced by the arrival of the pickup, rumbling to a stop beside us. The driver's side window slid down, and the driver – an older guy in a brown coat and red flannel hat – leaned out to survey the damage.

Cami called up to him. "Hey, can you give me a ride?"

The guy frowned. "I'd love to, but—"

"I'll pay you." As she spoke, she reached into the pocket of her coat and pulled out a wadded plastic shopping bag along with the envelope I'd given her just last night. She tucked the bag under her arm, and then reached into the envelope. She yanked out a hundred-dollar bill and lifted it in his direction. "Please? I'm in a hurry."

I demanded, "To go where?"

She whirled to face me. "Away from you, that's where."

The guy in the pickup gave me a sour look. "You bothering her?"

Yeah. I was. But not in the way he thought.

I said, "I'm her boss."

At this, Cami made a sound – a half scoff, half sob. "Yeah. And I'm the Help." She turned back to the trucker. "Listen, I don't care where you take me—"

What the hell? I stepped between her and the truck. "But you don't even know this guy."

"Yeah. And I don't know *you* either."

"Cami—"

"Forget it." With her free hand, she reached for the package that she'd tucked under her arm. She wadded it up and thrust it into my hand. "Merry Fucking Christmas."

And with that, she sidestepped around me and rushed over to the truck's passenger's side. The driver pushed open the door and reached out to help her into the truck.

As he did, I called out to the guy, "I swear to God, if anything happens to her…"

The driver turned and gave me another look, this one more sour than the last. "Looks to me like it already has. *Asshole.*"

I was still standing there when his window slid up and the truck rumbled off, leaving me staring after it.

Fuck.

CHAPTER 54

Cami

Safe in Arden's kitchen, I put my face in my hands and groaned, "I'm *so* embarrassed."

The truck driver – who apparently had a daughter my own age – had taken pity on me. In spite of the weather and the fact that he surely had somewhere else to be, he'd driven me all the way to Arden's place, where I'd found Arden and Willow finishing up their baking.

As far as the driver, he wouldn't even accept my money, which made me feel guiltier than ever, even though I'd just lost not only my purse, but everything I'd abandoned in the SUV.

Sure, I realized that I'd probably be able to retrieve my things from the vehicle eventually, but as far as my purse, I wasn't terribly optimistic.

On the upside, I still had the remaining cash from Mason. But even *that* felt tainted by the spectacle on the roadside.

I'd made a total fool of myself.

Again.

I'd arrived on Arden's doorstep ninety minutes ago, cold and bedraggled. Now, I was warm and toasty, thanks to hot chocolate, a hot bath, and some fresh clothes from Arden's closet.

And yet, nothing could warm the cold ache in my heart.

Arden said, "But why should *you* be embarrassed? *He* was the one giving out mixed signals."

"Yeah, maybe," I said. "But I felt so stupid. You know you see those movies, where the guy rides up on his white horse and rescues the damsel in distress?" I gave a wistful sigh. "And they kiss, and it fades to dark? Happily-ever-after, right?"

Her voice was quiet in the kitchen. "I love those stories."

"Me, too," I said. "And that's what it was like – until I realized that his rescue had nothing to do with me at all, which makes me feel *especially* stupid, because I knew that from the get-go."

I blinked away tears of frustration. "It's just that when he said he came for me, I read it all wrong. And then, the way he kissed me…" I shoved a hand through my hair and groaned again. "I was *such* an idiot."

"For kissing him?"

"For kissing him *and* flipping out," I said. "Here, he risks his life to stop the car-jacking, and what do I give *him* in return? A total hissy-fit. And I *know* I should feel bad about it. And I do, honestly. But I also feel so stupid and angry." I winced. "I think I might hate him."

Somewhere on the opposite side of the house, Willow was laughing with Brody. The sounds were muted, but cheerful – a lot more cheerful than *I* was, that's for sure.

Still, I'd tried my best not to show it when I arrived, telling Willow only that I ran into some car trouble.

Boy, was *that* an understatement.

Arden said, "You weren't stupid. You were just caught up in the moment, that's all."

I shook my head. "I don't think so. I mean, yeah, I *did* get caught up in the moment, but that *never* would've happened if I didn't have real feelings for him." I forced a laugh. "Which only *proves* that I'm an idiot, right?"

I reached up to rub at my eyes. "Seriously, what kind of moron would fall for Mason Blastoviak?"

"I'll tell you who," she said. "Someone who sees the best in everyone."

She'd said something similar at the mall. And by now, I'd had some time to think about it. "I know what you're getting at," I said.

"But the truth is, I really *did* see a different side of him – a warm and funny side. And *really* thoughtful, too."

In the kitchen, Arden stared at me like I'd just announced that Mason was one of Santa's elves. With an awkward laugh, she said, "Are you sure we're talking about the same Mason?"

I knew it was a joke, but it bothered me just the same. Even today, he'd taken a huge risk to stop the SUV. *And what had he gotten in return?* Two damaged vehicles and a roadside spectacle.

I sighed. "I don't even know who I'm angrier at – him or myself. And I probably owe him *another* apology."

"But why should *you* apologize?"

"Because I keep losing my temper," I said. "It's not like me. And I can't seem to get over him, which is really stupid because we were never a couple in the first place."

Arden eyed me with concern. "Gosh, you *do* have it bad, don't you?"

When I replied with only a shrug, she said with obvious reluctance, "Well…I guess I should tell you something."

Oh, no. What now? Bracing myself, I asked, "What?"

"Mason called me looking for you."

In spite of everything, my heart gave a traitorous flutter. "Really? When?"

"Maybe an hour ago, when you were in the tub."

I shook my head. "And you're just telling me now?"

"Honestly, I didn't want to upset you. But you should know, he sounded *really* worried."

I tried to laugh. "Of course he is. He thinks I'm insane."

"It didn't sound like that to me," she said. "You want the truth?"

Judging from her expression, I wasn't so sure. Still, I nodded anyway.

Arden's tone was gentle. "He sounded like a guy in love."

I couldn't help but scoff. "Yeah. He is. With his family."

As soon the words left my mouth, I felt like a terrible person for saying them. Deliberately, I softened my tone. "You know what's funny? I actually love that about him, how protective he is and how much he cares for the people closest to him. But maybe..." I sighed. "...I was just thinking there might be a little room for someone else, you know?"

Arden's eyes filled with tears of her own. "Yeah, I know."

Great. Now I was spreading the misery. This was the last thing I wanted.

With forced cheer, I said, "Who knows, maybe he was calling to fire me. Or maybe he thinks I quit." I bit my lip. "Maybe I *should* quit. Or maybe I already did."

Regardless of the logistics, cussing out your boss was generally a pretty good sign that your job was over.

"Or *maybe*," Arden said, "you should sleep on it, and see how you feel in the morning."

It was good advice. And I took it with gratitude. I spent the night in Arden's extra guest room, where thoughts of Mason haunted my thoughts *and* my dreams.

But then, when morning came, I found myself more confused than ever. And why? It was because sometime in the night, Mason had managed to surprise me yet again.

CHAPTER 55

Mason

I opened the front door expecting to see Brody with Willow. Instead, I saw Brody's fiancée, looking as pissed off as I'd ever seen her.

Arden's long brown hair was in a loose ponytail, and she was wearing jeans and a thick winter coat along with heavy winter boots. *No gloves.*

It was the day after the car-jacking, and Willow had spent the night at Brody's place due to the blizzard, which hadn't let up until near dawn.

Now it was early afternoon, and although snow remained thick on the ground, the main roads were clear enough to be passable as long as you didn't get too crazy with the gas pedal.

But me – I was a different kind of crazy. I hadn't slept. I hadn't eaten. *And forget working.*

The house felt cold and empty. It would be easy to think that it was because Willow had spent the night at Brody's.

But it wasn't.

After all, this wasn't the first time Willow had spent the night away from home. And yet, it *was* the first time I'd wandered through the house like a mental patient, looking for signs of someone who wasn't there.

And that someone wasn't my little sister.

It wasn't the person on my doorstep either. I gave Arden a long, cold look. "Where's Brody?"

Uninvited, she stomped past me, saying, "Home."

I turned to follow her movements. "And Willow?"

Over her shoulder, she said, "The same."

I felt my jaw clench. It was Christmas Eve. A couple of hours ago, Brody had texted me asking if I'd be home around two o'clock. I'd assumed he wanted to drop off Willow. Instead, he'd set me up for an ambush.

Asshole.

As I watched, Arden stomped deeper into the house, calling out, "I brought cookies, not that you deserve them."

I shut the front door and strode after her. *I hadn't seen any cookies.*

As if reading my mind, she said, "They're in a baggie. I put them in my pocket so they'd get nice and crushed." She paused. "I hope."

"So that's why you're here?" I said. "To bring me crushed cookies?"

"Oh, please," she said. "If it were up to me, I wouldn't be bringing cookies at all. No. They're from Willow. We made them yesterday."

Willow had grown up without a mom – and without any aunts or grandmothers either. If I were in the mood to be reasonable, I might admit that it was nice that Arden took such an interest.

And she made great cookies. I knew, because every once in a while, Brody brought some into the office.

I'd even tried a few. *You know, for politeness.*

Arden stopped in the main living area and sank back into my favorite armchair. She motioned to the chair across from her and said, "Sit."

I ran a multi-billion-dollar company. I'd practically raised my brothers, and Willow, too, while I was at it. I wasn't accustomed to being ordered around, and didn't appreciate it now.

I gave her a hard look. "No."

"Fine," she said. "Then you can stand there while I tell you what I just learned."

I didn't like the way that sounded. "It's not about Cami, is it?" My stomach clenched. "Is she alright?"

"I'll get to that," Arden said.

Screw that. "No. Tell me now."

Arden rolled her eyes. "Well she's not dead in a ditch if that's what you're wondering."

The image alone was enough to make my blood run cold. "So she's alright?"

"Yes," Arden said. "Just like she was an hour ago when you called Brody to check on her."

I stiffened. "That's not why I called."

"It was, too, and you know it." She made a scoffing sound. "Oh sure, you pretended like you were checking for Willow's sake. But we all know."

"You know *what?*"

"The same thing *you* know, if you'll ever admit it."

I refused to go there. "So Cami – she's alright then?"

"More or less. She's on her way home."

Was she? I looked toward the driveway.

Arden said, "In case it wasn't clear, I meant her family's home in Petoskey."

Right. I knew that.

When I looked back to Arden, she added, "She left town maybe thirty minutes ago."

I frowned. "Driving what?"

"My SUV."

I didn't ask what Arden would be driving in the meantime. Brody had plenty of vehicles to go around. But I *was* curious. "So tell me, did she get her things?"

"You mean the things that magically appeared on our back deck sometime in the middle of the night?"

"Maybe," I admitted.

Yesterday, after everything had gone to hell with Cami, I'd been a busy guy. I'd had both damaged vehicles towed to the shop, and then

I'd purchased a new vehicle on the fly – a heavy duty pickup with its own snowplow.

Afterward, I'd gone out searching for Cami's purse.

From Brody, I'd heard about those two assholes tossing the purse out the window maybe a mile or two from the mall.

I'd started at the mall and worked my way back, walking most of the way. In the blowing snow, it had taken me hours to find it.

But I had. From what I could tell, nothing inside had been taken or damaged, including Cami's cellphone.

I'd boxed up the purse, along with the rest of the things I'd pulled from the smashed SUV. Finally, just before dawn, I delivered all of it to Brody's back deck.

Arden said, "The plastic sheeting was a nice touch."

Before leaving Brody's deck, I'd covered the stacked boxes with plastic to make sure that Cami's things remained free of snow.

But to Arden, my only reply was a noncommittal shrug.

She continued. "And it's funny that somebody – and we all know who that somebody was – did *all* of this in the middle of the night. During a blizzard. When *normal* people would be hunkered down in their homes."

"Yeah, well…some people aren't normal, are they?"

"If you mean yourself, trust me, you're gonna not get any argument from me – which brings me to the reason for my visit."

"Which is…?"

"I *know* what you did – and I don't mean recently. I mean six years ago."

Shit.

In a careful voice, I said, "Oh, yeah? What's that?"

"You kept me out of trouble."

I knew what she meant. During Brody's senior year of high school, there'd been a weekend explosion in the chemistry lab, resulting from the unfortunate combination of a gas leak and Brody's disposable lighter.

The gas leak hadn't been his fault, but the flame from the lighter? *Oh yeah, that had been Brody's doing.*

The explosion had happened on a Saturday afternoon, and Brody hadn't been alone. He'd been with his lab partner – the same girl who happened to be sitting in my living room right now.

I told her, "You're wrong. I kept *Brody* out of trouble."

After the explosion, Brody and Arden had been suspended, but there'd been talk of more serious ramifications – maybe a lawsuit, maybe criminal charges. *Maybe both.*

The whole thing was utter bullshit – which is why I'd applied pressure here and there to anyone who thought it was a good idea to railroad two minors for a freak accident.

In the living room, Arden said, "But it wasn't *only* him, was it? You kept *me* out of trouble, too."

Without confirming or denying, I said, "And where'd you hear this?"

"At the grocery store, just yesterday. I ran into an old teacher when I was picking up baking supplies. But that's not important. The point is, I know exactly what you did."

"Oh yeah? And what's that?"

"Threats, bribery, intimidation – whatever it took to keep us out of trouble."

"You mean to keep *Brody* out of trouble."

She gave me a dubious look. "Right."

"Don't be flattered," I said. "It was strategic."

"Oh, I'm not flattered," she laughed. "Sure, I'm grateful, but you're missing the point."

"Which is…?"

"You're not as heartless as you look."

"My heart's got nothing to do with it," I said. "It would've looked funny if he got off and you didn't."

"Uh-huh."

"Call it a twofer."

She gave me a long, penetrating look. "And the thing with Cami yesterday?"

"What about it?"

"It was for Willow, not Cami? That's your story?"

"More or less."

"So that makes Cami what?" Arden lifted her hands and made exaggerated air quotes. "Another 'twofer'?"

No. Cami wasn't the second half of anything. She was the sweetest – and yeah, the sexiest – person I'd ever known. She was the one who made me smile. She was the one who gave as good as she got. She was the one who made me think of things I'd never thought before.

She filled the house with something I'd never had, even as a kid.

God, I missed her.

And now she was the reason I couldn't eat or sleep, the reason I'd been kicking myself for doing what needed to be done – *and* the reason I'd resisted calling her, although God knows I wanted to.

I didn't even know if she'd be back.

In the living room, Arden persisted. "So *that's* what you want me to believe? That if it weren't for Cami being Willow's nanny, you wouldn't have cared enough to go after her?"

Shit. By now, *I* didn't even believe it. I reached up to rub the back of my neck. "Believe what you want," I said.

"Oh, believe me, I will. But here's another question. Is that what you want *Cami* to believe?"

No. I didn't.

And I did.

When I said nothing in reply, Arden kept on going. "Because she *does* believe it, you know. And I'm just saying, if it's not true, you're making the biggest mistake of your life." She pushed herself up from the chair as she added, "And you damn well know it."

And with that, she reached into the pocket of her coat and pulled out a plastic sandwich bag with maybe a half-dozen Christmas cookies

– some broken, some intact. She slapped the baggie into my hand and said, "See you tomorrow."

"What?"

"Christmas dinner. Remember? And just so you know, if you don't show up, we're coming out to get you."

"Who's we?"

"Me and Brody. Because whether you like it or not, *I'm* family, too. And I'm not going away."

"I never said I wanted you to." *And I didn't.* She made Brody happier than I'd ever seen him, which was several times happier than myself, especially now.

Arden said, "Yeah, well, you haven't exactly thrown out the welcome mat either. But that's alright. You'll come around eventually."

Hell, I was halfway there now.

Maybe more than halfway.

And maybe I should've told her, but my thoughts were too full of Cami. As I walked Arden to the door, I couldn't help but wonder what I might've given to see Cami on my doorstep. Or in my living room. Or hell, even in the pantry – naked or not.

Just before Arden walked out the door, she turned and asked, "You want some sisterly advice?"

I shrugged but said nothing.

With a tight smile, she said, "You might want to remember, not all women are like your mother."

I knew that.

But I also knew something Arden didn't. The story of my parents – it was more complicated than she knew. More complicated than Brody knew either.

Because unlike my two younger brothers, *I* wasn't blameless.

CHAPTER 56

Mason

Arden's visit made me think – as if I hadn't been thinking enough already.

I'd been a mess *before* she showed up. But afterward, I was utterly spent. On the upside, it wasn't Arden, or even Brody, who brought Willow home later that afternoon.

It was Chase, who'd apparently decided it would be a good idea to spend the night in one of my guest rooms. Maybe it was for Willow's sake. Maybe it was for mine. Or hell, maybe it was for his own.

Chase – he was messed up, too, in his own obnoxious way.

Regardless, I was glad for his company – not for myself, but for Willow, who deserved a happier Christmas Eve than I felt capable of providing.

Sure, I had the gifts, and the premade dinner, along with maybe three dozen Christmas cookies, courtesy of Willow, who explained that the cookies in the baggie had been only a sample to show just how good they were.

On that, she was right.

Still, their taste held little enjoyment as I wondered what Cami was doing, and if she'd ever be back.

And if she *didn't* come back?

What then?

What would I do without her?

Not Willow.

But me.

It was a good question. But as far as the answer, I had no idea.

Later that night, I was sitting in the family room with Chase, not saying much of anything as I stared into the fire, wondering what the next year would bring.

At this rate, nothing good.

Already, Chase and I had put the presents under the tree and had eaten the cookies set out for Santa.

Now, we were sitting in silence – me because I was too lost in my own thoughts and Chase because he was more somber than I'd seen him in a while.

But then, he roused himself to say, "So what'd the nanny get you?"

My gaze shifted to the small plastic bag – the one she'd slapped into my hand on the roadside. I hadn't opened it. Instead, I'd set it under the Christmas tree with plans to wait – maybe for Christmas morning, or maybe for when she returned.

If she returned.

I looked back to Chase and said, "She's got a name, you know."

"Yeah. Cami the Nanny, right?" He grinned. "Is it just me, or does that sound like a porno flick?"

My jaw clenched. "It's just you."

"It is not," he laughed. "Or you wouldn't be looking so pissed off."

"Yeah, I'm pissed," I said. "I don't like the way you said it."

"Oh yeah? Why's that?"

"I just don't."

"Right," he laughed. "So, are you gonna get a new one?"

"A new what?"

"A new nanny," he said. "The way *I* hear it, the old one's not coming back."

"What?" I felt the blood drain from my face. "Where'd you hear that?"

"At Brody's place, when I picked up Willow. Brody and Arden were talking in the entryway."

"In front of Willow?"

"Nah, she was packing up the cookies. But you're gonna have to tell her sooner or later." He gave me a look. "I mean, if the nanny leaves, she's gonna notice."

My mouth tightened. "Stop calling her the nanny."

"Why?" he laughed.

"Because she's more than that." At the realization, my pulse quickened. "She's family." *Or at least, I wanted her to be.*

How in the hell had I not seen it sooner?

Chase gave me a dubious look. "Oh yeah? Does *she* see it that way?"

Fuck.

No. She didn't.

My fault. Not hers.

But I could *make* her see it – and maybe figure things out for myself along the way.

Suddenly I didn't want to wait.

I stood. "I'll be back in a bit, alright?"

CHAPTER 57

Cami

In my darkened bedroom, I stared at my cellphone. Mason's text was still on the screen. It said, *"Can you talk?"*

I bit my lip. *Yikes.* Where had I read *that* before?

I was *so* longing to hear his voice, but the thought of actually talking to him after everything that had happened – well, I wasn't quite sure I was up for it.

I texted back, *"About what?"*

His reply came in an instant. *"Us."*

Us?

I scoffed under the covers. There was no "us," unless he meant our boss-employee relationship. And even *that* had taken a serious beating.

When a couple of minutes passed without me texting him back, he texted again. *"Say yes. You know you want to."*

It was similar to what he'd texted me a few weeks ago. The first time, it had been funny. Now, all I felt was anger, mostly at myself. *Because he was right.*

I *did* want to.

And that was the whole problem. Almost from the beginning, I'd been all too willing to fall into his arms, into his bed, or cripes, into his pantry.

I was just about to tell him to forget it when I considered recent events. Mason had not only come to my rescue. He'd *also* managed to deliver all of my things – including my purse – to Arden's place in the middle of a raging blizzard.

It was ironic in a way. Even the phone I was using now – I wouldn't have it if it weren't for Mason.

But had I thanked him?

No. Not even by text.

This wasn't like me.

Plus, I still owed him an apology. Correction – *multiple* apologies. Even now, when I considered how I'd cussed him out on the roadside, I couldn't help but feel totally ridiculous.

A guy rescues you, and you yell at him? That wasn't exactly normal, was it?

I sighed. The sooner I got this out of the way, the sooner I could move past whatever I was feeling.

In the end, I didn't bother texting him back. I just hit the call button and waited for him to answer.

I didn't need to wait long. In fact, he answered so quickly, I couldn't be certain that his phone had rung at all.

His voice was quiet in the night. "You called."

"Yeah, well, I figured we had to talk *sometime."*

"Good," he said. "Because I've got a question."

With my heart in my throat, I whispered, "Alright."

"Are you coming back?"

In spite of all my good intentions, disappointment coursed through me. "So you're asking if I quit?" I forced a laugh. "Maybe I should ask *you* if I'm fired."

"You're not."

"Alright. Then I don't quit." Whether for Willow's sake, or because I was a glutton for punishment, I was still determined to finish out my term.

If nothing else, it would look good on a resume – or at least that's what I kept telling myself whenever my resolve wavered, which it did. *All the time.*

Regardless, I'd be smart to stick it out. Mason Blastoviak was a household name. With his name on my resume, I'd almost certainly get a good job in the fall.

And then, I could be done with Mason for good.

The thought should've made me happy. And maybe it would've, if not for the ache in my heart when I considered the prospect of not seeing him again.

As far as Willow, I'd get to see *her* through Arden.

But Willow's oldest brother? *Him, I'd be smart to avoid.*

As my thoughts churned, Mason remained silent. Obviously, he was out of things to say, now that he'd gotten what he'd called for – news that he wouldn't need to go nanny shopping any time soon.

Still, as long as I had him on the phone, I figured I might as well say what needed saying. "By the way, thanks for delivering my stuff, especially the purse. And I'm sorry for not thanking you sooner."

"Forget that."

"No. I mean it," I said. "I know you must've gone through a lot of trouble, and even though it wasn't for me personally—"

"You're wrong."

"What?"

"It *was* for you," he said. "And only you." With a rueful laugh, he said, "I doubt Willow wanted your clothes."

It wasn't just my clothes. It was Christmas presents for my family, all of my makeup and toiletries, my favorite pillow, and so much more. And to think, he'd even retrieved my purse from heaven-knows-where.

Even in *good* weather, that wouldn't have been easy.

Still, I'd be foolish to assume anything about his intentions. *Those days were gone.* "Well, regardless, I really appreciate it."

Bracing myself, I continued. "And as long as we're talking, I'm really sorry for flipping out. I don't know what got into me. I mean, it's not exactly normal to cuss out your boss."

He was silent for a long moment before saying, "Your boss?"

"Yeah. My employer." I tried to laugh. "You know, the guy who signs my direct deposits? Anyway, I *know* I made a total fool of myself."

"That's not true."

He was wrong. Still, it was nice of him to say. I wanted to say something nice in return. But there was nothing I *could* say, not without making an even bigger fool of myself.

Into my silence, he said, "Cami?"

"Yeah?"

"You're not the fool. *I* am."

Oh, God. So now he was pulling out his own version of, *"It's not you. It's me?"*

How humiliating was this?

"Anyway," I said, "I just want to let you know it won't happen again. So you don't need to worry, alright?"

His voice was tender in the night. "I'm not worried."

Of course he wasn't. He wasn't the worrying type. But me? I was worried enough for both of us.

Soon, I'd be returning to work. *Could I seriously get over him while living in the same house?*

Yes. I could.

Hopefully.

And if I were smart, I decided, I'd end this conversation now, before I said something I shouldn't.

So, with as much dignity as I could muster, I said, "Alright. Then I guess I'll see you next year." And with that, I ended the call before *he* could, if only to keep from looking desperate.

Technically, "next year" was only a week away. Until then, I decided, I'd be smart to put Mason out of my mind.

As if that were remotely possible.

CHAPTER 58

Mason

When I returned to the family room, Chase was sitting on the sofa where I'd left him. But his appearance had changed.

From the open doorway, I stopped to stare. Over his red sweater, he was wearing the ugliest necktie I'd ever seen. The thing was bright yellow with streaks of purple and gold.

I shook my head. *No.* It was *purple* with streaks of pink.

Shit. The damn thing was changing colors right in front of me. I felt my eyebrows furrow. And unless I was seeing things, it was glowing in the dark – except the room wasn't dark enough for me to be sure.

I reached over and flicked off the nearby light-switch. The lights went out, leaving only the light of the fire – *and* the flashy tie.

Oh, yeah. It was glowing, alright. Glowing *and* pulsing in random colors.

When I flicked on the lights, Chase grinned at my reaction. "I know, right?"

I had to laugh. "Where'd you get that thing?"

He pointed vaguely toward the Christmas tree. "I found it in a bag."

I stopped laughing. "What?"

Chase reached beside him on the sofa and picked up the familiar shopping bag. It was the small plastic one that Cami had thrust into my hand the last time I'd seen her.

I glared at my brother. *The fucker.* He was wearing *my* Christmas present.

Through clenched teeth, I told him, "That's *mine.*"

He laughed. "Fine. It's all yours." And with that, he wadded up the plastic bag and tossed it in my direction.

It landed at my feet, but I made no move to retrieve it. "I don't mean the bag," I said. "I mean the tie."

"Oh, come on," he said. "You'd never wear this thing."

Normally, he'd have a point. But this wasn't a normal tie. *It was a gift from Cami.* "That doesn't mean *you* get to wear it."

"Aw come on," he laughed. "Why should it go to waste?"

My eyes narrowed. *He was messing with me.*

One thing about Chase, yeah, he was flashy, but he still had a good fashion sense – or at least that's what all the bloggers said.

I gave the tie a longer look. The thing really *was* ugly, flamboyantly ugly, the kind of ugly you couldn't ignore if you tried, especially in the dark.

Obviously, *Cami* had been messing with me too. And I could think of nobody on this Earth who'd have the guts to do such a thing, with the possible exception of the guy wearing *my* Christmas gift.

I strode toward him and held out my hand, palm up. "Hand it over."

He grinned. "Make me."

"I mean it," I told him.

"Yeah? Well, so do I." And *then*, what does he do?

The fucker whistles.

That did it.

One way or another, I was getting that tie.

CHAPTER 59

Cami

I glanced around the crowded nightclub. This wasn't where I'd planned to spend New Year's Eve, but Livia had been incredibly persistent. Apparently, she had something to celebrate, and didn't want to celebrate alone.

In the end, I'd been unable to resist – and not only for curiosity's sake. Livia and I had been friends for most of our lives. And sure, we'd had our ups and downs, but we always made up in the end.

The truth was, I liked her, even in spite of her quirks. *I mean, we all had them, right?*

So here I was, back at her favorite local club, wearing my little black dress, and meeting her for drinks and dancing to welcome in the new year.

Like me, Livia was in Petoskey for the holidays. On the phone, she'd told me very little – only that it involved a big career change and that I'd never guess in a million years.

As for myself, I was struggling with my own career choices. Soon it would be January 2nd, and I'd be returning to Mason's place to resume nanny duties.

I missed Willow – and Mason, too, if I were being completely honest.

But this, too, was a problem. I still had feelings for him, and they weren't going away.

We hadn't talked – or even texted – since our midnight conversation on Christmas Eve. But I *had* talked to Arden several times, including just this morning.

She'd had some news of her own. Apparently, using mall surveillance footage, Mason had identified the car-jackers, who turned out to be none other than Willow's former nanny, Veronica Wallace, along with her occasional boyfriend, a guy who went by the nickname of Buster.

According to Arden, Mason had gotten the full story of what had happened straight from Buster himself, who Mason had tracked down personally.

After some not-so-friendly persuasion, Buster had told quite a story.

Apparently, Veronica had spotted the nanny-mobile while out Christmas shopping and had decided it would be hilarious to steal the vehicle – whether to make me look bad as revenge for the slapping incident, or because she wanted to scare me off so she could reclaim her old job.

Regardless of her motives, she obviously hadn't thought things through. For one thing, her accomplice was so idiotic, he couldn't even remember Willow's name, much less Mason's attitude toward anyone who messed with his family.

Sure, *I* wasn't family. But Willow was.

And I was apparently her favorite nanny.

I guess that had to count for something, right?

As my thoughts churned with memories of Mason, I scanned the crowded nightclub in search of my friend. Finally, I spotted Livia near the main bar, surrounded by several admirers, including Chopped Liver – the guy from our *last* club visit, back in September.

When Livia spotted me, she gave me a happy wave and set down her drink before heading in my direction, even as I waded through the crowd to meet her halfway.

After greeting me with a fierce hug, she pulled back to say, "So, you wanna hear my news?"

"Sure," I laughed. "I mean, that's the reason we're here, right?"

"Nah. That was just an excuse."

I wasn't following. "Sorry, what?"

In reply, she lifted her left hand and waggled her fingers. On her ring finger was a huge diamond ring. But that wasn't the *only* sparkly thing I saw. She was *also* wearing an emerald ring on her pinkie and a giant sapphire on her index finger.

With a laugh, she said, "So…What do you think?"

If this were anyone but Livia, I'd be offering congratulations. But I'd made such a mistake before, and she *hadn't* been happy.

Bracing myself, I gave it my best shot. "So…you're hand-modeling again?"

Her smile faded, and she dropped her hand. "Excuse me?"

"You know. For your dad's jewelry store?"

She gave a snort of disbelief. "Oh, please. That job sucked. It was *so* boring."

I wasn't quite sure I agreed. Regardless, it was time to pull out my second guess. "So, you're…?"

"Getting married!" She gave a happy squeal. "He proposed on Christmas Eve!"

"Oh." I blinked a few times before summoning up the biggest smile I could muster. "Congratulations!"

She laughed. "I know, right?"

Now, this is where it got awkward. If I *had* to guess, I'd say that the lucky guy was almost certainly Lorenzo, the father of the two teenagers across the river.

But the last time I'd talked to Livia, she'd mentioned nothing about a serious relationship. In fact, I'd had the distinct impression they weren't even a couple, not officially, anyway.

Still, I kept my smile plastered in place as I asked, "So, is it…?"

Her eyes filled with excitement as she practically yelled, "Mason!"

I froze. *Wait, what?*

CHAPTER 60

Cami

As I stared at Livia, I waited desperately for the punchline – for her to tell me that she was just kidding, or that the rings were simply borrowed from her dad's shop.

I was still waiting when an unfamiliar male voice from somewhere to my left said, "Hey, you wanna dance?"

I turned to look. It was Chopped Liver. And *this* time, he wasn't looking at Livia. He was looking at *me*.

By now, several seconds had passed since Livia's startling announcement. I still hadn't found my voice when Chopped Liver held out his hand, as if preparing to lead me out onto the dance floor.

His hand was still there when another male voice – this one *very* familiar – said, "Forget it. *She's mine.*"

I whirled to look, and there he was – Mason, holding at least a dozen yellow helium balloons by their strings, along with a giant bouquet of yellow roses.

But that wasn't the only thing that made me stare.

It was the necktie – the one I'd given him on the roadside. He was actually wearing it, along with a tailored business suit that looked a million times more traditional than the rest of his getup.

As for as the tie itself, Mason had apparently activated the power switch because even now, the hideous thing was glowing and pulsing, almost in time with the music.

I gave a quick shake of my head. Okay, this *had* to be a dream – or maybe a nightmare, because honestly, I still had no clue what was happening.

Oh sure, I recalled telling Mason that I loved yellow balloons and roses. And I *also* recalled buying him that tie.

Now, here he was with all three of those things, looking so sinfully delicious that I couldn't help but stare.

And yet, this would surely be a nightmare if he'd come for someone else, especially someone I considered a friend. But that *couldn't* be the case, because for one thing, he thought Livia was crazy.

As I stared up at him, those two magical words lingered between us along with the scent of the roses. *She's mine.*

Somehow, I managed to stammer, "Do you mean me?"

He moved closer, and his eyes filled with something that could only be love. In a voice that was nearly a caress, he said, "Who else?"

And with that, he handed me the roses, along with the balloons, whose strings were tied together by a shiny yellow bow. In that same tender voice, he said, "If you'll have me."

Oh, boy.

The balloons were big and festive, and the roses were the most beautiful of any I'd ever seen. As I clutched them tight against me, I felt my eyes fill with unshed tears.

I wanted to hurtle myself into his arms. And yet, lingering confusion made me pause. *What about Livia?* When I gave her a quick glance, she looked to Chopped Liver and said, "Sorry, she's taken."

Mason said, "Got that right."

A soft breath escaped my lips. "Oh."

Around us, everyone was staring, even Chopped Liver, who still wasn't leaving. He looked to Mason and said, "Hey, aren't you that guy from the show? You know, with the tools?"

Livia laughed. "Of course he is. This isn't the first time you've seen him, you know."

"Yeah, but…" The guy was still staring. "It's the first time I've seen him do *that.*"

Livia asked, "Do what?"

His eyebrows furrowed in obvious confusion. "He's smiling."

I looked back to Mason. *Yup, he was smiling, alright.* And it was one of those rare and wonderful smiles that went all the way to his eyes.

As I clutched the roses tight against me and gripped the strings of the balloons, I looked to Livia and said, "But wait, so that engagement thing, it was just a joke?"

She frowned. "Why would you say that?"

"Because you said you were engaged to Mason."

"Oh, that?" she laughed. "No. I was just calling him over."

"Oh." *Of course.* This should've been obvious. But in my own defense, all this was so very unexpected that my head was still spinning.

Livia gave her fingers another waggle. "I've got a guy of my own." In a much lower voice, she added, "And besides, *your* guy never offered."

My guy.

Oh, wow. I loved how that sounded.

I looked once again to Mason, and I swear, everything faded into the background as our gazes locked and held. He flicked his head toward the dance floor and said, "So, how about it? You wanna dance?"

At this, I actually giggled. "I'd love to."

Livia spoke up. "I'll find some water for these." And with that, she carefully took the roses from my grip and looked to Chopped Lover. "Hey, find me a big vase of water, will you?"

I didn't catch his reply, because already, Mason was sweeping me into his arms. We never even made it to the dance floor. Instead, I lifted my face to his and kissed him like I meant it.

And he kissed *me.*

All around us, the crowd broke into raucous applause, punctuated by one long and very loud wolf-whistle. I pulled back, expecting Mason to be irritated, not just by the whistle, but by the all the attention.

But to my surprise, he looked just happy as before. With a tender smile, he gathered me close against his chest and whispered into my hair, "I love you, Cami O'Neal."

My heart swelled with happiness. *I knew it.*

I mean, I'd seen it in his eyes, but to hear him say it out loud was something else entirely. Maybe this *was* a dream.

I pulled back to gaze up at him. "You do? But I thought you didn't believe in it."

"I didn't." His voice softened as he added, "Until you."

I was still holding the balloons. And Mason was still holding me. And I was pretty sure that I was once again holding my breath – not because I meant to, but because I was so surprised and happy, I was finding it hard to breathe.

And then, with a soft exhale, I said the thing I'd been wanting to say for longer than I'd *ever* admit. "I love you, too, Mason Blastoviak."

He grinned. "I know."

Now I couldn't help but laugh. "Wait, how would you know?"

"You must," he said, "if you're willing to put up with me."

I was willing to do more than *that.* Willing *and* eager.

But I didn't want this moment to end, so I hurtled myself back into his arms and kissed him like the world was ending.

And even if the world wasn't truly ending, the year definitely was.

We stayed in the club for the countdown to midnight, when we kissed all over again, even as balloons of all colors, along with rainbow confetti, fell from the ceiling and onto the crowd below.

This crowd included Livia, who later reiterated in the ladies room that she was truly engaged. *It was no joke.*

In fact, she said, Lorenzo would have been here with her now, except that he'd gotten delayed by snow in Switzerland.

It was funny to consider that I'd never met the guy, and I couldn't help but marvel at the speed of their engagement. But according to Livia, it was love at first sight – on his part, if not hers.

She got that a lot.

But this was the first time I'd ever seen *her* fall in return. And she seemed to be truly happy, so I was happy, too, except for one concern.

"But the kids…" I said. "You told me they're monsters. You're not going to try to put them in boarding school or anything, are you?"

"Oh, please," she said. "As if they'd go. And besides, they've actually grown on me."

"Really?"

"Oh, yeah," she said. "They've got real spirit."

I smiled. "Yeah. And so do you."

"I know," she laughed. "And you *do* realize what *this* means?"

"What?"

She gave a happy squeal. "Now we'll be neighbors forever!"

That word – *forever* – I liked the way it sounded, but it seemed terribly premature to assume anything. After all, Mason and I had only just confessed our love.

Who knew where we'd end up?

I couldn't say for sure, but I did know where I wanted to go *next* – anywhere in the world, as long as he and I could be alone.

CHAPTER 61

Cami

Whether from champagne or love, I was just a little bit tipsy. So it was a good thing that Mason was holding me tight against him, even as we crossed the threshold into his hotel suite.

I'd already texted my parents and let them know that I'd be staying with a friend. I didn't say which friend, because I hadn't wanted to take the time to explain.

All I'd wanted was to be held in Mason's arms, to kiss his lips, to run my hands over his naked body, and to take all night to explore each other all over again.

Technically, Mason wasn't a friend. Or at least, he wasn't *only* a friend. I stopped just inside the open doorway to his suite and breathed, "Wow."

With a smile in his voice, he said, "Wow, what?"

I glanced around the luxurious space. The suite had its own living area, complete with a gas fireplace and furniture that looked way too nice to actually sit on.

I knew there had to be a bed around here somewhere, but for the life of me, I couldn't see it. Then again, there *were* two doors leading to who-knows-what.

With a laugh, I said, "This is bigger than my first apartment in college. And I shared *that* with two roommates."

He laughed. "Only two, huh?"

I turned to face him. And as I gazed up into his amazing eyes, I felt a surge of warmth and eagerness. "And you know what?"

He smiled. "What?"

I couldn't help giggle. "I'm *so* glad they're not here."

"Oh yeah? Why's that?"

With my foot, I nudged the door shut behind us and said, "Because I'm *so* gonna get you naked, and there's no way I want them seeing *that*."

He grinned. "Who says I'm not gonna get *you* naked?"

The truth was, it wouldn't take a lot to get me naked. I was wearing only the little black dress with black high heels, along with the usual undergarments.

But Mason? He was still wearing his suit *and* the tie – which had stopped glowing and flashing maybe an hour ago. Either the battery had died, or the tie had a limited shelf life.

I didn't know, and I didn't care. I was just so stupidly touched that he'd worn the thing.

I reached between us and gave the tie a playful tug. As I did, I noticed a little rip along the edge. "Oh, no," I laughed. "What happened here?"

With a sheepish grin, he said, "Don't ask."

Now, I seriously wanted to know. "Did something happen?"

"Yeah," he said. "I had to fight Chase for it."

I stared up at him. "You're joking."

"No joke," he said. "You should've seen us Christmas Eve."

"Really? What happened?"

"Ask me later."

"Why later?"

"Because," he said, sweeping me up into his arms, "I'm gonna carry you to the nearest bedroom and have my way with you."

Oh, man. I was loving the way that sounded. Still, I couldn't help but tease, "Are you sure there's a bedroom? I mean, this place is pretty big."

"Trust me," he said, cradling me tight against his muscular torso, "I'll find one."

It didn't take him long either.

Just as I'd suspected, at least one of the two mystery doors led to a spacious bedroom. Leaving the door open behind us, Mason carried me straight to the king-size bed as I kicked off my shoes and let them fall wherever.

I felt giddy and light, and so very happy, I couldn't seem to stop smiling. And I wasn't the only one.

Mason looked happier than I'd ever seen him, even as he laid me gently across the bed and gazed down at me with an expression that took my breath away.

In a quiet voice, he said, "You're my dream-girl, you know that?"

I smiled. "And you're my dream *guy*." With an embarrassed laugh, I said, "Actually, I think you've been my dream guy for a while now."

He smiled back. "You know what that makes me?"

"What?"

His gaze softened. "The luckiest guy in the world."

As I stared up at him, there were so many questions I wanted to ask. *What had prompted this change? When had he decided that he loved me? And where would we go from here?*

But the way *I* saw it, we had plenty of time to talk later. What I wanted *now* was something I'd been thinking about all night.

From the bed, I beckoned him closer. "You're so far away."

"Not for long." And true to his word, he pushed off his shoes, shrugged out of his suit-jacket, and removed the tie.

And although he let his jacket fall to the floor, he laid the tie across the nearby armchair, making me smile with sentimental sappiness.

When Mason joined me on the bed, I turned toward him and gave a happy sigh as he pulled me into his arms and kissed me just the way I liked.

His lips were warm and welcoming, and I felt his hands caressing my back, and then move lower, skimming the thin fabric of my little black dress.

When he reached underneath the skirt and caressed my backside over my silky panties, my breath hitched, and my pulse jumped.

I pressed my hips tighter against him, and felt his erection surge against my stomach.

I smiled into his kiss. *He wasn't the only one who was primed and ready.*

Already, my insides were warm and slick with yearning. I wanted him so bad, I could practically taste it.

Beyond eager now, I pulled back and reached between us. With trembling fingers, I fumbled for the top button of his white dress-shirt. When I finally managed to undo it, it only left me hungry for more.

I wanted him shirtless, and then pantless. But more than anything, I wanted him inside me.

As I fumbled for the next button, he reached around me and unzipped the back of my dress. As the dress loosened, he moved his hands to my shoulders and nudged down the straps, exposing my black strapless bra as he leaned forward to kiss my collarbone.

With his teeth, he nudged down the bra just enough to expose my nipples to his mouth and his tongue. As he took a hardened nipple into his warm mouth, I gave a little whimper of longing.

This turned into a soft moan as he suckled my nipple with the perfect amount of pressure – not too much, and not too little.

As his mouth worked its magic, he yanked down my panties, not all the way, but enough so I could feel his warm hands on my bare ass and feel his thumbs skimming the intersection of my thighs.

When he moved one hand closer to the front and found that special spot with his thumb, I gave another whimper of pleasure and need.

Suddenly, it was like both of us were so eager, we'd lost all sense of time and space. By the time I reached the last button of his shirt, I was almost panting with anticipation.

I sat up and practically yanked the shirt from his muscular torso, and then went straight for his pants. I fumbled for the button, and then the zipper. I gave his pants a hard yank and watched with eager anticipation as he shoved them all the way down and tossed them onto the floor.

His pants had barely hit the carpet when he yanked my dress over my head and tossed it aside. Without skipping a beat, he went for my undergarments even as I went for his.

When at last we were both naked, I climbed on top of him with all of the pent-up eagerness I'd been feeling all night.

I straddled his hips and reached between us, stroking his massive erection, savoring the feel of him and the sound of him as he responded to my touch.

By now, I was literally aching with need. I wanted him inside me, and I didn't want to wait.

From the look in his eyes, neither did he. His hands caressed my hips and stroked my sides, making me shiver with warm anticipation as I positioned his erection at my opening, and then finally, blissfully, lowered myself onto his length, making both of us moan in sweet satisfaction as he filled me completely.

And then, I rode him with all the wild abandon of someone who'd been deprived for far too long.

Because I *had* been deprived – of him, of his body, of his kisses and his company.

I loved him.

And he loved me.

As our hips moved in harmony, I couldn't stop marveling at his perfect face, his perfect body, and the perfect happiness I felt in my heart as we climaxed at nearly the same time.

Afterward, he pulled me close and cradled me tight against him as our breathing returned to normal, and something like sanity returned.

Into my ear, he whispered, "You're the sweetest thing I've ever known."

"So are you."

He chuckled into my hair. "Yeah, right."

"It's true," I laughed.

His tone grew teasing. "I'm glad *you* think so."

I *did* think so. In fact, I *knew*, so.

And eventually, I decided, so would he.

CHAPTER 62

Cami

The next day, Mason surprised me yet again by not only escorting me back to my parent's place but actually staying to visit, much to the delight of my family, who were still more than a little star-struck.

But Mason, to his credit, was a terrific sport about the whole thing, even when the crowd at our house grew to nearly forty people, consisting of neighbors, relatives, and fans of the show.

Afterward, rather than returning to Mason's hotel suite, we spent New Year's night in my old bedroom, where we actually behaved ourselves.

Mostly.

On January 2nd, the day I was scheduled to return to work, I rode back with Mason rather than returning alone.

With Mason behind the wheel, we traveled in Arden's SUV, leaving Mason's own vehicle in Petoskey to be picked up later by heaven-knows-who.

An hour into our drive, I couldn't help but say, "I've got a question."

He smiled in profile. "Oh yeah? What's that?"

"What changed your mind?"

"About what?" he asked.

"About everything," I said. "Love, family…" I snickered. "The tie."

"About the tie, there was nothing to change." He laughed. "Well, other than getting it from Chase."

"But you never finished telling me," I said. "What happened with that, anyway?"

"I'll tell you what. The lunk-blaster tried to steal it."

I laughed. "No way."

"Believe it," he said. "I had to wrestle it away from him."

I was finding this hard to believe. One thing about Chase, he was a very smart dresser. But that tie? It was truly atrocious, even *with* a dead battery. "You're joking."

"No joke," Mason said. "But this time, *Chase* has the black eye."

My laughter faded. "Oh, my God. "You didn't seriously hit him, did you?"

"Me? Nah." Mason shrugged behind the wheel. "He bumped it when the couch tipped over."

"But wait, why would the couch tip over?"

"Because Chase didn't want to give it up."

I just had to tease him. "The couch?"

"No," he laughed. "The tie. And I know what you did there."

I smiled. "Oh yeah? What's that?"

"You're messing with me." He grinned. "And you know what?"

"What?"

"I think I like it."

As I gazed at him from the passenger's seat, I couldn't help but marvel at his easy demeanor. With mock suspicion, I said, "Who are you, and what have you done with Mason Blastoviak?"

"Me? I didn't do anything." With a smile, he said, "It was all you – with some help from your friend."

"You mean Livia?" This was the obvious guess. In the ladies room, Livia had also confessed that she'd invited me out for New Year's Eve as a special favor to Mason, who'd been determined to surprise me.

And boy, had he succeeded.

Livia, too.

I smiled with fondness for both of them. Even with their quirks, life was so much better with both of them in it, especially Mason.

In the driver's seat, Mason shook his head. "Not Livia," he said. "Arden."

Now *that* surprised me. "Arden? How so?"

"Let's just say she got me thinking."

"About what?" I asked.

"Family," he said. "Meaning my own."

"Oh?"

"Listen, there's something I want to tell you. But it stays between us, alright?"

I nodded. "Sure."

"About Willow – and my brothers, too – the fact we've got no parents. Well…the thing is, some of it's my fault."

That didn't make any sense. "But how could it be *your* fault?" I said. "You're the one who kept the family together."

"Sure, when I wasn't tearing it apart."

As I listened, he went on to tell me that just before his mom announced she was pregnant with Willow, Mason had caught her cheating on his dad.

I stared from the passenger's seat. "You don't mean in the act, do you?"

"No. But pretty damn close. I mean, shit, I caught the guy yanking up his pants coming out of my parent's bedroom."

I shuddered at the image. "Gosh, I'm so sorry. So, what happened? Did you confront her about it?"

"Her *and* him," Mason said. "As far as the guy, I told him if I *ever* caught him around the house again, I'd kick his ass. *And worse.* And you can guess how my mom loved *that.*"

I bristled with outrage on Mason's behalf. "Yeah, but she was married – to *your* dad. What did she expect?"

"I'll tell you what she expected – to not get caught." He gave me a long, meaningful glance. *"Or* to get pregnant."

And just like that, the pieces slid into place. "Oh, my God. You don't mean Willow has a different dad? Does she know?"

Mason gave a bitter laugh. "Hell, you don't even know."

I hesitated. "Sorry, I'm not following."

"Lemme back up," he said. "My parents. They had this love-hate sort of thing. My mom – she had a real wild streak. And my dad – he had a temper, not all the time, but it would build up, you know?"

I knew the type, not from my *own* family, thank goodness. With real sympathy, I said, "That sounds *really* explosive."

"Got that right," he said. "Anyway, they'd get together, split up, and do it again a few months later. But the *last* time they got together – maybe a year before Willow was born – they seemed to be making a real go of it."

"But wait, you just said she was cheating."

"Yeah, well. I guess Mom got bored."

Ouch. "So she took up with someone else?"

"Yeah. This fighter from Miami. A real has-been."

From Arden, I already knew much of the story. Still, I was dying to hear Mason's version.

He continued. "But to her? The guy's a celebrity, someone exciting to see on the sly." With a sideways glance, he said, "You'd be surprised how much that means to some people."

I wouldn't be *that* surprised. After all, I'd known Mason long enough to see that fame could be a real aphrodisiac. Wherever Mason went, women stopped to stare, and not only because he was so ungodly sexy. "So the fighter – *that's* who you caught with your mom?"

He nodded. "And that's what busted up the family."

"But wait, how could that be *your* fault?"

"Oh, you're gonna love this," he said in a tone that suggested otherwise. "See, my dad, he gets suspicious, thinking my mom's up to her old tricks. And he starts asking questions."

I could only guess where this was going. Bracing myself, I said, "You don't mean he's asking *you?*"

"Who else would he ask?" Mason gave a hard scoff. "See, I'm not a kid anymore, right? So he's asking me 'man-to-man' if there's anything going on."

I couldn't even imagine how awkward that would be – or what I'd do in the same situation. "So…you told him?"

Mason's voice grew quiet. "Yeah. I told him. Not flat-out, but let's just say I didn't cover for her." Mason shook his head. "And hell, he probably knew already."

"But then it's not your fault at all," I said. "And even if you *did* tell him, that's your mom's fault for cheating, not yours."

"Maybe. But you haven't heard the rest."

I frowned. "There's more?"

Again, Mason nodded. "So later that same night, my mom announces she's pregnant. And my dad – he flies off the handle, because he knows damn well it's not his kid."

The way he talked, he'd seen this with his own two eyes. "And you were there?"

Mason blew out a long, unsteady breath. "Yup.

"How about Brody and Chase?"

"They were gone. I don't remember where, but it was a good thing, because things got ugly – more than usual, too. And one thing leads to another, and Mom's yelling at my dad, telling him it's *his* fault she's stuck making money on the side–"

"Wait, what kind of money?"

Mason's jaw clenched. "The old-fashioned kind."

I sucked in a horrified breath. "Oh." But then, hoping for the best, as if there *were* such a thing, I said, "So…that's why she was cheating? I mean, for the money?"

"With the fighter? No."

I was still trying to figure it out. "So, with other guys then?"

"Some," he said.

"What do you mean some?"

"Some for the money and some for the fun." He grimaced. "After a while it was easy to gauge who was who."

"How?" I asked.

"By how good-looking they were." Mason gave a bitter laugh. "Or weren't."

By now, I was so disturbed, I hardly knew what to say. Still hoping to find *some* silver lining, I persisted, "But with the other guys, was it to help support the family?"

"No. To support her habits."

Yikes. "So…did Brody and Chase know what was going on?"

"No. And they still don't. And that's why this stays between us."

"But why?" I asked.

With a ghost of a smile, Mason replied, "You think I want *them* as jaded as I was?"

In spite of everything, I almost smiled, too.

Was jaded.

As in the past tense.

Now *that* was a silver lining. I told Mason, "I won't say a word. I promise."

He gave me a sideways glance. "And that includes Arden, too. You know that, right?"

I did. Given Arden's relationship to Brody, Mason's concern was totally understandable. "You don't need to worry," I assured him. "I won't tell a soul."

And yet, I *was* reeling. "So *that's* why your dad left while she was pregnant? Because the baby wasn't his?"

"Supposedly."

I gave Mason a perplexed look. "What do you mean?"

"So my dad takes off, and my mom has Willow – except surprise, surprise, it's my dad's kid after all."

My jaw dropped. "What?"

"Yeah. Isn't *that* a kick in teeth?"

"Yeah, but…Isn't that *good* news?"

"Sure," he said, "if my dad were still around. But he's not."

"But if he's gone, how could you be sure that Willow was his?"

"We weren't," Mason said. "Not a hundred percent. But my dad, he's got this rare blood type. Me, too. And even though we can't be sure, we're sure enough." He paused. "And she's definitely not the fighter's."

"For sure?" I asked.

Mason nodded. "Zero chance."

"So your dad must've been happy then. I mean, someone told him, right?"

"Yeah," Mason scoffed. "Me."

"So...was he happy?"

"He should've been."

I hesitated. "But he wasn't?"

"No. And he wouldn't come back either."

"But why not?"

"Because Mom's gone, and Dad says he's got better things to do than raise another guy's kid."

"But you just said—"

"Yeah, well, he didn't believe me."

"But so what?" I said. "He could've gotten a full blood test. And there's even DNA. I'm just saying, it wouldn't have been *that* hard to prove."

"You wanna know what *I* think?"

"What?"

"I think he liked it when the kid wasn't his."

I didn't get it. "But why?"

"Let's just say, responsibility wasn't his thing."

"Oh." I tried to think. "So he was just using that as an excuse?"

"Probably. Either way, he was done. And the fighter, *he* doesn't want another guy's kid either, especially a baby. So he tells my mom it's either him or us."

I felt my fingers clench. *What an asshole.* "Seriously?"

Mason shrugged. "That's what Mom said."

"When?"

"The last time we talked."

"In person?"

"No. On the phone from Miami. She tells me that she loves the guy and can't give him up." His voice hardened. "*Won't* give him up."

"But what about her kids?" I said. "Doesn't she love *them* too?"

"Maybe, but not enough. Same with my dad."

By now, I was so angry, I could hardly see straight. "Just what were they thinking, anyway?"

"Hell if I know," he said. "All *I* know is that neither one of them would step up."

Hearing this, something squeezed at my heart. Quietly, I said, "So *you* did."

"Hey, someone had to."

There was a time, and it wasn't terribly long ago, when I'd thought Mason didn't have a heart. But now, I knew the truth. His heart was bigger than anyone knew, even his own brothers.

With a smile, I said, "You wanna know what *I* think?"

"What?"

"I think they were all incredibly lucky to have you." My voice softened. "Especially Willow."

"Yeah, well…I'm lucky to have her, too. She's a great kid."

I was still smiling. "Yeah, she is. Isn't she?" But then, my smile faded. "So, did you ever find out for sure who her dad is?"

Mason nodded. "I got it tested maybe five years ago."

"And?"

"And she's my dad's daughter alright."

"You know what? I don't think so." Again, I smiled. "I think she's *your* daughter, sure not biologically, but you've been a terrific dad." I hesitated. "And as long as we're talking, can I ask you a question?"

"Anything."

"Well, you've been a 'dad' for so long, does that mean…" *Gosh, how to put this?* "Like, do you want kids of your own someday, or…?"

At this, he actually smiled. "With the right girl." He turned and gave me a wink. "Hell yeah."

CHAPTER 63

Mason

At the company headquarters, I was sitting behind my desk going through some paperwork when I heard Chase ask, "What the hell are you doing?"

When I looked up, he was standing in my open doorway looking disgruntled for the second time this week.

"Working," I said. "What are you doing?"

He frowned. "You're not working."

The hell I wasn't. "What?"

"You're whistling."

I scoffed, "Yeah, right."

"It's no joke." Chase was still frowning. "I heard you in the hall."

A few months ago, I might've told him he was nuts. Me – I'd never been the whistling type. But these days, I couldn't say for sure that he was wrong.

Today was the first day of spring, and I had big plans with a certain someone – someone who loved kids and cookies, roses and balloons, ice cream and champagne.

And me.

She even loved Willow – not because of the nanny gig, but because over the last few months, we'd become something like a family.

We'd stopped dwelling on the end of Cami's employment term. Instead, we'd been talking about teaching jobs here in Bayside or maybe more courses toward her master's degree. *Either way, Cami wasn't going anywhere, not if I could help it.*

Lucky for me, she saw things the same way.

These days, we shared the same bedroom, the same ideas about love, and the same hopes for the future.

It was long past time to make it official.

I smiled at my desk. *Huh*. Maybe I *had* been whistling.

Chase was still in the open doorway. With an accusing look, he said, "And stop smiling. It's freaking me out."

I grinned up at him. "Oh yeah? Why's that?"

"Because you do it all the time."

"Yeah, so?"

"So I'm not used to it."

By now, he *should* be used to it. I'd been smiling for months – sure, not all the time, because, hey, I still had a business to run.

And besides, Chase was the charming one, not me – well, normally, anyway. But he wasn't looking so charming now as he said, "Shit, maybe *I* need a nanny."

Chase didn't need a nanny. What he needed was a swift kick in the ass. Over the last few weeks, he'd been getting plenty, thanks to the marketing blitz that was driving his foul mood.

But hey, this was his area, not mine.

He'd figure it out.

As for myself, I had somewhere to be, and I didn't want to be late. With a smile, I stacked my papers and stood. If I were a better guy, I would've resisted tweaking the smart-ass brother who'd been tweaking me for years.

But the way I saw it, payback wasn't all bad.

So yeah, I whistled on my way out.

Hey, someone had to, right?

CHAPTER 64

Cami

I'd just pulled into Mason's garage, and I knew something was up the moment I got out of my car. It was the time of day I'd normally be bringing Willow home from school. But Arden had surprised both of us by swooping Willow up in the school parking lot for an impromptu Easter cookie bake-a-thon.

Until now, I hadn't even known there *was* such a thing as Easter cookies.

But I did know they'd be delicious, because when Arden and Willow got together, they *always* were.

As far as this particular bake-a-thon, Willow had loved the idea, and I'd agreed on the spot. These days, I didn't even need Mason's permission. *Arden was family. And in a way, so was I.*

Even though I was still technically the nanny, I wasn't feeling like an employee at all. Mason and I weren't hiding our relationship – not from Willow or from anyone else, including his brothers who I was becoming fonder of every day, even Chase, who was probably the biggest trouble-maker I'd ever met.

As far as Mason, he and I still clashed occasionally like any couple, but for some reason, it only seemed to make our relationship stronger. No matter how spirited our discussions became, we always ended up in exactly the same place – in each other's arms.

Now, standing in the garage, I couldn't quite figure out what was different. But *something* was. And then it hit me. It was the scent of flowers – and not just *any* flowers. *Roses.*

I smiled. For the last few months, Mason had been surprising me with them on a regular basis.

My gaze strayed to his favorite car, parked right next to the nanny-mobile. Obviously, he'd left the office early and – judging from the scent of the flowers – had just gotten out of his vehicle and carried the roses inside.

I was still smiling. *Was I lucky or what?*

Turns out, I had no idea.

When I entered the house and made my way into the main living area, I felt my eyes widen in surprise.

The whole area from floor to ceiling was practically overflowing, not just with yellow roses, but with yellow balloons, floating above practically every surface. It was like something out of a dream or a maybe fantasyland, and I stopped to stare in open wonder.

And then, I laughed. "Oh, my God."

From directly behind me, I heard his voice, sweet and tender, say, "You're home."

Home.

Oh, how I loved that word. And even though I would always love my parent's home in Petoskey, this place had become my home, too – not because it was so nice, but because of the people who lived here, Mason and Willow.

I whirled to look, and there Mason was, standing amidst all the yellow roses and balloons.

With a laugh, I asked, "How come I didn't see you?"

He grinned. "Because I was hiding."

"Oh yeah? Why?"

"Call it the element of surprise."

I couldn't help but recall that he'd said something similar months ago about surprising me the first time in Petoskey, when he'd offered me the nanny job.

So of course, I just *had* to tease him. With mock suspicion, I said, "Are you *sure* you don't mean an ambush?"

"I mean *something*," he said.

I glanced around in open wonder, marveling at all the balloons and roses. "It really *is* something out of a dream." I looked back to Mason. "You're crazy-wonderful, you know that?"

"Crazy's right," he said. "If you mean crazy about you."

With my heart overflowing, I closed the distance and fell into his arms. "I know exactly the feeling, except I'm crazy about *you*." I pulled back to ask, "So, what do you think of that?"

"I think I'm a lucky guy."

"So what's the occasion?"

His gaze warmed. "You can't guess?"

It wasn't my birthday or Valentine's Day, or anything resembling an anniversary. But there *was* something I'd been dreaming of for a while now. With a sheepish grin, I said, "I'm not sure I should."

He smiled. "Want to know what *I'm* sure of?"

"What?"

"I love you, Cami."

My breath hitched. "I love you, too."

The words had barely left my lips when Mason got down on one knee and held out something he must've been hiding in his hand. It was the most beautiful diamond engagement ring I'd ever seen.

He held it up between us and said, "You're the family I've always dreamed of, even if I was too blind to see it at first. But I know what I want, and I hope you want it, too. Because I've got a question…"

And I had an answer.

Boy, did I ever.

A moment later, I had the chance to give it when he asked, "Will you marry me?"

"Oh, boy." I swallowed a lump so big, it almost made it hard to speak. But somehow I managed to say, "Yes. A million times, yes."

I watched through misty eyes as he slipped the ring on my finger and kissed my fingertips one by one before standing and pulling me into his arms for one of his mind-blowing kisses.

By the time we pulled back, I was breathless and so giddy I was having a hard time collecting my thoughts. And even though it hardly mattered, I just had to ask, "The cookie thing, with Arden…"

He grinned in obvious satisfaction. "All planned."

I grinned back. "Well, aren't *you* devious."

Slowly, he shook his head. "Not devious. *Lucky.*"

"Maybe you're devious *and* lucky. But me? I'm just lucky."

With a smile, he pulled me back into his arms and whispered into my ear. "You're a lot more than that."

And so was he.

And somehow, I just knew that regardless of what life threw at us, we'd get it through it together. Because we were family – and would *stay* a family.

Forever.

THE END

ABOUT THE AUTHOR

Sabrina Stark writes edgy romances featuring plucky girls and the bad boys who capture their hearts.

She's worked as a fortune-teller, barista, and media writer in the aerospace industry. She has a journalism degree from Central Michigan University and is married with one son and a pack of obnoxiously spoiled kittens. She currently makes her home in Northern Alabama.

ON THE WEB

Learn About New Releases & Exclusive Offers
www.SabrinaStark.com

Printed in Great Britain
by Amazon

48829381R00215